THE RAKE

It was a magnificently wanton position, displaying every inch of her ready charms and leaving the open holes of her vagina and anus pointed at the ceiling. Her hand was back between her legs, cupping her mound, with one finger rubbing at the centre in a lazy, sensual manner. Swallowing hard, he walked quickly across to her and placed a candle to the entrance of her vagina. She sighed as it went in, but made no increase in the pace of her masturbation. Charles placed the second candle by the first, easing it into her vagina.

'In my breech, Charles,' Judith sobbed, 'and then light them.'

'Light them?' he queried even as he pulled a candle free of her vaginal opening and put it to her anus.

'Yes, then watch me in my pain,' she demanded. 'Come, do it!'

THE RAKE

Aishling Morgan

To list all those who have assisted – wittingly or unwittingly – in the creation of The Rake *would be a mammoth task. It would start with long-departed French nobles, include historians, wine-merchants, re-enactors and modern-day rakes, and finish with many spectacularly naughty girls and boys. Particular thanks, though, must go to Ishmael, James and Spencer, all of whom allowed me to bully them into reading and commenting on the manuscript in under a week.*

Nexus

This book is a work of fiction.
In real life, make sure you practise safe sex.

First published in 1999 by
Nexus
Thames Wharf Studios
Rainville Road
London W6 9HT

Typeset by TW Typesetting, Plymouth, Devon

Printed and bound by
Cox & Wyman Ltd, Reading, Berks

ISBN 0 352 33434 7

GLOSSARY

Aldermen – roast geese or turkeys hung with strings of sausages.

A parcel of old crams – nonsense or bombast, literally information that is as much use as rotten crab apples.

Bell swagger – a noisy, coarse bully.

Bene darkmans – good night, in the sense of enquiring after, or wishing for, the success of a nocturnal venture.

Biter – in full 'a wench whose cunt is ready to bite her arse', meaning a rampantly lascivious girl.

Bob-tail – any willing girl, but especially one who wiggles her bottom to excite male admiration, also a girl much given to playing with herself.

Breeches bewrayed – breeches soiled through excessive drink or fear.

Bull – one crown.

Buttered bun – a recently used vagina, similar to the modern expression 'sloppy seconds'.

Clean – skilled, particularly at a manual activity.

Cockish wench and a puppy's mamma – roughly equivalent to the modern expression 'hot bitch'.

Crew – a criminal or disreputable gang.

Dell – a young, but ripe girl, in some contexts a virgin.

Dog's portion – a sniff and a lick, said of men who hanker unsuccessfully after women.

Dowsers – powerful fists capable of knocking an opponent senseless.

Dubber – a professional picklock, also the actual tool.

Dust – money, especially in the form of winnings.

Frog's wine – gin.

Gambling hells – fashionable gaming houses.

Hog – one shilling.

Miss Laycock and Robby Douglas – the vagina and anus respectively.

Mobility – the mob, as opposed to nobility.

Nipperkin – a vessel containing half a pint, designed for especially strong ale.

Parting my beard – penetrating a woman's vagina.

Partridge eye – pale red or dark pink wine from the Loire valley.

Rum piece – a physically attractive woman, 'rum' meaning good and not odd.

Touranjou/Tourangelle – male and female inhabitants of the Touraine respectively.

Traps – watchmen and thief takers in general.

Upright man – the leader of a criminal gang.

For a more detailed study of period slang see *A Classical Dictionary Of The Vulgar Tongue* (Captain Francis Grose, 1785; 2nd ed. 1788) and *1811 Dictionary of the Vulgar Tongue* (various inc. 'Hell Fire Dick', 1811; unabridged reprint 1984, Bibliophile Books).

One

At the Château de Montrichard, the midsummer ball of 1788 was in full swing; yet, rather than participate in the revels, Henry Truscott viewed the dancers with a glassy-eyed stare. Anyone watching him would have thought him drunk or maybe exhausted, but the truth was that his entire mind was fixed on one of the dancers. She was Eloise de la Tour-Romain, daughter of the Comte Saônois. Her dress was a magnificent creation of pale green silk, heavy with flounces and sewn with bows and roses of subtly contrasting hues. The dress matched the jade of her eyes and piled red-gold curls of her hair, both features that added to the exquisite delicacy of her face, along with a small, proud nose, and a pert chin. Her lips were full, the lower perhaps a little fuller than its neighbour, creating an impression of a permanent sulky pout which Henry found particularly alluring. Lower, her flawless neck swept down to the upper surface of apple-like breasts whose *embonpoint* threatened to spill from the restraining silk. A trim waist served to exaggerate the fullness of her chest, while the flare of her skirts barely hinted at womanly hips and entirely concealed the charms of her bottom and legs – charms which Henry found no difficulty in imagining. All of her, from immaculately coiffured hair to dainty shoes, gave the impression of warm, haughty beauty – of a poised, disdainful shell concealing immense passion.

1

Sadly, she was so far above him socially that to do more than pass a polite greeting to her would be regarded as an intolerable breach of etiquette. This did not stop him wondering what it would be like to push her gently down into a kneeling position and lift her magnificent brocaded skirt, along with its spray of supporting petticoats, baring her undoubtedly splendid rear. He would then kiss the smooth pink globes, working slowly towards the centre her knees came apart to make available every crevice of her divine bottom. She would sigh in her rising passion as his tongue began to explore her . . .

'Deuced fine filly, isn't she?' a masculine voice broke into his reverie.

'Eh, what?' he replied, turning to see his friend and the only other Englishman in the room, Charles Finch. 'Er . . . yes, she is rather.'

'I understand,' Charles continued, lowering his voice to a conspiratorial whisper, 'that she is available . . . at a price.'

'You're teasing me, Charles,' Henry replied. 'A member of her family, prostituting herself? Why, the idea's ridiculous.'

'Not so, not so,' Charles continued. 'She takes – it would seem – a peculiar delight in extracting money from admirers. Also – so I believe – the Comte is somewhat less than generous with his wealth. Indeed, he is an out-and-out miser by all accounts.'

Charles fell silent as he took a sip of champagne, Henry returning to his reverie. Well, why not? The worst that could happen would be for Eloise to scream the house down and have the footmen give him a sound thrashing before ensuring that his name was disgraced throughout polite European society. His family, led by his priggish elder brother Stephen, would then probably make him take service in the colonies, or at the least confine him to their Devon estate in the Torridge valley.

Yet it was a gamble, and gambles were the stuff of which Henry's life was made.

'Then you will excuse me, Charles,' he addressed his friend. 'I have a proposition to make.'

Henry rose to his feet, pausing a moment to adjust the set of his bottle-green coat and set a strand of his thick brown hair in a convenient mirror before securing a flute of champagne from a footman with a practised gesture. Eloise, he saw, was executing the complex steps of one of the most modern dances, the upper curves of her not insubstantial breasts quivering deliciously as she moved. Her partner was some ageing grandee, tall, stick-thin and wearing an elaborate wig that added close to a foot to his height. This, Henry realised, was going to be a problem. There would not be a moment in the evening when she was not either partnered by some pompous noble or else surrounded by a throng of attentive suitors, few of whom he knew more than slightly, and none of whom would want to make the necessary introductions. Henry thought for a moment and then found the answer. It was bold, reckless even, but undoubtedly sound. Returning to his seat, he explained his plan to Charles, whose initial look of incredulity quickly gave way to laughter.

'Henry,' his friend quipped, 'you shall either be hung or succeed magnificently and become the talk of the London clubs, though I'd not care to place money on which!'

Henry merely smiled and sat back to wait his moment. It came within ten minutes, Eloise detaching herself from the dozen or so young beaus paying court to her and sweeping gracefully from the room. Henry followed, leaving Charles with the information that a competent physician lived in the Rue Gaumont. As he had surmised, Eloise mounted the splendid double staircase and took the passage that led towards the guest wing of the Château. He followed at a discreet distance,

3

noting the room she had entered and walking nonchalantly down the corridor. After a moment came the sound he was waiting for and he took his fate in his hands and pushed the door boldly open.

The daughter of the Comte Saônois stood by the fireplace, skirts raised to her belly, knees akimbo and cunny held wide to emit a golden stream into the receptacle beneath her. For the briefest instant the tableau held, Eloise's mouth open in shock, Henry's eyes fixed on the soft bulge of her belly and the luxurious tangle of curls surrounding the open, pink divide between her legs.

'Sir!' Eloise exclaimed, dropping her skirts without thought to the consequences. 'Ah! No!'

'Do excuse me,' Henry began, bowing politely. 'It was not at all my intention that you should spoil your beautiful dress.'

'And so, what was your intention?' Eloise retorted, her perfect English delivered in a tone of icy hauteur.

'Well,' Henry continued, 'it is my experience that women are often more willing to give what has been seen than what has not, if you follow my meaning.'

There was a pause as Eloise registered utter outrage, her cheeks flushing and her eyes growing round. Henry could see that she was about to scream for assistance.

'A moment,' he cautioned, 'before you call the footmen, bear in mind that – not to be over-delicate – you are standing in a pool of your own piddle: hardly a respectable position for the daughter of a count, do you not think?'

Eloise glanced down at the tell-tale stain on the pale green silk of her dress and the pool that was expanding slowly on the floor beneath her. She paused, torn between her embarrassment and the need to have the cause of it dropped into the river after a richly deserved beating.

'Bastard!' she contented herself with. 'Get out!'

4

'A moment, please,' Henry continued. 'I wasn't suggesting you should surrender yourself to me merely for the satisfaction, though I assure you it would be an experience not lightly forgotten. No, I had in mind the sum of fifty guineas, in gold.'

Before Henry could react, she had stepped back and picked up the chamber-pot into which she had been discharging the results of the evening's champagne. Realising her intention, he ducked frantically, only her poor aim saving him as he grappled for the door and flung himself into the corridor.

'Damn!' he swore to himself, brushing at a damp spot on his sleeve. 'Still, the Devon air will do me good.'

Eloise de la Tour-Romain stood at her window in the Château de St Romain as a maid fussed over the buttons of her gown. Directly beneath her, the village huddled at the base of the crag on which the Château was built. Beyond it, vineyards rose in a bowl of golden green foliage to the foot of the cliff that enfolded St Romain like a curled protecting hand. To her left was the break in the cliffs and the great spread of the vineyards of Auxey and Meursault, with the brighter green of the Saône flood plain in the distance. Much of what could be seen was the property of her family, and the view normally gave her a feeling of serene comfort. Now, it produced only dissatisfaction and a curious sense of irritation.

She had been plagued with similar feelings ever since the ball at Montrichard. Her outrage at Henry Truscott had been genuine. Not only had he quite deliberately barged into her room while she was in the process of filling her chamber-pot, but he had offered fifty guineas to take his pleasure of her. Her shame and fury at him seeing her nakedness and at soiling her gown had been as nothing compared to her feelings at being offered such a miserable sum for an erotic liaison – as if she, the

5

Demoiselle Eloise de la Tour-Romain, were a common strumpet!

It was true that the vulgar, lecherous and elderly Marquis d'Aignan had made a less than discreet offer of money for her chastity after she had rejected his clumsy advances. She was also aware that he had been doing his best to propagate a rumour to the effect that she had accepted. There had been other lovers too, and by no means all had left on agreeable terms, while many had been obliged to part with handsome gifts in return for her favours. Some had even paid money in advance, yet only a discreet handful and never such a miserable sum.

Therefore the Englishman's assumption was less surprising than it might have been, yet it still left her burning with an indignation that had barely faded over a month. To make matters worse, there was her inner knowledge that the experience had been exciting. Henry Truscott, unlike the Marquis, was no decaying fop with rheumy eyes and liver spots on his skin. Indeed he was anything but, being well built, handsome and undoubtedly bold. Nor did he have any of the foppish effeminacy that marked so many of her male acquaintances. Indeed, he disdained both a wig and powder. He had also been right about the effect on her of his having seen her cunny; it had made her want to yield, a piece of self-knowledge that drove her to a state of tooth-grinding rage.

Yet, after a week of high temper she had been forced to acknowledge her feelings, if only to herself. With her most trusted maid standing guard at her door, she had pulled up her shift one night and put her fingers to her cunny, rubbing the hard bump of her clitoris as she thought of how things might have been, had Henry Truscott been bolder still. Rather than make his outrageous offer, he might simply have come forward into the room, pushed her down on the bed, pulled up her pee-soaked skirts and mounted her without preamble. Her breasts would have been pulled roughly free of her bodice as his cock found the entrance to her cunny. Then she would have been full, her vagina stretched around his prick as he took her vigorously on the bed, as indifferent to her half-hearted squeals of protest as to the dampness of her pee that would be soaking into her belly and his chest.

Her climax had been exquisite, yet it had only served to deepen her sense of chagrin and she had sworn to inflict on him the same depths of shame, frustration and longing that she herself had suffered. The question was – how? To admit to what had happened was unthinkable, and so it was impractical to visit ordinary justice on him. She had toyed with the idea of hiring rogues to give him the drubbing he so richly deserved; yet, while satisfying, it was not a revenge that would suit the crime.

As she stared out across the Burgundian countryside, her thoughts were once more running on the impertinent Englishman, only to be brought sharply back to the moment as her maid accidentally pinched the skin of her back.

'Natalie!' Eloise snapped, her anger transferring instantaneously to her maid.

'I beg pardon, M'selle,' Natalie responded hastily as Eloise turned to face her.

'Stupid, clumsy girl!' Eloise stormed. 'Get on your knees!'

For a moment, Natalie's face registered the strange blend of fear and longing that Eloise had long come to recognise, then the little maid fell quickly to the floor. That the maid enjoyed being punished, Eloise knew; yet the knowledge in no way reduced the satisfaction of doing it. Indeed, Natalie's immediate acceptance of even the most painful and degrading of punishments only inspired Eloise to push the boundaries of what she would do.

7

'You are an imbecile,' Eloise stormed at the grovelling maid. 'A coarse, graceless peasant! Can you not even do so simple a thing as button my gown?'

'I ... I'm sorry, M'selle, I ... I slipped,' Natalie stammered.

'Quite! Did I say you could speak?' Eloise retorted. 'Now, fetch the chamber-pot out from under the bed.'

'No, M'selle, please, not that!' Natalie begged.

'Yes, that,' Eloise sneered, 'and for your protest you may expect twice as many strokes as usual. Now fetch it out!'

Eloise watched with immense satisfaction as the trembling maid crawled to the bed and drew the chamber-pot out from underneath it. It was a ritual they had played out before, and Natalie knew only too well what she had to do. Placing the pot in the exact centre of the floor, she knelt over it, her pretty face no more than a foot above the china lid. With her lips set in a petulant moue, she removed the cover and, as a wicked smile turned up the corners of Eloise's mouth, Natalie lowered her face into the chamber-pot.

Deliberately taking her time, Eloise walked to her dressing table and picked up a heavy, long-handled hairbrush of silver and badger's hair. Smacking the smooth side thoughtfully against her hand, she went to stand above Natalie, looking down on the humiliated maid with every evidence of pleasure.

'Turn your skirts up,' Eloise ordered coolly.

Natalie obeyed, her face still deep in the chamber pot as she reached back to take hold of her skirt of plain blue wool. Bunching the material in her hands, she lifted it, exposing her shift. With the skirt on her back, she pulled up the shift, revealing pert buttocks well parted to display a tight ruddy-pink anus nestled in a bed of dark hair and a pair of pouting, hairy cunny lips.

Eloise admired the view of her maid's naked rear. Natalie was slight, her bottom a round ball of firm flesh, the cheeks now quivering slightly in anticipation of the coming beating. Nor was that her only reaction. Her anus was pulsing slightly, the puckered hole alternately opening and squeezing shut, intermittently revealing a dark centre, a sight that filled Eloise with both disgust and delight. Natalie's reaction to the prospect of punishment also showed in the state of her cunny, the lips of which were already somewhat swollen, while a single, tell-tale drop of white fluid had formed at the entrance to her vagina.

Smiling broadly to herself, Eloise brought the hairbrush down across the hapless maid's bottom, making the flesh bounce and drawing out a squeak and a sob. The smack left dark flushes on the pale tan skin of Natalie's bottom, a semi-circle on one buttock and a vaguely triangular shape on the other. Eloise chuckled, taking open pleasure in the maid's suffering. Once more she brought the brush down across Natalie's quivering nates, aiming lower to mark the rounded tuck of the maid's bottom. Again Natalie yelped and again the brush left its imprint in the soft flesh of its target.

Eloise laid the brush on Natalie's upturned skirts and stepped near to the maid's head. Natalie sobbed, knowing what was going to happen, her breath suddenly coming in sharp pants. Eloise reached down slowly, calm and poised as she took hold of the shivering maid's hair and twisted a handful of it into her grip. Natalie responded with a broken sob, a sound that mingled despair and excitement.

For a moment, Eloise paused, savouring Natalie's surrender, stretching out the moment of torment to extract every drop pleasure from the plight of the maid. Natalie was shaking hard, her breath coming in little ragged puffs that blended with her sobs. Slowly Eloise applied pressure, forcing Natalie's face down, inch by inch, towards the surface of the pale gold liquid that filled a good third of the vessel. The maid gave a choking gasp, only to be abruptly silenced as her face was pushed into the contents of the chamber pot.

Eloise laughed, a light, silvery sound that came in striking contrast to the lewd bubbling noises that the unfortunate Natalie was making as her head was held down in her mistress's waste. Then she began to sing, teasing Natalie with the suitably adjusted words of a popular ditty:

'Soeur Talia, Soeur Talia. Buvez-vous? Buvez-vous?
Sonnez les sanglottes. Sonnez les sanglottes.
Paf, paf, paf. Paf, paf, paf!'

Her words were punctuated with smacks of her palm to the maid's bottom, and only when she had finished did Eloise release her grip in Natalie's hair. The maid came up, spluttering and gasping, her mouth open wide. With a quick motion, Eloise thrust Natalie's face back into the chamber-pot, catching her unawares, only to immediately release her and jump up with a delighted laugh. As the maid gagged and spat out the contents of her mouth, Eloise was already reaching for the hairbrush. Giggling with a girlish glee, she smacked the brush down across Natalie's bottom. A second smack followed without pause, then a third, then more, and the maid's buttocks began to wobble rhythmically under the punishment.

Grinning merrily, Eloise set to work on Natalie's bottom, her anger and frustration forgotten in the delight of spanking the naked quivering cheeks. The maid's squeals rang loud in the chamber, further adding to her mistress's delight. When Natalie sneaked a hand back between her thighs and began to masturbate, Eloise gave another peal of laughter. With her own excitement rising quickly she watched the maid's fingers work among the moist pink folds.

The quality of Natalie's sobs and whimpers changed,

expressing less pain and humiliation and more helpless
ecstasy, until she had begun to give the low animal
moans that Eloise knew signalled the onset of her
climax. Changing to a hand for the purposes of slapping
the maid's now glowing bottom, Eloise pushed the
handle of the hairbrush deep into Natalie's cunny.
Natalie lifted her bottom to accept it and called out her
mistress's name as the wide silver handle filled her
vagina. The slaps rang louder as Eloise redoubled their
force and then Natalie was begging, not to stop, but for
harder and yet harder smacks. Eloise brought her palm
down full across her maid's nates, slapping upward in
the way she knew would bring Natalie to the peak of
rapture. The maid cried out loud, once more called
Eloise's name and started to come in earnest, panting
and thrusting up her buttocks for her mistress's smacks
with all the wanton abandon of a she-cat on heat.

Aware that it was now she who was the servant,
Eloise felt a flush of resentment. Grabbing Natalie's hair
once more, she quickly thrust the maid's face back into
the chamber-pot. The maid's cries of pleasure were at
once reduced to a bubbling noise, yet she continued to
come, writhing under Eloise's slaps as she rubbed
frantically at the firm nubbin at the centre of her cunny.
Eloise watched, continuing to spank and hold Natalie's
head down but with her eyes fixed on the rhythmic
pulsing of the girl's gaping vagina and pouted anus. She
could feel her own juices, moist between her thighs, and
with that came the thought that, were she to adopt so
undignified a position, she would look little different to
the maid, count's daughter or not.

As Natalie came down from her orgasm, Eloise
released her head. Without saying a word, Eloise led her
maid to the wash-stand and helped to clean her face.
Still silent, Eloise pulled up her skirts and sat on the
edge of the bed, presenting Natalie with her open cunny.
Without hesitation, Natalie sank to her knees and

11

buried her face among the curls of Eloise's sex, finding the clitoris and starting to lick.

Eloise stroked Natalie's hair as her pleasure rose towards orgasm. Her words were loving, apologetic, then pleas to be treated the same way herself, to have her own bottom stripped for beating and for it to be done with her own face pushed into a night-soil pot. As Eloise came, she screamed out Natalie's name and then they were in each other's arms, cuddling together and kissing – no longer mistress and maid but lovers.

It was not a condition that could persist for more than a few minutes, and Eloise quickly regained her haughty composure, Natalie her air of willing obedience. Now feeling cheerful and strong, Eloise ordered Natalie to tidy up and once more turned to the window. The landscape of Burgundy now seemed as beautiful and tranquil as it ever had, a sight that increased her sense of confidence and power. Far below, a peasant was coming in from among the vines, his back bent under the weight of a great hod of grapes that represented the start of the vintage. For a moment he looked up, his eyes meeting hers with a look that brought to her mind the simile of a snail looking up to a dove – the hopeless yearning of a creature considering something that it could never, never aspire to. With that thought came the idea for a simple – and suitable – revenge on Henry Truscott. It was perfect, and also held out the faint yet tantalising possibility that it might not mark the end of their acquaintance.

In England – to Henry Truscott's surprise and satisfaction – the expected scandal never came and he had soon returned to his carefree round of clubs, brothels and gambling hells, the beautiful daughter of the Comte Saônois reduced to a frustrating memory. So when a porter at the club in which he was taking a leisurely after-lunch cognac handed him a letter sealed

12

with mauve wax and scented with a perfume reminiscent of exotic fruits, he had no idea as to its origin.

'If that's from a trollop, she's a deuced expensive piece,' Conrad Clive remarked from the neighbouring chair. 'What's the game, Harry?'

'I really have no idea,' Henry replied, breaking the seal and unfolding the letter. For a moment he read, his expression changing from alarm, through delight, to frustration.

'Something up,' Conrad remarked to the assembled young idlers and club hangers-on within earshot.

'Damn little tease!' Henry finally exclaimed, tossing the letter on to the table with an irritated gesture. 'As if I could find such a sum.'

Conrad picked the sheet of paper up and scanned it briefly.

'I say, listen to this,' he announced, evading Henry's half-hearted attempt to snatch the letter back. '"To Henry Truscott Esquire, from the Demoiselle Eloise de la Tour-Romain. Sir, on regaining my composure following your most dishonourable behaviour, I set out to identify you and was soon rewarded with the information by your friend Charles Finch, in return for a small favour." I say, I bet the old whoremonger drove a hard bargain! "I must apologise for becoming unsettled when last we met, and trust that the damage to your coat is no worse than that to my gown." Whatever have you been up to, Harry? "On calmer reflection, I have decided to consider the offer you made to me as you left. I will be yours to use in whatever way you please –" I say! "– to have naked, or partially naked, or dressed in any manner that amuses you. To display myself in any way that may please you, however revealing of my private person, exposing my body as if I were bitch or mare. To surrender to you each orifice of my body and to use my fingers, tongue or whatever you wish to favour you, in any way you command."

13

Good God! "To allow myself to be tied with rope or secured by chains and my body forced into unnatural positions. To allow myself to be beaten across the buttocks and breasts with hand, strap, cane or whip. To serve your lust as if I were your property." I say! "Should this offer be acceptable to you, send a simple note of reply and I will arrange a rendezvous. The price of my favours is ten thousand English pounds, either in gold or the new notes of promise." Ten thousand pounds! Good God!'

Conrad finished the letter and collapsed back in his chair, then began to laugh. His laughter deepened and became louder, until he began to draw looks of disapprobation from those club members not privy to the joke.

'Priceless!' he managed when he had finally overcome his mirth. 'This French piece certainly knows how to tease our friend! Imagine, promising the earth and then setting the price at ten thousand pounds! Superb!'

'I am glad you find it amusing,' Henry replied sourly. For a moment, he sank into a gloomy silence, only to rise and stride from the club without a word.

In a remote but well-appointed hunting lodge in the Perseigne Forest, Eloise de la Tour-Romain sat swaying to and fro on a swing. Her manner was pensive, yet a slight flush to her cheeks and the little nervous kicks with which she kept the swing in motion revealed both excitement and apprehension. Despite her surprise when the Englishman had accepted an offer that was primarily intended as a taunt, she had determined to go through with the assignation. She was unable to deny her interest in him, her pique at his effrontery being diluted by an erotic thrill at the memory of how he had seen her filling her chamber-pot.

On the not overly frequent occasions that she had prostituted herself for her amusement and the delight of

14

controlling her eager lovers, she had always made the choices, and their lovemaking had been more typical of that of concerned suitors than of men taking their fill of a girl paid to surrender her favours. Henry Truscott, she imagined, would not be so gentle and over-eager. Firstly, she had made it clear that she was his to do with as he pleased, an offer she had been sure he was in no position to accept. Secondly, the way he had broken into her room, clearly deliberately, so as to catch her in a position not only of erotic display but deeply embarrassing to her, spoke of a distinct streak of malice. Still, she reflected, whatever he chose to put her through, she knew that the ultimate satisfaction would be hers.

Yet the possibilities of what he might choose to do were both intriguing and disturbing. For one thing, he might choose to whip her, inflicting on her the sort of punishment she so often meted out to her servants. Applying physical discipline to the exposed buttocks of her inferiors was a pleasure in which she took great delight, yet the thought of it being her bottom that ended up naked and sore filled her with both alarm and a curious feeling of need. Alternatively, he might make her dance nude or adopt lewd poses before having his way of her, a choice that, while less painful, would be equally humiliating.

A sharp rap on the door gave her a sudden start. Composing herself on the swing, she watched as the strapping footman she had brought along as a safeguard opened the door and Henry Truscott stepped through. If he felt unease at the presence of the footman, he managed to hide it, striding confidently into the room and bowing to Eloise with no more than a hint of mockery.

'Good evening, Mademoiselle de la Tour-Romain. You look enchanting, if I may say so, yellow so suits your complexion. Watered silk, is it not?'

15

Eloise found herself blushing involuntarily at the compliment, taking an instant to absorb the sting in the tail of his remark.

'Good evening to you, too, Mr Truscott, though I fear I cannot return the compliment. Yet I suppose being English excuses your taste, to some degree,' she managed in return.

'*Touché*,' he replied, 'but enough raillery. I have ordered my man to drive round to the stable, where I trust you will join me, in accordance with our agreement?'

'The stable?' Eloise replied with a pang of discomfiture. 'Very well. Christian, the brazier.'

'The brazier?' Henry asked, only to meet a meaningful smile from Eloise.

They walked slowly to the stable, each pondering the other's actions. By the stable door stood a servant of Henry's, a tall, burly man who effectively neutralised Christian.

'Todd Gurney,' Henry stated, indicating the man, 'is an ex-farrier Sergeant, and not a man to be trifled with. I say this purely to avoid any mistakes on the part of your own manservant.'

Eloise made no reply but glanced to the big man, who returned a knowing leer. Christian was big and by no means ill-formed, but Todd Gurney stood perhaps a hand's breadth taller still and showed a decidedly solid musculature. Behind him loomed the dark bulk of a heavy wagon, its details impossible to make out in the faint moonlight. To the front stood a brass-bound chest, which Henry indicated with a flourish.

'Is it your habit to travel by farmer's dray?' Eloise asked mockingly as she opened the chest to inspect the bundles of notes stacked carefully within.

'I judge my mode of conveyance to suit the occasion,' Henry replied casually. 'At a ball, a smart gig. At the races, a carriage. Here . . .'

Eloise felt another brief rush of blood to her face but chose to ignore Henry's remark, instead instructing Christian to light torches and heat the coals in the brazier until they glowed yellow.

'You will find me quite faithful to my word, Mr Truscott,' she addressed Henry. 'Yet you must appreciate that there must be some limit on how long you may slake your bestial lust on my person. So, as we proceed, Christian will feed your bank notes on to the brazier. When the last bundle is consumed, we stop.'

'You intend to burn ten thousand pounds?!' Henry managed, his expression registering incredulity.

'Why not? It seems as good a way of marking time as any.'

'But ... but ... dash it, I mean, I had to put my estate up for security on that, at a ruinous rate of interest, I might add. You can't just burn it!'

'There is still time to cancel our agreement.'

'No, but I mean ... Oh, the hell with it, but by God I'll take my money's worth!'

Eloise gave a coy smile and signalled to her servant. Christian took a bundle of notes from the case and held it poised over the brazier.

'Well if that's the way of it, I think we shall begin by warming your pretty bottom,' Henry announced, his air of distress gone as rapidly as it had risen. 'Gurney, unload the wagon.'

Eloise took a step back, only to have Henry catch her arm and pull her roughly over to a stump that was used for wood-cutting. Holding her firmly, he made himself comfortable and then took her across his knee, making sure that she could see what his valet was up to while her bottom was spanked. With her head down and her bottom up, Eloise felt a lump rise in her throat from a sharp twinge of humiliation at her shameful position. This became quickly worse as she felt her skirts and petticoats lifted and the cool air on her bare thighs and

17

rump. Her bottom was naked, showing not just to the lecherous Henry Truscott but also the two servants!

Henry began to caress her buttocks as she watched Gurney use a pitchfork to unload straw from the wagon. The servant seemed oblivious to the sight of her naked bottom, yet lying over Henry's lap with it bare filled her with both an agonising shame and an excitement that was in itself equally shameful. Many a time she had put other girls in similar positions and had always been aware that her naked buttocks and cunny would look little different from those of the meanest serving girl. Yet no man had ever had the courage to spank her, and she had never anticipated being forced to adopt so undignified a position. Now, though, it was about to happen. Her buttocks were naked and her arm was twisted into the small of her back, rendering her helpless while he stroked and fondled her flesh. Now, whether she liked it or not, she was about to be spanked – to have her bare buttocks slapped up to a glowing pink, as if her rank and breeding were nothing – to be beaten like any common girl, with her skirts thrown up and not an ounce of modesty left to her.

As Henry tightened his grip, she wondered whether she would react like Natalie, wriggling and moaning as her cunny moistened with the rising pain. Determined not to make any such lewd display, particularly with both Christian and Henry Truscott's servant watching, she braced herself.

With her head bowed and the scene around her illuminated by the flickering orange torchlight, she waited for her punishment. Henry, however, seemed in little hurry, continuing to explore her bottom with the proprietorial thoroughness of somebody who has paid for a commodity and intends to make the best of it. She felt her cheeks pulled apart and knew that he was making an inspection of her bottom-hole and the rear of her vaginal pouch. As her anus tightened involuntarily, she gave a sob at the thought of her most intimate parts being so closely admired. A finger traced a slow line between her labia and back to her anus, making her shiver. An instant later, a hard smack caught her unawares. She gave a little cry and a gasped at the sudden sharp pain, his next smack catching her before she had time to regain her composure. Then it started in earnest, her first spanking, with a strong male hand smacking down on her bare bottom both as punishment for her and for his amusement.

As Henry warmed to his task, Eloise could feel her bottom bouncing rhythmically under his hand. He was whistling a tune as her flesh warmed and reddened, a casual act that somehow made the pain and indignity of being spanked worse still for her. Soon she had given up any attempt at the aloof composure she had intended to maintain and began to kick and squeal with no more restraint than any of the serving girls she had so frequently seen spanked, or indeed spanked herself. She knew that her motions made her thighs and buttocks part, displaying both vaginal and anal charms in an immodest show that filled her with shame. Yet her pain was too great for restraint; nor could she deny the gradual feeling of arousal that came from that very exposure and the feeling of being punished. It went on until her head was spinning and her bottom seemed to be a great, fat ball of hot pain, only for the punishment to stop as suddenly as it had begun, leaving Eloise panting over Henry's knee, legs akimbo, without thought for the resulting lewd display of her rear view.

'Warm enough, I think,' Henry remarked cheerfully, as if her spanking had been a mere idle diversion – pleasurable but of no great consequence.

All she could manage was a sob, which altogether failed to express the depths of her feeling at what he had done to her.

'Now, before we proceed,' he continued as he pulled

her to her feet and took her hand, 'perhaps I should explain what I intend so that you may feel the full effect of it. Though I have little doubt that when you penned your letter, your intent was to torment me, I also surmise that the suggestions you made are things that you would in truth delight in. It is clear that you are quite wanton and enjoy playing the whore, yet in most ways you are very much the lady and a few careful questions have revealed that above all things you detest actually doing any work, especially work that involves getting your dainty hands dirty. It was your suggestion that I treat you like a mare that gave me an idea, an idea which I do hope you will appreciate.'

Eloise's cheeks burned with blushes at his words, from outrage at those parts that were untrue and yet more in reaction to those parts that were true. Allowing Henry to lead her, she stumbled towards the stable door, into which his servant had already disappeared. Reaching it, Eloise's trepidation rose as she saw the servant standing grinning next to a pile of utterly filthy straw. Both she and Henry glanced at the brazier, where Christian was adding another bundle of notes to the flames with an air of placid indifference.

'Best not waste time,' Henry said with a worried glance at the diminishing pile of notes. 'Come on, you little jade, strip. Gurney, fetch my dog-whip from the cart.'

Henry caught a curious look from Eloise as she began to disrobe. She started with her bonnet, then the buttons of her dress, fumbling them open behind her back and taking her time until he made a threatening gesture with the leather whip. Unable to go faster, she was forced to beg for his assistance, which he gave with a chuckle of amusement for her evident discomfort. With the dress undone, it fell easily to the ground, along with her petticoat, forming a puddle of yellow and cream silk from which she stepped. Her chemise and under-petticoats followed, falling one by one until only her shift remained to cover her modesty. She made to start on her stockings, but Henry stepped forward, grabbed the hem of her shift and whisked it smartly up over her head.

Eloise gasped as her body was exposed, blushing and covering her ample breasts in sudden confusion. Henry merely clicked his fingers and gestured to her stockings and shoes, which she immediately began to peel away with trembling fingers. Each shoe was kicked off and each stocking was peeled down, Eloise standing back and placing her hands on her head to Henry's order as the second stocking fluttered to the dirty ground.

She was naked, not wearing so much as a stitch, her glorious curves causing Henry's pulse to quicken. Full, round breasts hung over a trim waist and rounded belly, each tipped with a large, hard nipple of darker flesh. Her sex was covered in thick curls in a tight V between her slightly crossed thighs, each of which was teasingly plump, yet in no way flabby. Henry motioned for her to turn, revealing her fleshy pear-shaped bottom, the cheeks glowing red from her spanking. Her eyes were downcast and her lips set in a sulky pout as she looked back over her shoulder, though Henry was unable to tell how much of her apparent bashfulness was acting.

'Take the pitchfork and shovel the straw into a stall,' he ordered, 'and work fast or I shall give you a taste of my dog-whip across those fine haunches.'

Eloise picked the fork up and bent to her disagreeable task, her big breasts lolling forward as she stooped to lift a fork-load of straw and muck. Henry licked his suddenly dry lips at the sight and unbuttoned his fly to flop his half-stiff member into his hand. She tossed the load into the stall and bent for another load, this time with her back to him so that the full glories of her bottom were revealed. He flicked the dog-whip casually

21

across her rump, drawing a squeak of protest and leaving a redder line on the already flushed skin.

She was soon covered in sweat and grime, her breathing coming heavily from the unaccustomed work. Henry continued to stroke his cock, occasionally glancing at the burning money. Her hair came loose as she worked, falling in a cascade of red-gold that Henry noted with approval as entirely natural.

'Now kneel in it,' he commanded when she had shovelled the last fork-load into the stall. 'Part your knees and push your bottom well up.'

Eloise obeyed, panting as she assumed the blatantly exposed position.

'Magnificent,' Henry breathed as he got down behind her and put the head of his cock to her open vagina. 'You have a backside a man could kill for, wench; now get your face down in the straw.'

Once more, Eloise obeyed, her whole body burning with indignation as she pressed her face into the filthy straw. It was true that the act was perhaps less degrading than that which she had put Natalie through so often, but Natalie was a mere maid. She was the daughter of a count. Yet, for all that, like Natalie, she was unable to suppress her feelings of sexual arousal at the casual power displayed in using her so wickedly.

She sensed him kneel down behind her and then felt his cock bump her cunny. His penis slid into her – slipping inside with an embarrassing ease – and he set off at a frantic pace, evidently mindful of the rapidly expiring time. Eloise began to groan as he took hold of her hair with one hand, the other sliding between her buttocks to find her anus and sinking the ball of his spit-wet thumb into the tight hole. She squealed as her bottom was opened, then groaned once more as he again began to ride her, only now with his thumb stuck well into her anal ring.

For a long while he continued to push into her, making her dizzy with pleasure. Only with difficulty did she fight the urge to reach back between her thighs and find her cunny. Determined not to show her excitement, she clenched her fists in the straw. Yet it was impossible to control her breathing and also stop herself moaning or crying out each time he increased the pace of his cock within her vagina. Half praying he would come quickly and half hoping he would take forever, she knew that her ability to hold back was reaching its end.

He slowed suddenly, and for a moment she thought he had come. Yet his cock remained rigid as he pulled his thumb from her anus. She sighed in resignation as his erection slid free of her vagina and was placed at the entrance to her rectum. He pushed and her bottom-hole opened like a flower under the pressure, Eloise relaxing the muscle to what was by no means her first experience of having a man's cock put to her bottom. He pushed it in, producing animal grunts from Eloise as her anus was penetrated. With his cock fully up, she sighed deeply, unable to restrain a show of her pleasure at having a thick penis filling out her rectum. Slowly, forcefully, he began to bugger her, making her squeal and then to give little ecstatic moans as his thrusts became harder. His front began to slam against her bottom, making the cheeks bounce and reminding her of her recent spanking. His pace quickened and, for a moment, it hurt, making her gasp and expel her breath in a sudden burst. He grunted and gave a yet harder shove, forcing his cock deeper still up her bottom as she realised that he was coming.

Henry felt his cock jerk in the tight, warm sheath of Eloise's rectum. Gritting his teeth in self-control, he grabbed the base of his penis and pulled it free. Even as the thrill of orgasm hit him, he had begun to pull her round by her hair. Pushing his penis into her open mouth, he came, filling it as his cock jerked once more. Eloise began to suck; all trace of the haughty lady vanished as she gulped down his sperm. Again and again his penis spasmed in her mouth, his come bursting from around her lips when her mouth could take no more. He put his head back and let out a long moan of utter contentment as his orgasm came to its peak, then blew his breath slowly out as it subsided. For a long moment after coming, he kept his cock in her mouth, still enjoying her gentle sucking motions. Finally, he pulled away, leaving a trail of come and spittle hanging from her lip.

As Henry sank on to his haunches, Eloise rolled on to her back, her legs wide apart as her fingers sought her vulva. The three men watched as she masturbated herself, rubbing frantically until she reached her climax with a piercing scream, indifferent to the exhibition she was making of her body, naked and soiled on a bed of foul straw. Having come, she rolled to one side and pulled her legs up, keeping her hand between her thighs, but presenting her bottom rather than her belly to the onlookers.

'A minute or so, yet,' Henry remarked.

'More?' Eloise asked, turning her head to look at him in surprise.

'Oh, nothing of consequence, but I usually take a glass of brandy at these times. Gurney has a flask; you may serve it.'

Henry congratulated himself as he saw that she was smiling as she moved into a kneeling position and took the flask and glass from Gurney. He sipped warm, fiery fluid as the last few notes burnt to ash, admiring her delicious body as she knelt in submission, her knees open and her hands crossed in her lap, damp hair falling in lank strands across her breasts.

Yet, as the final shred of ash lifted in the heat of the brazier, Eloise made no move to rise, instead remaining

24

kneeling as if awaiting further orders. Henry exchanged a glance with his servant.

'May I, sir?' Gurney asked respectfully.

'Pray do,' Henry replied with an indulgent gesture.

It was clear that Eloise no longer cared as she lifted her breasts obligingly to make a slide for the servant's cock. He pulled it free of his breeches, already engorged with blood. Placing it between Eloise's sweat-slick breasts, he began push it backward and forward. As Gurney's erection disappeared between the soft pillows of Eloise's chest, Henry turned to her discarded clothing, which was strewn indiscriminately across the stable floor. A brief search revealed a garter of yellow ribbon, which he appropriated as a trophy. A grunt from behind him signalled Gurney's climax and he turned to find Eloise kneeling with a coy, satisfied smile on her face and her big breasts now wet with sperm as well as sweat. With a polite inclination of his head he showed her the garter he had taken and slipped it into his pocket.

Half an hour later, Henry had left and Eloise was once more the poised young noblewoman. She laughed to herself as she prodded at the remains of the bundles that had been burnt. Each had been so much paper with a single real note placed on top, exchanged for the real money while Henry had been paying attention to her body rather than to Christian. He had burnt only a few good notes, nothing compared to the ten thousand pounds she now had and which would finally bring an end to her father's control of her purse. Henry, by contrast, had little chance of paying the debt back and was more than likely to end his days as a pauper. True, he had given her immense pleasure – more by far than he realised, of that she was sure – yet he had truly paid a price.

She reached for the chest in which the real money still

lay. Extracting a sheaf, she ran her fingers along the edge in pure bliss.

Two miles away, Henry Truscott took a deep pull from his flask and turned to Gurney.

'Well, thank you, Todd. I trust that you enjoyed the performance?'

'Not at all bad, sir,' the big man replied. 'It's I who should be thanking you, in truth; after all, you could have picked any one of a dozen men to do the job.'

'Ah, but not so well. Who else among your fellows could also act as manservant and bodyguard?'

'None, I dare say . . .'

'Precisely; besides, you have connections in the world of art, and there is no art more useful than forgery.'[1]

Two

As Henry Truscott pushed open the door of the Pheasant, a great gust of noise assailed his senses, along with pipe smoke, strong smells of beer and tallow and a dozen less forceful aromas. The house was crowded, with its usual half rough, half supposedly genteel clientele and the inevitable smattering of lawyers. As he began to push his way in, a gale of drunken laughter came from the smaller of the taprooms, followed by a genial shout.

'Ho, and here's the duddering rakehell and no mistake! Harry, are you game for a bet?'

Henry turned, making out the drink-reddened features of his friend Conrad Clive among a group of men he knew more or less well. Greeting them, he pushed between two earnestly conversing students and into the small room.

'Here's the game,' Conrad announced as Henry approached. 'We dance the college hornpipe and down nips of Pharaoh, man for man. The last to fall takes the pot!'

'Who'll match a guinea?' Henry responded immediately and began to dig in his pockets for the coin.

Several men answered his challenge, few being willing to appear mean by failing to match the stake. With the pot standing at nine guineas, Henry moved to the counter and signalled the landlord, a heavy-set man who greeted him with a familiar grin.

'Nine nips of stingo and a cup of milk in a blackstrap bottle,' Henry demanded, lowering the tone of his voice for the later part of his order.

The landlord ducked into the back room to tap the beer, quickly returning with the order on a tray. Henry raised the port bottle to his lips and drained it in full view of the company, then set it back down on the bar with a thump.

'As I say,' Conrad Clive called out, 'Harry's a buck of the first head. Who else would down a pint of port to keep fair with his fellows?'

A space had already been cleared in the centre of the room, barely adequate for the nine of them to attempt a hornpipe. As Henry placed the tray on a table, a tune was struck up, to be met with a roar of eagerness as the company attempted to manage the dance. Henry joined in, yelling and kicking out with the best of them.

As he had anticipated, his fellow sportsmen quickly began to fall by the wayside, three collapsing in gales of drunken laughter before managing to down their first nip. With the floor awash with spillage, the second round was called up and distributed, the dance continuing to the manic piping of the flute and the laughter of the assembly. Two more men collapsed before reaching the end of the second nip, one slipping in the beer and one simply slumping to the floor in a drunken stupor.

The remaining four stayed upright for their third, fourth and fifth nips, each now dancing proudly and attempting evolutions of increasing complexity as their confidence rose with their intake of alcohol. Conrad Clive finally resigned as the sixth nip was handed out, sinking back on to a bench with his boisterous laughter broken by urgent pants. Henry downed his nip and called out for more, forcing his remaining competitors to follow suit. One – a lank fellow who Henry knew only as Long William – shook his head and sat down, turning his half-empty pot upside down over his head in

28

the ritual gesture of defeat. The other – the stout, fleshy legged Squire Robson – downed his nip with every evidence of gusto and held out his hand for more.

For three more rounds Henry danced opposite the squire, those others who remained conscious clapping and calling out encouragement. Finally, instead of downing his tenth nip, Robson sank puffing to his knees, admitting defeat with an exhausted hand gesture. Victorious, Henry downed his last beer, scooped the pot up and called for port all round. His generosity was answered with a chorus of claps and cheers, Conrad Clive seizing up the first of the black bottles to be placed on the counter and raising it in a toast to Henry.

An hour later, Henry drained the last of his third pint of port. Conrad had been singing the praises of a new brothel in Clerkenwell, and Henry had been becoming increasingly tempted to sample its merchandise. The pleasures of the inn had begun to pale as his drunkenness had risen and Conrad's boasts had become more vivid. Henry's need for a girl had risen in counterpoint, until he had determined to make the best of his winnings and decided to leave.

'Well, I'm for this bawd's house, then,' he announced, rising unsteadily to his feet. 'Who's for drink and who's for cunt?'

Only three of his companions took sensible notice of his question, and their response was only to laugh and pass an incoherent but evidently crude jest.

'Think on this, you greenhorn crew,' Henry responded jovially. 'You can swill till you're under the table, but while you're lying in the gutter with your breeches bewrayed, I'll be up to my elbows in some sweet-cunted young doxy. Now, who's with me?'

Again the response was nothing more than drunken nonsense, so he turned his back and made for the door.

Henry staggered out into the night. A cold fog had blown in from the river, dampening the pervading smell of horse dung but adding a yet more fetid tint. Sight was also difficult, with the flickering oil lamps barely able to penetrate the fog. Clasping his handkerchief over his face, he steadied himself, his senses reeling from the drink he had taken aboard. Within the Pheasant, the sounds of drunken revelry continued unabated, providing a strangely distant background noise in contrast to the quiet of the street. With somewhat over six guineas remaining in his pocket, he was in a position to pick and choose, and so set off in the direction of Clerkenwell with vague, lustful ideas of trying three wenches at once, or possibly four.

As he made an unsteady progress down the lane, a muffled noise and a swirl in the mist ahead alerted him to the approach of a stranger. Drawing to the left of the way, he loosened the grip of his swordstick, ready to respond as circumstances dictated. For a fleeting instant, he wished he had drunk rather less, only for the thought to dissolve in the face of overwhelming lust as a quite evidently female figure stepped towards him.

She was of moderate height – little over five feet – and blessed with curves that her heavy cloak did little to conceal. Dull, uneven light from an oil lamp and yet dimmer light from nearby windows showed an upturned nose and freckles beneath large bright eyes, while he could make out suggestions of a pale neck and ample chest within the shadows of her cloak.

'My God, but aren't you the white ewe?' he managed, certain that, for all her apparent innocence, no respectable girl would be abroad on such a night.

Her answering giggle confirmed his suspicions and made his prick stir in his breeches. Suddenly, the temptations of Clerkenwell seemed less appealing.

'So what would your name be?' he asked, doing his best to restrain the urge to grab hold of her on the instant.

'Peggy, sir, Peggy Wray,' she answered in a sweet,

simple voice that spoke more of the counties than of London.

'Well, Peggy,' he continued, abandoning all pretence of subtlety or decency, 'would a half-bull suffice for an introduction to Miss Laycock and Robby Douglas?'

Once more she giggled and, when he extended the crook of his arm, she took it and pressed herself close to him. A noise to his rear alerted him and he swung round, once more putting his hand to his swordstick. Nothing moved and, after a moment, he relaxed, transferring his hand to one of the girl's well-fleshed buttocks as he moved on.

Peggy Wray knelt on the floor, her face pressed into Henry Truscott's crotch as his cock came slowly to erection in her mouth. Their lovemaking had started with a passionate eagerness and then foundered on Henry's inability to maintain his erection. On entering her lodgings, she had been tipped over her bed and had her skirts thrown up, the instant she had shed her cloak and bonnet. Expert hands had popped her breasts free of her bodice as she giggled and made a vain attempt to slow his frantic pace. He had paid no attention, briefly exploring her breasts and then burying his face between her buttocks to lick indiscriminately at her vulva and anus until her giggles had turned to soft moans of need.

He had then mounted her, setting off at a furious pace that left her breathless and squealing, only to suddenly stop and sit back heavily in a chair. Thinking he had come, she had turned to find him red faced and puffing while he massaged the half-stiff penis that protruded from his fly. Glad of the opportunity to take time over the experience, she had smiled and crawled over to him, squeezing his cock between her breasts before going down to take it in her mouth. Her skirts were still up, affording him a view of her naked bottom as he stroked her hair and allowed her to use her skills on his penis.

31

Finally she had had the desired result, a large, firm penis standing proud from his lap, two-thirds of its length in the warm wet cavity of her mouth. Its taste was slightly salty and distinctly male, overlaid with the richer flavour of her own juices from its brief immersion in her vagina. She pursed her lips around the shaft, making gentle sucking motions as her tongue caressed the rubbery flesh of the taut foreskin. He moaned and swallowed, tightening his hold in her curls and pressing her face more firmly on to his erection.

Her big breasts were dangling naked beneath her chest, one cupped in the palm of her hand so that she could feel its weight and caress the nipple, the other loose and swaying gently back and forth with the rhythmic motions of her head. Her vulva and the cleft of her bottom felt wet and a touch cool, especially around her anus, which he had left wet with spittle. Having offered the full intimacies of her body, including the enjoyment of both her vaginal and anal openings, she was unable to suppress a shiver of half-frightened anticipation at the thought of the thick cock in her mouth being pushed into the tight rosebud between her ample cheeks. Yet, for all her qualms, she was determined to accept him in her bottom and so experience the deliciously helpless, full sensation that only came with surrendering her anal opening to a man's cock.

His balls lay in her other hand, moving sluggishly in their sack as she stroked and teased. He had taken over the motion of her sucking, closing his hands gently around her head to slide her mouth up and down on his penis at his own pace. Pleased by the gesture of control, Peggy thrust her bottom higher, keen to demonstrate to her lover that she was truly his to do with as he pleased. He gave a low moan of pleasure at the sight, pushed his penis slowly to the very back of her throat one more time and began to ease her head back.

'On the bed with you, little one,' he growled as his cock came free of her mouth, 'face down and arse to the sky.'

Henry took his cock in his hand, stroking it as he watched Peggy Wray climb into the position he had demanded. Her plump breasts were completely free of restraint, dangling beneath her chest and quivering with her giggles as she got on to all fours. The folds of her dress concealed her midriff, yet not sufficiently to hide the shape of her waist, nor the full, buxom flare of her hips. Behind, her bottom was a plump ball of white flesh, coming completely bare as she once more pulled up her dress and shift. She sank down, squashing her heavy breasts against the cover of the bed and lifting her bottom to full prominence. Her face was turned towards him, her eyes bright with passion and her tiny mouth set in a mischievous smile. Suddenly, the urge to have her became overwhelming.

Her giggles turned to a squeak of mock alarm as he scrambled up on to the bed behind her. With her knees open, her glorious bottom was well spread, her big cheeks wide to show the smooth pink skin between them. At the centre, her anus was a puckered ring of flesh a tone pinker than the pale skin around it – also wet, puffy and highly enticing as a potential sheath for his cock. A firm bar of clear flesh separated her anus from the first swell of her cunny, which was swollen and wet with juice, clearly more than ready to accept a cock. Her lower belly was plump and well grown with fur, the outer lips of her vulva being particularly full while the inner were neat and pink, running to a moderately large clitoris, the pinkish-white tip of which was peeping from beneath its fleshy hood. The whole was magnificently feminine.

He smacked his cock against her bottom, then pressed it to the centre, rubbing the glans among her meaty folds. She sighed and pushed her bottom up, a drop of white fluid oozing from her vagina as she altered position. Moving up on to his knees, Henry placed the head of his cock against her hole, pressed and watched it go in, Peggy's wet, eager vagina accepting it with ease. Her sigh echoed his as the full length of his erection slid into her, only stopping when his balls met the warmth of her vulva.

Lying his body on to her back, he mounted her, taking a fat breast in each hand as she rose a little to allow him access. Feeling her full bottom squash out against his front, he began to push, with his cock inside her just enough to allow the sensitive flesh of his foreskin to penetrate the entrance to her vagina again and again. Immersed in Peggy's soft femininity, Henry quickly lost all control of his intentions to take his time with her. Gone were his ideas of having her strip and dance naked for him; forgotten was his goal of using her vagina only briefly and then buggering her at a leisurely pace until he came within the tight confines of her back passage. With a grunt of passion, his cock exploded inside her, draining sperm deep into her cunny without thought for the consequences.

For a while, he held his penis in her, still mounted on her back with her plump breasts in his hands. Rising slowly, he sank back, his cock pulling from her vagina, which was left gaping open as if desperate to be filled once more. As soon as he was clear of her, she rolled over, spreading her thighs and sinking her fingers into her cunny. They came out sticky with come. As she began to rub at herself with one hand and massage a breast with the other, Henry felt a flush of pride that he had managed to bring a presumably experienced street girl to such a height of ecstasy that she needed to masturbate after he had come inside her.

Yet that was undoubtedly what she was doing, and he obliged by reaching out a finger to tickle her bottom-hole as she started to come. The muscles of her thighs and belly locked and he felt her anus pulse. Popping the top joint of his finger into the little hole, he felt the muscle tighten, relax and then tighten once more as she came. Impressed by her display of raw passion, he watched until her body had subsided and she was left limp and panting on the bed, her satisfied smile showing the depth of pleasure she had taken in the experience. He had had no particular intention of returning to the family's town house in Petty France anyway, yet as Peggy gave a contented sigh and held out her arms to be hugged he became determined to manage another bout, if not two, and stay until the morning.

Later, once Peggy had completed her douche and been prevailed upon to provide refreshment, they sat together on the bed, Peggy naked, Henry in only his shirt. She was stroking his penis as he alternately sipped wine and took mouthfuls of the coarse bread and hard cheese that she had provided. Although his cock showed little signs of returning to life, he was enjoying her touch and was confident of managing another bout in due time, meanwhile being content to talk, munch food and sip wine. After the strenuous effort of mounting her and two hours without a drink, he had become sufficiently sober to take at least some notice of his surroundings.

'I must say,' he ventured, 'you do yourself deuced well at the game. Mind, you're a game pullet, and no bawd nor pimp to cheat you of your earnings, I'll wager, but still . . .'

Her response was to lean gently over and transfer his flaccid cock from her hand to her mouth. Henry sighed as she began to suck and took another mouthful of bread, washing it down with the wine.

'Rum wine, too; frog's wine's more the go usually,' he continued. 'What is it? Not claret – too strong and rich – Burgundy, I imagine, and worth fifteen the dozen, perhaps twenty. I know a girl from Burgundy, a cockish wench and a puppy's mamma to boot, for all that she's the daughter of a count . . .'

A cough sounded from the direction of the door. Henry spun round, pushed Peggy away from his lap and grabbed for his swordstick in one smooth motion, only to trip on his discarded breeches and sprawl on the floor. A light laugh sounded from behind him as his arms were grabbed and pulled into a grip that brooked no resistance.

Eloise de la Tour-Romain stepped daintily into the room, her mouth set in an amused smile. On the floor, the massive Christian had Henry Truscott in a firm grip, the Englishman's struggles availing nothing against his opponent's greater bulk and sobriety. Peggy Wray sat on the bed, her shift clasped to her bosom, her expression an uncertain smile. Behind Eloise, Natalie came into the room, immediately giggling at the sight of Henry's naked buttocks protruding from beneath his shirt-tails.

'Bind him well, Christian, then turn him over,' Eloise ordered and lowered herself on to a corner of the bed.

Christian made quick work of binding Henry's hands and feet, ignoring his threats and curses and quickly rendering him helpless. His own handkerchief was used for a gag, stifling his complaints, while a loop of cord secured his bound wrists behind his body. Finally the Frenchman stood up and rolled his victim over with a foot, leaving Henry to glare furiously at his captors.

'So, Mr Truscott,' Eloise said, giving his naked genitals a pointed look of distaste and then throwing his hat over them, 'we meet again, only this time the advantage is mine. But I am being thoughtless; with a gentleman like yourself, I should at least make introductions. Christian I believe you have met, while obliging me to your depraved tastes in the Perseigne

Forest – an incident that I feel sure you remember as vividly as I. Little Natalie is my lady in waiting and has been with me since childhood. Peggy Wray I only took into my employ last week, yet she has already proved her worth. She, incidentally, is the daughter of a Southwark wine merchant who has had the misfortune to fall into distress.'

Henry turned his head, throwing a furious glare at Peggy, who responded by quickly lowering her gaze. Eloise laughed to see his impotent fury and gave him a gentle nudge with the tip of her boot.

'Now, before we proceed,' she continued, deliberately mocking his way of speech, 'perhaps I should explain what I intend so that you may feel the full effect of it. Following your nasty little game in the Perseigne Forest, I discovered that the notes you had provided were false. No, do not protest – I did not burn them. I never intended to burn them, that was simply a device to ensure that the experience left its mark – for both of us. Had they been of worth, I would have been satisfied with the exchange. Only they were not of worth, were they, Mr Truscott?'

Eloise stopped and smiled at the look of rising alarm on Henry's face.

'Do not fear,' she went on, her tone increasingly mocking. 'Your body is in no danger, only your pride. Natalie, Peggy, make him proud.'

At Eloise's order, Natalie sank immediately to the floor, Peggy following suit somewhat less hastily. The little maid removed Henry's hat to once more expose his genitals and took his now shrunken cock gently into her hand. He gave Eloise a look of impotent fury in return, at which she simply laughed. Natalie had already begun to stroke his cock as Peggy sank to the floor beside her. As the two girls' fingers began to caress his genitals, Henry lay back, evidently resigning himself to the indignity that was being put upon him.

37

Eloise stood watching as Henry's cock slowly filled with blood. For all his condition, the girls' fingers were provoking a response, and when Natalie bent down to take the tip of his cock in her mouth, this response quickened. Seeing his increasing excitement, Eloise began to pull up the front of her skirts, exposing nothing but allowing herself to place her hand on her cunny. She began to rub gently, feeling the soft swell of her mound beneath her fingers as she watched Henry's cock expand in her maid's mouth. Peggy was toying with his balls and had her fingers ringed around the base of his cock, tugging it gently into Natalie's mouth with the foreskin held down so that the maid could work on the sensitive tip.

Soon Henry was fully erect, his cock standing proud from his prone body, the head glistening with Natalie's saliva. His face showed a mixture of pleasure and worry, bringing Eloise a delicious feeling that combined vengeance, lust and a reassertion of the pride that he had taken from her in the forest.

'I hardly think he should be allowed to watch this,' she announced coolly as an idea for a further humiliation entered her head. 'Peggy, sit upon his head. I am ready, Natalie.'

Both girls moved away from Henry's middle. Natalie giggled as Peggy flung her leg across his chest and lowered her plump behind on to his face, smothering him in fleshy bottom and completely denying him his ability to watch. Eloise came forward, pulling her skirts up as she straddled the recumbent Henry to reveal the ripe mound of her cunny with its moist, pink centre. She lowered herself into a squat and took Henry's cock in her hand, squeezing the hard shaft and then beginning to rub the tip against her vulva. Placing it to the mouth of her vagina, she eased herself down on to him, sighing deeply as she filled with cock.

Making herself comfortable, with her skirts spread

out over his body and the floor, she began to ride, bouncing gently on his cock to get the feel of it inside her. In front of her, his face was almost entirely hidden beneath the naked Peggy, only his chin projecting from under the plump swell of her cunny. His features, she knew, would be entirely smothered beneath Peggy's large bottom, his lips pressed to her cunny around his mouthful of handkerchief, his nose pushing against her anus.

It was a delightful thought, while the sight of Peggy's full curves were by no means unexciting. The girl's full thighs were spread on either side of Henry's head, while the gentle swell of her cunny and stomach moved slightly at the sensation of being sat astride a man's face. Her breasts looked huge, hanging forward as she rested herself on her arms, their big, dark nipples fully erect. The shy, abashed expression on her face completed the image, bringing Eloise's enjoyment of the situation to a fine peak. Having other people pleasure themselves in ways that also embarrassed them always excited her, and now she had the double pleasure of both Henry and Peggy.

She began to bounce faster and then gave a laugh of pure joy as Henry, no longer capable of restraint, began to make little bucking motions inside her, doing his best to make his cock move in her cunny. Pulling her skirts up at the front, she put a finger to her vulva, finding the clitoris and starting to rub as she concentrated on her pleasure. She had conquered the man who had obsessed her since the day he had punished and degraded her in the Perseigne Forest. He had spanked her until she howled and kicked. He had forced her to strip naked and shovel dirty straw. He had mounted her from behind and he had had his cock up her bottom. He had made her so excited that she had played with herself in front of him and accepted his servant's cock between her breasts. Ever since, she had been in turmoil, alternately dishing out cruel and arbitrary punishments to her hapless maids and playing with herself helplessly over the thought of how it had felt to be spanked, to be humiliated, to be buggered as she knelt naked among the dirty straw – all that and then cheated.

Now, though, she was in charge once more, mounted on her persecutor's cock, taking her pleasure of him as she wished while his face was smothered between the fat buttocks of the girl she had hired to help seduce him. It had been easy, Henry responding to Peggy's beauty and ample charms like a prize bull put to a heifer.

With her finger moving in little firm circles on her clitoris, she started to come, her gaze locking on the point where Henry's face disappeared beneath Peggy's bottom as her climax began. She moaned, long and deep in the back of her throat, then began to give choking sounds almost like sobs and finally a long, high squeal of pleasure as the muscles of her vagina clamped tight on his penis and her back and neck arched with the ecstasy of orgasm.

Beneath her, Henry was trying desperately to reach his own climax, bucking and wriggling in his attempts to get enough control to come. Sensing his pleasure and frustration, Eloise dismounted quickly, ignoring her body's need to remain full of cock while she came slowly down from the peak of her orgasm. She moved back, lifting her skirts carefully clear of his erection, which was sticky with her juices and looked fit to burst. Christian gave a coarse laugh at the sight, Natalie a knowing giggle. Henry remained still, although Eloise was unsure whether from an attempt to show disdain or in the hope of her taking mercy on his swollen member. Rising to sit on the bed, she accepted a glass of Burgundy from Natalie.

'Poor little Henry,' she said when she had taken a refreshing sip. 'So manly, and so helpless, and look at that big, hairy thing, so hard and so fierce. It is lucky he can't get up, isn't it, girls? Or he would surely mount us all. Ah, but he would like that, wouldn't he? The great brute would enjoy us kneeling, I think, three pretty bottoms all bare for his attention, all round and naked for his amusement. Tickle his balls, Peggy, but don't let him come.'

Peggy obeyed, rocking forward to touch the taut sac of Henry's scrotum. Eloise laughed again as his cock jerked in response to the girl's touch. Her climax had taken the edge off the burning need for revenge that she had felt for nearly three months, but she was enjoying Henry's plight immensely, especially because of his all too plain state of sexual arousal. Intent on taking her time, she sat back and took another sip of wine.

'So,' she said, 'how do we progress? The pleasure you took in my body, I think we may regard as paid for. Which leaves only matters of my pain and indignity and, of course, your servant. Let us deal with that first. Peggy, take his gag out.'

Peggy Wray rose from her seat on Henry's face. Her emotions were mixed. Eloise had taken her from debtor's jail, a hell from which she had had no prospect of release. Her resultant feelings of loyalty were intense and, to her, Eloise's word was law. She knew that she had been chosen for her looks and because she spoke French, yet the fact remained that, without Eloise's assistance, her future would have been bleak indeed. On the other hand, Henry had treated her with a cheerful, friendly lustfulness and she found it difficult to feel the vengeful ill-will towards him that Eloise required. She already felt guilty for tricking him, and only the fact that Eloise's attitude was one of malicious playfulness rather than outright aggression had allowed her to continue playing her part. Yet, as she struggled with the knot that held his handkerchief into his mouth, her decision to go on was driven as much by lust as by duty.

41

'You now have a choice,' Eloise was saying to Henry. 'Either you may satisfy both my maids with your tongue, or we shall trouble you no further, but simply drop you back to your town house in Petty France, where I believe your brother Stephen is in residence – as you are, that is. Which is it to be?'

'I'll lick your maids, damn you!' Henry responded, as Peggy pulled the handkerchief free of his mouth.

'Such words!' Eloise responded in mock alarm. 'So be it, then. Peggy, sit on his face.'

Peggy moved forward, settling her bottom across Henry's face and leaning a little forward so that his tongue could work on her properly. She moaned as he began to lap at her clitoris, then felt herself blushing. Other than Henry – whose sight was effectively blotted out by the cheeks of her bottom – everybody was looking at her, admiring her naked body as she began her stated intention of coming to orgasm over Henry's mouth. Neither Eloise nor Natalie were making any attempt to hide their interest, while the burly Christian's impassivity was given the lie by the size of the bulge in the crotch of his breeches.

Returning their gazes with a nervous and excited smile, she moved a little further forward, allowing herself to reach out for Henry's straining penis. She began to stroke it as he licked, delighting in the sensation of the hard shaft in her fingers and the firm tongue on her vulva. She had watched Eloise take her pleasure of Henry, and the sight had added to her own arousal. Yet Eloise had retained her clothes, showing nothing of herself until she had exposed her cunny for the final ride to orgasm. Mounted on Henry, Peggy felt both rude and bashful, showing everything and showing it in a way that made it very clear that it was she who was taking her pleasure of the man beneath her.

Yet her need to come was quickly overriding all her other feelings. His tongue was working directly on her clitoris, using an expertise that none of the other men she had known had even approached. Lost to pleasure, she leant forward and took Henry's cock in her mouth, starting to suck on the hard shaft as her orgasm approached. His penis felt huge, a massive, virile thing, about to erupt come into her mouth.

Then, even as she started to come, a hand locked in her hair and pulled her head sharply back, depriving her of the wonderful cock she had been sucking. Too far gone to stop, she came in Henry's face, rubbing her cunny hard over his mouth as the ecstasy of orgasm went through her. Her back arched in bliss, a bliss made stronger by the hand cruelly twisted into her locks. For a moment she saw Eloise's face, full of delight at her helpless ecstasy and at her own power in controlling the scene. Then she was coming down from her climax and filling with shame and embarrassment at the sheer wantonness of her own behaviour.

Henry swallowed a badly needed breath as Peggy lifted her bottom from his face. His fury at being tricked into submission had not abated, yet the girls' manipulation of his senses had put him in a state where his need for orgasm was a desperate craving that overrode all other concerns. Twice he had been brought to the very edge of orgasm, both while inside Eloise's vagina and in Peggy's mouth. He had also had his face smothered in Peggy's bottom and his mouth was full of the taste of her juices.

Yet, even as Peggy moved back to the bed, Natalie was moving towards him, giggling with delight at the prospect of what she was about to do. She had taken her dress off and bunched her petticoats around her waist, leaving her naked between waist and stocking tops. Unable to resist, he could only wait as she threw a slim leg across his shoulders and poised her pert backside directly over his face. Her neat buttocks were parted above him, her cunny swollen and ready, the centre pink and moist in a bed of richly grown black hair, her anus pouted and slightly open.

He quickly moistened his lips in anticipation of her vulva, only to have her sit herself down with not her vagina but her anus directly over his mouth. As a delicate hand closed on his penis, he resigned himself to licking the tiny maid's bottom and poked his tongue out as she settled her weight on his face. He heard her squeal of delight and pleasure as the tip of his tongue penetrated her anus, going in with an ease that suggested that many a cock had been there before his tongue. The head of his penis was taken carefully between her fingers and thumb as he began to tongue her bottom-hole. It was a tormenting touch that kept him firmly erect and yet which denied him orgasm, and as she began to masturbate herself with her free hand he came to realise the extent to which it was possible to be tormented. His whole body seemed about to explode and the muscles of his cock had began to jerk of their own accord, always at the very brink of orgasm but never actually there.

Natalie's taste was strong in his mouth, mingling with Peggy's. His head was spinning with drink and sex, blotting out all reality less immediate than Natalie's bottom and the furious straining of his cock. She was laughing as she rode him, and rubbing her buttocks in his face to force him to lick deeper into her anus. Then suddenly the quality of her movements changed, her laughter turning to moans and her bum-hole contracting on his tongue. The maid cried out, calling not his name, but for Eloise, and as she did so her fingers tightened on his cock, squeezing the head. He jerked, pushing the tip of his penis into her ring of fingers, desperate for friction. For an instant he was coming and then her hand had been snatched away and all he was left with was the derisive peal of Eloise's laughter.

* * *

Eloise watched Natalie dismount. Henry's face was red and wet with sweat and the two girls' juices, his expression one of agonised need. His cock was a rigid rod, the tip purple and glossy with the pressure of the blood within. Thoroughly pleased with the condition he was in, she reached down and ran a long fingernail slowly up the length of his penis. He groaned and his cock jerked, a drop of clear fluid squeezing from the hole at the tip. His arousal was blatant, a state that she was sure he found every bit as erotic and uncomfortable as she had her own enforced servitude.

'For the sake of mercy, make me come,' he growled between gritted teeth as she gently pinched the head of his penis between thumb and forefinger.

'No,' she replied. 'I shall not.'

'I let you do it, you wanton bitch!' he spat.

'I know, but I choose not to allow you,' she answered coolly. 'I have something else in mind to finish our pleasant little evening together.'

'What?' he demanded.

'Heat the blacking Christian,' she ordered, ignoring Henry, 'we mustn't allow our friend to take chill.'

Henry's squirms immediately became more pronounced, and his eyes showed a look of desperate pleading.

'No more than warm,' Eloise laughed, 'perhaps enough to smart as much as might a firm spanking.'

Christian nodded acquiescence and produced a large pot of boot-black from the recesses of his coat. Opened and placed over the candle, it began to melt, while the girls watched in keen anticipation and Henry's struggles became ever more desperate.

Finally it was ready, and Eloise took the pot from Christian, using Henry's handkerchief to shield her hand. Instructing Christian to hold Henry's legs and the girls to pin his shoulders, she knelt, and, locking her eyes with his, poised the pot of half-liquid boot-black over his straining genitals. He made a desperate feint to the side, but to no avail. Slowly Eloise tipped the pot, a heavy blob of boot-black forming at the lip, growing, bulging, swelling and then oozing over the edge to fall directly on to the taut skin of his penis.

Henry gave a despairing jerk and then stopped abruptly, his face registering profound relief as he realised that the boot-black was no more than warm. Eloise felt a rush of pure glee at his response and burst out laughing, her hand shaking with her mirth as she upended the remainder of the pot over his genitals. It came out slowly, a viscous slick of oily black.

'Bitch!' Henry gasped as Eloise drew back.

'Rub it well in, Natalie,' Eloise laughed, 'and let the poor boy come, it will serve his shame all the better.'

Natalie put her hand to Henry's genitals, smearing the blacking liberally over his cock and balls, then down between his thighs to get at his buttocks. With her right hand cupping his sac, she began to use her left to masturbate him, using deft, short strokes with her dainty hand squeezed tight around the solid glossy pillar of his erection. He groaned, his eyes closed in ecstasy. The tension in his body increased, each muscle hard and distinct in a way that sent a new thrill to Eloise's sex. Then he came, his semen erupting in a powerful jet that splashed over his genitals and belly and caught Natalie in the face.

The little maid gave a squeal of alarm and delight, continuing to pull at his cock as more of the thick white fluid came from the tip, spurting, then oozing until her hand and his cock were thickly coated in a rich mixture of come and blacking.

'Magnificent!' Eloise exclaimed, clapping her hands in sheer joy. 'Christian, throw him in the street, just like that!'

'Eloise, have mercy!' Henry protested vehemently. 'Did I make your shame public? Did I leave you bound and helpless in a freezing street?'

'Demoiselle de la Tour-Romain, to you,' Eloise

replied, 'and yes, you did make my shame public, for I am aware that the story has been making the rounds of London's clubs and coffee houses for some while. As to a freezing street, I fancy that the morning will see no more than a light frost. All this is of no great matter, though. You are going in the street because the idea amuses me.'

Henry lay half in and half out of the deep shadow of a doorway. He was naked but for his shirt, tied securely and smeared with boot blacking from his belly to his buttocks, also with semen. It had already been close to dawn when they had dumped him and now the London sky was a pale, opalescent grey, presaging another cold, damp day.

His efforts to get free had failed, despite the frantic tugs and wrenches at his bonds. The cold, his exposure and undignified condition, all were minor inconveniences in comparison to the possibility that the first people to come across him might be one of the vicious crews who worked the area around Gray's Inn and Clerkenwell. Despite the fact that he had nothing worth taking, he was painfully aware that such people might view his helpless state as an opportunity for risk-free violence.

The sound of a voice caught his attention and he rolled round. Three figures were coming towards him, indistinct in the morning mist. They were evidently masculine, and walked with assurance. For a moment, Henry felt a wave of panic and then relief flooded through him as the smart, evidently expensive cut of their tricorn hats became evident. By a frantic jiggling of his shoulders and hips, he managed to wriggle a little further out into the lane, the details of the men's conversation becoming evident as he did so.

'. . . yet in the long term the masses, the hoi polloi, as it were, must prove incapable of government . . .'

Henry's feelings of relief turned abruptly back to

panic as he recognised the earnest, droning tones of his brother Stephen's voice. Desperately, he tried to reverse his direction.

'. . . the ability to govern requires more than simple will,' Stephen's voice continued. 'That some families have risen over the years to high estate is no accident . . .'

'By my faith! Look at that fellow!' one of the others interrupted.

Henry abandoned his attempts to regain the now comforting shadows of the doorway. Allowing his head to sink back to the pavement, he resigned himself to discovery.

'Doubtless some rogue set upon by his fellows,' Stephen was saying as the men hurried forward. 'Such is the drunkenness and debauchery of the lower orders, these days – Great heaven! Henry!'

Three

In the rural fastness of the Torridge valley, autumn passed to winter, winter to spring, spring to summer with a tenor that owed much to nature and little to man. For Henry Truscott, presented with the stark choice of remaining in Devon or being cut off entirely, the time passed with a monotony only partially alleviated by the willingness of the local girls. For company he had his father, John Truscott, once a great buck but now reduced to a sad shell of a man by the onset of senility. Although fond of the old man – with whom he had much in common – Henry found his company both hard work and saddening. The only other people on the estate were Thomas and Martha Catchpole, steward and housekeeper respectively, an elderly couple of unswerving loyalty to the family. To Henry, their sole virtue lay in having learnt to turn a blind eye to the most outrageous of happenings, a characteristic that had come from a lifetime of keeping house to John Truscott and subsequently to Henry himself.

With few visitors and little interest in politics, Henry remained in blissful ignorance of events beyond the neighbourhood, let alone in such far-off places as France. On the rare occasions that his mind did turn to that country, it was to dream of ever more elaborate stratagems for taking his revenge on Eloise de la Tour-Romain – stratagems that were as impractical to carry out as they were satisfying to contemplate.

* * *

In the far off Château de St Romain, Eloise would have given a great deal for the air of bucolic peace which Henry so resented. Despite the attempts of her family to remain aloof, it had been impossible to ignore the ever more threatening rumblings of discontent among the populace. The comte, brought up to regard his status as a God-given right, found the idea of such rebelliousness both shocking and terrifying. His daughter – by nature both braver and yet more arrogant – regarded it as outrageous to the point of impossibility and made every effort to behave as if the *ancien régime* were good for another thousand years. Even the storming of the Bastille and the summoning of the States General for the first time in close to two hundred years failed to do more than increase her sense of indignation.

Intent on escape from the realities of life, she came increasingly to spend time among the woods and crags of the Morvan, the great expanse of wild land to the west of Burgundy. A considerable area of this was the property of her family and offered the seclusion of a landscape unchanged by the squalid considerations of modern life. Deep in the forest, some seven miles from St Romain, a thickly wooded valley sheltered a stream. The course of this was uneven and broken by several deep pools, the deepest and most beautiful of which had been Eloise's favourite place of refuge since childhood.

Here, accompanied by Natalie Moreau and Peggy Wray, she would spend whole days – swimming, relaxing or playing gentle games that not infrequently became erotic in nature. A sultry day towards the middle of August found the three of them there. With their horses hitched among the trees a little way down stream, they had began to make their way up among the tumble of boulders that acted as a natural dam to the pool. Eloise was ahead, her skirts held up to allow her to jump from rock to rock, making a display of leg and lower thigh that would have been quite improper anywhere less private. Natalie and Peggy followed more slowly, each burdened with the wines, delicacies and accessories that Eloise considered indispensable to an outing.

Reaching the highest of the rocks, Eloise jumped down to the area of flat grass that bordered one side of the pool. All around her the warm air was rich with woodland scents, while birdsong and the tinkling of the stream were the only sounds. To her it was Arcadia, a place detached from the strictures of decorum, a place where she might do exactly as she pleased.

'Do hurry,' she called back to the two girls. 'I wish to bathe and you must help me with my dress.'

'Yes, mistress,' Natalie called back, her voice showing a trace of strain as she struggled to lug a heavy pannier on to the rock.

'Put it down there,' Eloise ordered, indicating the centre of the small piece of greensward. 'Peggy, undress me while she lays things out.'

The English girl placed her own pannier by Natalie's and hurried forward. Eloise turned her back, allowing Peggy to get to the buttons of her dress and begin the process of undressing her. As she was stripped, Eloise made no effort whatever to help, instead allowing Peggy to take off each garment. The sensation of being disrobed was pleasant, and made more so by her ability to command and control Peggy. Following her delightful revenge on Henry Truscott, Eloise had chosen to keep Peggy on. Not only did the English girl show a depth of loyalty that accorded with Eloise's self-esteem, but her plump curves invited both caresses and punishment.

When Eloise had first taken Peggy to bed, the maid had been shy and reluctant. By a mixture of cajoling, teasing and simply taking what she wanted, Eloise had slowly worn down Peggy's resistance. Now the once coy girl was now as willing to share cuddles and caresses as

Natalie, if less accepting of the erotic humiliations that Eloise so loved to inflict. Peggy's first beating had been a traumatic affair, with plenty of tears as she knelt on the floor of Eloise's room with her big white bottom bare and raised for punishment. She had squealed and blubbered while her buttocks were turned red, but ended shivering and needful in Eloise's arms, alternately apologising for her misbehaviour and begging for the privilege of licking her mistress's cunny.

Eloise stood naked, revelling in the feel of the sun and air on her body, unashamedly naked, with her nipples already stiff from the touch of Peggy's fingers on her skin. Stepping forward, she dipped a toe experimentally into the water, finding it cool and fresh.

'Undress and join me,' she ordered, turning back to where the maids stood watching.

They obeyed quickly, giggling as they helped each other strip while Eloise waded out in the pool and submerged herself in the cool, clear water. Rising and turning, she watched the maids come to the edge, their arms around one another's waists in a gesture of casual intimacy. Both had fine bodies, yet they could scarcely have been more different. Natalie was tiny, with pert breasts and sweetly rounded hips separated by a narrow waist and a soft belly that showed as no more than a gentle bulge. Her skin was a rich olive and thickly grown with black hair over her sex. Large brown eyes and a slight flare to her nose hinted at Spanish or even Moorish ancestry. Peggy, by contrast, was pale-skinned, golden-haired, freckled and decidedly plump. Big, heavy breasts and a chubby bottom were saved from being excessive only by their youthful firmness, while her belly and thighs were sleek and rounded. Despite their differences, both girls produced a sexual reaction in their mistress, a reaction that she fully realised was partly physical and came partly from their submission to her will.

When all three girls were in the water, they began to play, freely yet with the maids showing a deference to Eloise that she considered natural. Naked together, their play became increasingly erotic, pinched nipples and buttocks becoming commoner and then giving way to more open, intimate caresses. Finally the three came together, Eloise's hands finding the others' bottoms and squeezing a wet cheek in each.

Without a word they climbed from the pool, coming together in a tangle of wet, eager limbs, their mouths meeting and their fingers burrowing into crevices without restraint. As if by a natural force, Eloise moved to the middle, taking the girls' heads and putting them to her breasts so that they could suckle. As firm, eager lips closed on Eloise's nipples, Natalie's fingers found the cleft of her cunny, parting the lips to find the centre of her pleasure.

Delighting in the warm, maternal feeling of being suckled by two girls, Eloise lay back, intent on taking a long, leisurely climb to her orgasm under Natalie's expert fingers. When it finally arrived, it signalled the onset of an hour of uninhibited play, the three girls enjoying each other's bodies without reserve. Slowly, without conscious effort by any of them, their play came to revolve increasingly around Natalie's enjoyment of sexual chastisement. On discovering that no glasses had been packed, Eloise ordered Natalie into a kneeling position, regardless of the detail having been as much Peggy's responsibility.

The application of one of Eloise's discarded slippers quickly had the small girl's bottom cherry red. As always, her moans and the openness of her vagina betrayed the maid's sexual response, while increasing Eloise's desire to punish and humiliate. Ordering Natalie to push her bottom up, Eloise took the bottle of wine that they had opened.

'As you have neglected the glasses, you must be the

glass yourself,' she teased and began to pour the rich yellow wine into Natalie's open vagina.

Peggy giggled at the sight and came quickly forward as the wine began to spill from the mouth of Natalie's gaping sex. Eloise laughed as the English girl began to lap, only to break off as the sound of a branch snapping cut through the air.

Looking up, she saw a horse coming through the trees towards them. Her angry rebuke faded on her lips as she saw that the rider was Christian, who she felt could be relied upon not only for discretion, but also to add to the pleasure of their sex play. He waved at them with a lack of propriety that immediately irked Eloise. Yet, given her complete nudity, it seemed hard to demand formality and she waved back, acknowledging his right to join them.

'Good day, Christian,' she called in greeting. 'Dismount your horse and mount Natalie instead; she will benefit from your use. You may use your whip on her, too; the experience will teach her a valuable lesson.'

'I've had her many times,' Christian responded, 'and I see she has already been spanked. No, if I am to dally, I'd rather put my member to your own proud cunt, Eloise.'

Eloise stopped, aghast at his reply. Many times she had taken pleasure in his large, powerful body, but always it had been as mistress and servant. He would lie to be mounted, obedient and patient while she bounced up and down on the rigid pole of his cock. Now his tone was very different, and closer to a threat than anything. Yet her arousal was high, and her cunny badly in need of the filling of hard penis that his presence promised.

'If you must, then it seems I can do little to prevent it,' she responded, effectively offering herself while privately vowing to have him whipped for his temerity at a later date.

'Get in a line, then, with your arses up,' he ordered.

'I'll have your cunts one by one, to be sure no girl misses her share.'

'Do as he says,' Eloise instructed Natalie and Peggy, who moved to comply, with giggles and arch looks at Christian.

Kneeling naked between her maids with her bottom raised, Eloise felt a strong sense of submission. The pose was rude, showing cunnies and bottom-holes to him in a flagrant display of female sex.

She waited, shivering slightly as he dismounted and moved behind them, inspecting their spread rears and dangling breasts with a proprietorial detachment that fuelled her sense of subjugating herself to his raw lust. Turning her head, she found him with his cock already in his hand, stiff and long over Peggy's plump behind. Annoyance that the maid should be given preference to her flared in her mind, only to fade as he sank down behind her. She felt her thighs pulled open, then the head of his cock at her vaginal opening.

She gave a little yelp as it was pushed unceremoniously in, then sighed as her vagina filled, her status put aside for the pure joy of kneeling to accept a man's cock in her vagina. He began to push, making her moan and whimper with pleasure, only to pull out as suddenly as he had entered her. Instantly feeling deprived, she put her hand back and began to stroke herself, sure that once he had had his fill of Peggy and Natalie, he would return to take his climax over her.

Eloise continued to frig as Christian mounted Peggy, humping her chubby behind until she was squealing and clutching at the grass in her ecstasy. After a while, he pulled free, leaving his cock standing proud and glistening with both girls' juices as he moved quickly behind Natalie. Eloise watched the expression of expectant pleasure on the little maid's face, only to see it turn suddenly to surprise. With eyes open wide and mouth round and gaping, Natalie gasped, gritted her teeth and then once more gasped.

'Ow, Christian!' she exclaimed and Eloise realised that the big man had penetrated not the maid's vagina but her anus.

For several minutes Natalie was buggered, Eloise watching in fascination as the expression on the maid's face changed, from surprise to resentment to an abandoned, breathless bliss. Knowing only too well the powerful effect of having a cock in her rectum, Eloise could only watch and wonder if she herself was going to be served the same way. Christian had never buggered her, yet this was a new game, and one that relied on her acceptance of his lust. Still toying with her clitoris, she felt her pleasure rise at the thought of being buggered, especially while her two maids watched it done to her.

With her sense of anticipation nearing breaking point, she waited. Christian stopped, and began to withdraw from Natalie's anus. The maid was left panting on the grass as the footman moved to Eloise. She stuck her bottom up, acquiescent to the penetration of her anus, only for Christian to reach forward, grab her by the hair and pull her sharply back towards his cock.

'Suck it clean, Eloise,' he snarled, his voice deep and commanding, entirely different from his normal tones of deference and respect.

She felt a catch in her throat, but her mouth was opening of its own accord and she knew that she could not resist. Gaping wide, lost to everything but her wanton pleasure, she accepted his cock in her mouth and began sucking. He laughed at her response, still holding her hair as her mouth filled with the rich tang of her own juices mingled with those of Peggy and Natalie.

Eloise could hear Christian's laughter as he fed her his erection, a triumphant, scornful sound that mocked her inability to control herself in her ecstasy. Then he grunted, jerked and sperm flooded into her mouth, adding a salty, male flavour to the tastes of bottom and cunt.

'Swallow, you little whore,' he demanded, forcing his penis to the very back of her throat.

Eloise gulped, felt the slimy come at the back of her mouth, then gagged as the head of his cock was jammed down her throat. Again it jerked, his come erupting deep to fill her gullet and the rear of her nasal cavity. He pulled back as she began to choke, withdrawing his penis to leave her gasping for air with his sperm bubbling from her mouth and nose. Deliberately, carefully, he wiped his cock on her cheek and nose, then stood up.

She sank forward on to her face, then rolled slowly over, her hand all the while working against her vulva. With her eyes tight shut and her mouth wide she began to make the final touches that would bring her to orgasm. As the pleasure built in her head, her mind focused on the way he had taken her, making her kneel between Natalie and Peggy with her buttocks in the air, just like the maids, just as if she were no more than one more common serving girl. He had fucked her, then Peggy, buggering Natalie purely for the pleasure of subsequently putting his cock in her, Eloise's, mouth. She had accepted it, all of it, sucking on his cock and masturbating, hearing him call her a little whore as he came in her mouth.

Eloise came, her head ringing with Christian's derisive, knowing laughter as her spine arched in orgasm. Her tongue was sticking out, slimy with his sperm as she hit a long drawn out peak of shame and ecstasy. Then, at the very peak of her bliss, she opened her eyes, finding Christian standing above her with his half-limp cock in his hand. His face was set in an amused sneer and she realised what he intended even as the urine sprayed from the end of his cock.

A great burst of outrage welled up in her as the hot fluid splashed on her breasts, but she was still coming, too far gone in the ecstasy of orgasm to do anything. As he moved his cock to splash urine on her vulva, she felt another peak rising. His laughter increased in volume as her back arched once more and she screamed out her pleasure as the pee splashed over her furiously rubbing hand.

Three more times her cries rang out, echoing in her own ears as she rode her orgasm. Then she was coming down, subsiding limply on to the grass, indifferent to Christian slowly playing his stream of pee over her naked body. She no longer cared. Her degradation was complete. He had urinated on her while she was coming, in just the way she had so often treated Natalie. Even when he let the last trickle fall into her open mouth, she made no resistance, merely pushing her tongue up to make it bubble up over the side rather than down her throat.

Lolling her head to the side in utter defeat, she found the two maids kneeling together, their arms around each other as they watched their mistress in open-mouthed disbelief. Suddenly the reality of what she had done crowded in on Eloise, replacing her blissful, trance-like state with anger and indignation. Sitting quickly up, she spat out her mouthful and looked round for Christian, trying to find words to express even a fraction of the depth of her outrage.

He was already by his horse, one foot in a stirrup.

'I came only to deliver a message,' he said, calmly meeting her furious gaze, 'so I'll not stay, for all the possible pleasure of another go in your well-fleshed cunt, or perhaps up your fat backside.'

'I . . . I'll have the skin from your back for that!' she yelled, finding her voice.

'I'm sure you would,' he laughed, 'but you won't. You are no longer the Demoiselle of St Romain; you are merely another over-eager slut. The assembly has declared all ancient privileges void and all men equal, and so you no longer have the power to order me whipped, nor any other. But this is all beside the point. I have come to say that your father has decided to flee the Château. He is making for Switzerland, and if you wish to join him you had best hurry. Myself, I am for Dijon and the army, so farewell.'[2]

He pulled himself quickly on to his horse and sped away, leaving Eloise sitting splay-legged and speechless on the grass. Her mind burnt with the shame of her own submission; yet, as his final words sank in, her anger took on a new target. Her father was fleeing, leaving lands that the family had held since 1015. The act was unthinkable, a betrayal that made Christian's appalling insolence and her own helpless delight in being used by him utterly insignificant.

Forcing the servant from her mind, she rose and hastily made her way into the pool. As she washed her body clean, she became set and grim, determined firstly to attempt to stop her father leaving and secondly, if that failed, to ensure that the Château remained tenanted.

Eloise stared down from her window in the corner tower of the Château St Romain. Beneath, where the village ended and the road to Auxey began, a knot of artisans and peasants had gathered, principally *vignerons* and field hands, but with a student and the local cooper among them. Their attitude was very different from the obsequious stupidity she regarded as typical. Instead they were surly, aggressive and anything but respectful. Having already felt how once obedient servants could change at the hands of Christian, she had no illusions as to their loss of proper obedience. Nevertheless, to her mind they were more misled than malicious.

The student, Emile Boillot, and the cooper, Jean Faugres, were the ringleaders, and those who Eloise blamed for what she saw as the subversion of her people. The former was the son of a villager and fresh from the turmoil in Paris. A thin body with an overlarge head and a small mouth that seemed permanently pursed all went to add to what she considered a most distasteful whole. He claimed to be something called a Jacobin. The word meant nothing to Eloise, yet he seemed to derive considerable self-importance from this fact. It was also he who had brought the proclamation of the assembly in Paris to the area. A letter he carried, and of which he made much in his speeches, authorised him to impose the requirements of both the Declaration of the Rights of Man and the bill that abolished feudal law. Indeed, it was the presentation of a copy of this letter to Christian at the Château gates that had made her father finally decide to flee.

The latter was a huge, bearded man, a Touranjou by origin and someone who in Eloise's view had never shown adequate respect to her family and, more importantly, to herself. Indeed, she strongly suspected that, had it not been for the penalties attached to such an act he might well have forced his sexual attentions on to her. Unlike Boillot, Faugres carried no official sanction for his actions, yet his sheer size and force of personality had always made him a leader in the village.

For the week since her father's departure, the two men had been haranguing the villagers on a daily basis, something that Eloise had done her best to ignore. Now it was impossible, because instead of choosing to assemble by the church, they had done so at the base of the cliff, directly below her window. Furthermore, the remarks of the student Boillot were directed at her and becoming increasingly exaggerated and increasingly personal.

'. . . there she sits in her castle,' he was saying, 'surrounded by luxuries – dresses worth what a good man might make in a year. She eats from golden plates while we eat from clay! Do you know that she has a maid merely to wash her feet?'

There was a pause, with the crowd's murmurs reaching up to Eloise. Stung by his words, she nevertheless held herself back, allowing Natalie to continue brushing her hair as Peggy finished buttoning her dress. Boillot's words hurt, the more so for being lies. She had no idea what a peasant might earn in a year, but was sure it could not be so little as the value of a mere dress. Nor was the family's plate gold, being plain silver for the most part. As for the maid, she had never had more than three personal maids, and more usually two, which she had always regarded as an example of her father's meanness towards her. Yet all of this was irrelevant. She was a de la Tour-Romain, they were peasants – her position was a right, a right given and sustained by God over some eight hundred years.

'But her gluttony is nothing to her lust!' Boillot's voice rang out once more from below. 'She is depraved beyond words, as you all doubtless know! Who has not heard of the pool in Chaume woods, where she bathes naked and indulges in the most vile of acts with the wanton trulls who serve as her maids? Who has not heard the screams of pain and howls of unnatural pleasure that ring nightly from her window? So debauched is she that she would offer her arse to the devil himself for the sake of a new indulgence!'

The final remark was greeted with gusts of laughter as well as sounds of disgust, bringing the blushes to Eloise's cheeks. Finally, her resolve to pretend that nothing was happening broke and she leant out of the window to confront her tormentors. Boillot, directly below her, had failed to notice, but others had not.

Someone shook a fist at her, the wife of a *vigneron* and a woman who Eloise had always regarded as meek and respectful. Taken aback by the naked anger of the crowd, Eloise steeled herself, determined to put a stop to the foolishness by sheer élan.

'People of St Romain,' she said in a loud, clear voice

that betrayed nothing of her inner turmoil, 'I, the Demoiselle de la Tour-Romain, stand before you as your rightful liege, to whom your fealty is owed, both by the law of France and by right of birth. For near eight hundred years my family has held this land, land given by Robert the Second, and held by right not just of man but of God.'

None responded, the entire crowd gaping up at her silently, a reaction that Eloise took as representing suitable submission to her authority.

'Now, hear my words and then return peaceably to your homes,' she continued. 'This foolishness has gone far enough. It is no more than the wicked chattering of lawless men, born of jealousy and hatred for all that is true and right. I know that at heart you are good people, with respect for your natural superiors and obedience to the will of God. Yet you are simple, and easily led by the voices of unrest and greed. Rest assured that the discontent of the country will be subdued, as it has been so often before when the disaffected have attempted to suborn the will of the good people of France. When this happens, I will speak for you and plead clemency. For now, all I ask is that you bring in those tithes currently due and put into custody those who seek to poison your minds, the traitors Boillot and Faugres. That is all, my people; now, return to your homes.'

She finished and stood looking proudly down, expecting them to start dispersing. None moved, and every eye was on her, including that of Emile Boillot, who had turned his face up to meet her eyes.

'Your power is gone, Citizen Delatour,' he said evenly. 'The days of the *ancien régime* are gone. Leave now, and I will give you leave to join your father in Switzerland, else who knows what will become of you?'

'You? Give me leave?' Eloise retorted in disbelief, her anger rising both at his words and at the refusal of the crowd to obey her very fair and reasonable speech. 'This is my home, Boillot! Do you hear? Mine! As is your own filthy hovel and every stick and stone in this village. You have no right!'

Boillot laughed and turned his face to the crowd. Her anger burst like a bubble in Eloise's head, suffusing her with a red rage that had her tearing at the casement. Turning into the room, she looked around in fury, ignoring the cowering Natalie and Peggy, who were hovering uncertainly in the doorway. Casting about for a suitable missile, her eyes lit on the chamber-pot, a heavy lidded vessel of green and white china. Seizing it up, she turned back to the window and, with an incoherent scream of pure fury, hurled it down.

The student looked up at her scream, his expression of righteous indignation turning to horror for an instant before the chamber-pot struck. There was a crash and a clatter of pottery shards on stone, the thud of Boillot's body as he fell face forward to the ground, and then silence.

For a moment, the crowd remained silent, and motionless: then, as one, they gave vent to a great roar and began to move up the road in the direction of the Château gates.

Jean Faugres stood before the gates of the Château St Romain, great legs set apart and arms raised to the furious crowd before him.

'Yes,' he boomed, 'she shall have justice, the same justice that she and her family have given us! As Emile taught, we must have an equal law for all, with a tribunal of citizens to try her. That is the way of justice!'

Angry murmurs greeted his remarks, but as many nods of agreement. For some time, he had been attempting to impose his control on the villagers and was at last succeeding.

'Besides,' he continued, 'with deliberation, we may decide a fate suitable for her crimes, may we not?'

This time, the shouts of agreement outnumbered those of dissent and he knew he had won. Eloise would now be incarcerated in the Château until it could be decided what to do with her, a period that he was sure would give him ample time to satisfy the lust he felt for her, a lust that until that moment had been as illusory of fulfilment as it was overwhelming.

On the cliff top above St Romain, Peggy Wray cowered, shivering among the scrub. At the moment when the crowd rose in anger, her will to remain by Eloise had broken. Running frantically from the Château, she had made the shelter of the scrub moments before the crowd had erupted from the road. Running blindly, indifferent to scratches and bruises, she had reached the far side of the bowl of cliffs, only then stopping to look back, full of guilt and fright. She had watched Jean Faugres harangue the crowd and divined that Eloise was to be incarcerated in the Château, yet she had no illusions about her mistress's eventual fate.

Flushed with guilt and sorrow, with tears running freely down her plump cheeks, she turned and made for the west, her mind full of vague thoughts of seeking help.

Four

Charles Finch paused at the park gate, made a final adjustment to his hat and strode on. His appearance, he knew, was immaculate. From highly polished boots to well-brushed tricorn hat, every detail was exactly as he wanted it. Griggs, his valet, had lavished over an hour of attention on the *ensemble* before Charles had left the house, and the hall mirror had shown the effort to have been well worthwhile. His coat, Charles felt, was particularly fine, cut sharply back at the hips after the French fashion and of a delicate powder blue that matched his eyes. This, he felt, gave him a dashing look that set him aside from the dozens of other smartly dressed young gentlemen who had also chosen the bright autumn morning to promenade in St James's.

Running his eye over the park he noticed the corpulent figure of Squire Robson, whose imposing bulk made him unmistakable even at a distance of some four hundred yards. Beside him – tiny in comparison – was another figure, evidently female and also winsome, even in the distance. Charles increased his pace, making for the pair with as much speed as he could without seeming inelegant. As he drew closer, the girl proved yet more appealing: slight, pretty, with red hair and a mischievous look. Her dress, a confection in green and black, also suggested expensive tastes and libertine morals, implying that she might make a companion of more than polite interest.

'Ah, Cuthbert, how d'you do?' Charles announced himself, deliberately using Squire Robson's hated first name in the opening sally of his attempt to transfer the girl's attention to himself.

'Charles, good morning,' the squire replied without any great friendliness. 'Charles Finch, Miss Judith Cates. Miss Cates, Charles Finch, a rake who you would fare well to avoid, given his penchant for sodomy – of girls, of course.'

Charles hesitated, taken aback by the sheer flagrancy of his adversary's retort. Squire Robson was not known for the subtlety of his wit, yet to make such a remark in front of a woman was boorish, even by his standards. Charles felt the blood rise to his cheeks as he struggled for a suitable rejoinder. Then, while still searching for words, he realised that Robson had made an error. Judith Cates – far from blushing or lifting her chin in distaste, as might have been expected – was looking at him with a sly, coquettish smile.

'Are you a libertine then, Mr Finch?' she enquired.

'I confess it,' Charles responded easily, his confidence rising in the face of her open flirting.

'Then it seems that you and I have a common interest,' Judith continued, her attention now fixed firmly on him.

'Humph, um. . . you must excuse me,' Robson put in. 'I must be at Le Roy's coffee house within the hour. Judith, Charles.'

The Squire left with a polite nod to each of them. For a moment, Charles watched, amused by Robson's ponderous but somewhat hurried walk. Sensing that he was in the presence of a better man, Robson had evidently decided to do the decent thing and leave the field clear. With a gay smile, Charles turned back to Judith Cates, offering his arm. She took it without hesitation and he began to lead her back in the direction of his house.

His feelings of personal satisfaction rose as they crossed the park. Twice he passed male friends, and both gave him glances that contained a great deal of envy and also respect. Judith Cates was also stimulating company, flirting with an easy, impish manner that had his cock hard in his breeches by the time they reached his front door. Griggs greeted them with a polite but knowing bow, and Charles ushered his new conquest upstairs, deeming it pointless to delay matters.

'Let us take a flyer first, my dear,' he suggested as the door closed behind them, 'and then perhaps something more leisurely.'

Judith giggled and bent to grip her skirts by the hem, taking hold of both dress and petticoats in one. Turning her back to him, she flipped them up, revealing her legs and bottom.

'Do I suit your taste, Mr Finch?' she asked as she looked back archly.

'Indeed you do,' he answered, already struggling to loosen his breeches.

She giggled at his haste, holding her pose and taking a shapely ankle in each hand with her feet planted some way apart. Charles freed his cock, pulling at it as he admired her charms. Her figure was slender, yet her pale-skinned buttocks had a pleasing fullness and stood high and proud. The lips of her cunny were clearly visible between her thighs, a small, plump apricot of flesh richly grown with hair as ginger as that on her head. More hair grew in the groove between her bottom-cheeks, yet the area around her anus was clear, as if freshly shaven. The bottom-hole itself was a pale pink star of puckered flesh, tempting him with thoughts of the tight, warm sheath it would offer.

Stepping forward, he placed his cock between her buttocks and reached beneath her belly for her cunny, drawing a squeal of pleasure from her as he began to rub at her clitoris. She sighed and squeezed her buttocks

67

around his cock, making a hot, fleshy tube in which he began to rub as he continued to fondle her. Looking down, he could see the shaft of his cock pressed firmly between her cheeks, half immersed in her flesh, the head protruding from the top of her cleft, swollen and purple.

Knowing that he would come in moments, he pulled back and put his erection to her cunny. The entrance was moist but not fully open, its firm flesh embracing the head of his penis as he pushed for entry. Judith gave a strained little grunt and reached back, pulling her buttocks apart to stretch her sex. His cock slid in, its full length easing into her until his belly met her buttocks.

He took hold of her hips and began to push, his senses swimming with the feel of his cock in her vagina and the sight of her slight body with her beautiful bottom naked and spread, emerging like the centre of a flower from the petals of her upturned dress and petticoats. She had taken hold of her ankles once more, making a tense bow of her body. The scent of her arousal was strong in the air, mixing with her perfume.

'Not in me, Charles,' she panted as his thrusts became harder.

Despite being on the edge of orgasm, he complied, pulling back and laying his cock down between her bottom-cheeks even as it gave its first jerk. For an instant he considered trying to force the head into her unlubricated back passage, using her anus as a safe receptacle for his semen. Then it was too late as his cock spasmed in his hand, spraying come liberally between her buttocks. He pressed his cock to her anus as the second spurt arrived, the come pooling in the tight pink hole as he drained himself slowly over her. Greased with his come, her ring opened, his cock pressing a little way in as he finished off. For a long while he kept it there, the tip of his cock nestling in the semen-filled bowl of her anal opening.

Judith groaned as he briefly popped his cock into her anus. The sensitivity of his flesh was close to unbearable, with her ring like a loop of fire around the neck of his penis. He sighed deeply, content in his experience as his cock slowly lost its hardness, yet anticipating more. Finally he pulled back, leaving Judith's anus as wide and wet as her vagina.

'My turn; put candles in me,' she sighed, her voice hoarse with need.

Pausing only an instant to get his breath back, Charles hastened to comply. While he prided himself on his ability to bring a girl quickly to heat, the strength of Judith's passion was impressive, and he had no wish to fail her. Striding quickly to a candelabrum, he pulled three thick candles free of their cups. Turning, he found that Judith had crawled on to the bed and was waiting with her bottom pushed up high and her knees well apart.

It was a magnificently wanton position, displaying every inch of her ready charms and leaving the open holes of her vagina and anus pointed at the ceiling. Her hand was back between her legs, cupping her mound, with one finger rubbing at the centre in a lazy, sensual manner. Swallowing hard, he walked quickly across to her and placed a candle to the entrance of her vagina. She sighed as it went in, but made no increase in the pace of her masturbation. Charles placed the second candle by the first, easing it into her vagina.

'In my breech, Charles,' Judith sobbed, 'and then light them.'

'Light them?' he queried even as he pulled a candle free of her vaginal opening and put it to her anus.

'Yes, then watch me in my pain,' she demanded. 'Come, do it!'

Charles prodded the base of the candle to her anus. The sticky hole everted as she pushed out to accept penetration, the candle sliding up easily to leave Judith as a beautiful but deeply rude double candlestick. Charles felt his cock stir at the sight, a response to Judith's wanton, exotic display. He also felt a trace of guilt, which came from the knowledge that the idea of her pain excited him.

As he struggled to light the remaining candle, she began to speak, her words coming soft and urgent.

'Let them burn, Charles,' she said, 'and watch me in my shame and suffering. Then, if you are able, take me again, at the finish.'

'I shall; by God, I shall,' he answered.

Once ready, he applied the flame to the two candles that protruded from the openings of Judith's body. Her masturbatory motions, which had not altered from their leisurely pace while he was lighting the candles, now became more urgent. He watched, enraptured as the first beads of wax formed on the candles, translucent drops that shimmered in the yellow light, growing, swelling with heat, until one gained more weight than it could support. It fell, landing on the bare skin around the girl's anus. She gave a little, sharp cry and bucked her bottom, dislodging another drop, this time on to the soft wet lips of her vulva. Again she cried out, and her finger began to move faster on her clitoris.

Charles, still holding the third candle, began to play with his cock. It stiffened, responding to the sheer power of female sexuality exhibited before him. In front of him Judith was writhing, squealing with the pain of the wax and wriggling her tormented backside, which only resulted in shaking more drops on to her tender skin. Her cunny and anus were spotted with wax, also her fingers, the richly grown hair of her sex and the pale, quivering globes of her buttocks. Her distress was evident as she cried and sobbed out her pain, yet so was her pleasure as her fingers worked harder and yet harder on her clitoris.

With his cock once more stiff in his hand, Charles

stood and moved behind her. Poising his candle over her bottom, he angled it, sending a double drip of wax on to the very peak of one white buttock.

'Yes, do it, you bastard!' Judith responded. 'All over me, on my nates, in my cunt!'

Charles continued to stroke his now erect cock as he began to drip wax over her buttocks. There was now a ring of congealed wax around the stretched-out ring of her anus and her cunny was full of it, caught between her soft pink sex lips and pooled in the hole around the candle. She was crying, but her masturbation had become frantic, a display of rude passion that had his member itching for her body.

Reaching forward, he pressed down on her back, forcing her buttocks into yet more conspicuous display. The motion put her cunny uppermost of her openings and sent a splash of wax on to the ridge of bare skin between vagina and anus. Judith squealed and bucked, but got back into the position he had wanted. She was weeping openly and sobbing hard as he put his hand back on his cock and moved his candle directly over her cunny. A drip fell on her inner lips, drawing a yet sharper cry of pain from her.

'That's right, in my cunt, in the middle,' she gagged as her rubbing motions became yet more frantic.

He lowered the candle, holding it over her frantically jiggling clitoris. A drop began to form, bulged out and fell, to splash directly on to the hard white bud of flesh. Judith screamed and Charles saw her vagina clench hard on the intruding candle. Again she screamed, both vagina and anus contracting fiercely. The candle in her bottom rose, momentarily stretching the skin of her anus up under its burden of wax. Then it began to squeeze from her bottom-hole, the emerging shaft glistening with the come he had put into her. As her orgasm hit its peak she arched her back, then began to buck frantically, spraying hot wax across her buttocks.

A drop caught Charles's cock, making him cry out at the sudden, hot pain. The candle in her anus began to topple and he quickly blew at it, extinguishing the flame even as her orgasm began to subside. Following suit with the other candles, he watched her sink slowly down from her climax, her vagina still filled with candle, her bum-hole gaping and red.

Charles's cock felt like a poker in his hand, iron hard and desperate for a sheath of soft girl flesh. Judith was sobbing and shivering, snivelling out her emotions into the bedcover with her bottom still pushed up and ready. Unable to contain himself further, Charles pulled the candle from her vagina and mounted her, quenching his burning cock in the velvet smooth wetness of her inside.

Judith sighed, allowing his weight to press her down on to the bed as his cock filled her. He kissed her neck and began to hump, feeling the firm globes of her bottom squash out against his belly as he sank into her. She sighed, a happy sound more of contentment than passion.

For a long while he rode her, bouncing on her little round bottom while his need to come rose slowly within him. She remained quiescent throughout, accepting the pleasure of his penis inside her perhaps more as an act of submission than of need. Only when the increasing urgency of his pushes signalled the approach of orgasm did she speak.

'In my breech, Charles,' she sighed gently. 'Sodomise me.'

Happy to grant a favour, he withdrew, placing his hand down to catch his cock as it came free. It was slippery with her juice and felt ready to explode as he placed the end to her anus. She pushed out, everting her bum-hole in what was evidently a practised motion. The head of his cock popped inside and she gave a little grunt at the effort of accommodating him.

'That's my girl,' he said, in response, and began to

force his erection slowly up her bottom, rocking back and forth to reduce the pain of anal entry and increase his pleasure at the act of putting his penis into her.

It went up slowly, Judith giving grunts and sighs as she struggled to accept him. Finally it was all in, the full length of his cock sheathed in the warm, soft flesh of her rectum. He began to bugger her, bouncing on the pillows of her bottom with his cock wedged firmly into the central hole.

Judith was quickly clutching the bedcover as she began to lose control of her body. Yet the turmoil of her senses made no difference. He was in her and on top of her, his cock up her bottom, regardless of her feelings. She was screaming again by the time he came, lost in a welter of ungovernable impulses centred on the penis invading her rectum.

She heard him grunt and felt the jerk of his cock inside her. Then there was the slimy sensation of his sperm around the opening to her bottom and she knew he had come in her rectum. His cock stopped moving and her senses began to return to order, leaving her gasping and shivering beneath his weight, sore, used but thoroughly satisfied.

For a long time they lay together, bathed in an intimacy born of their mutual depravity. Finally Charles rose and ordered basins of scented water and a bottle of champagne from Griggs.

Later, after an afternoon spent in bed and two more encounters of a less frantic and more conventional nature, she decided that the time had come to leave. Charles accepted without fuss, demanding only that she leave a garter as a memory of their pleasure.

'I did not say that there would not be another occasion,' she said cheerfully as she tossed the embroidered green ribbon to him. 'Merely that I had to go. As you may have realised, I am a kept woman and,

73

for all the ease of life thus afforded, I am obliged to make at least a show of punctuality.'

'A fine attitude,' Charles replied, struck by the incongruity of the fat, jolly Squire Robson keeping such a fiery mistress, let alone indulging in the undoubtedly perverse pleasure she had demanded. 'But tell me, the trick with the candles?'

'It is called the burning shame,' she informed him casually as she adjusted her remaining garter, 'and is generally used as a punishment applied by bawds and pimps to slovenly or insufficiently wanton girls. It has the advantage over the cane or strap of not leaving evidence of its application. Personally, I find it most stimulating.'

'So I see,' Charles rejoined.

Later that day, Charles was seated in his favourite chair at the club, smoking and sipping cognac while he enlarged on the delights of Judith Cates to a group of his friends.

'Judith Cates, you say?' Conrad Clive enquired as he joined the group. 'By God, but you're the cool one, Charles!'

'Why so?' Charles laughed in response.

'Well, the last fellow who tupped her ended up being put to bed with a shovel. He's a devil of a fellow, you know.'

'What? Bertie Robson? Nonsense!'

'Bertie Robson?'

'Yes, he was squiring her in the park this morning. I pinched her from him, easy as wetting the dunnegan! I don't suppose you're going to tell me he'll call me out, are you? Come, come, Conrad; he's no more than a buffoon!'

'No, no, not Bertie; she barely knows Bertie. She's Jinks's mistress. You know, Captain Jinks, fellow who was mixed up in that duelling scandal last year. Fellow called Hunt, it was. The seconds tried to patch it up, but Jinks wouldn't have it – shot Hunt dead. That was over her.'

'Oh, hell!' Charles breathed.

Henry Truscott stood before the doors of Truscott Hall, his hands thrust deep into his pockets. To every side, the Devon countryside sparkled with the dew of a bright autumn morning, while the sky was an unbroken vault of blue. In the distance a phaeton was approaching, a new and expensive-looking vehicle, which drew black looks from Henry. The passenger in the phaeton – he felt sure – would prove to be his brother Stephen, whose presence in Devon could only serve to curtail already limited pleasures. With his expression growing ever more morose, he watched the vehicle draw nearer, only for the driver to raise his hand in a familiar wave as it swung into the carriage sweep. Then, as the man alighted, Henry's face suddenly brightened in recognition of his friend Charles Finch.

'Charles!' Henry declared. 'You are a welcome sight indeed!'

'I heard of your mishap,' Charles Finch replied, 'and felt that you might appreciate a little company. Besides, in London, at present, I must watch my every pace.'

'Trouble?' Henry enquired.

'A mere splash in a pisspot,' Charles rejoined. 'I tupped a girl, only to find that she's the mistress of that loon Jinks. He wants a duel, but I'll be damned before I'll give him the satisfaction.'

'A duel? Over a mistress?' Henry sniffed disapprovingly.

'So I must be sure not to allow him the opportunity of making a challenge,' Charles continued, 'and where better than here?'

'How true,' Henry responded wistfully as he looked round over the green and peaceful scenery that spread away in every direction.

For a moment both men stood looking out over the Torridge valley, a view of small, steep-sided hills, wooded coombes and fields, decked in shades of green and the richer colours of autumn.

'So what sport is to be had?' Charles inquired after a moment.

'Rather little,' Henry replied. 'Father still drinks well enough, but he was ever a buck for the fashion and is currently following that set by our good King. At his age, he can neither ride nor wench, though he'd be game enough to try the latter, were not half the girls in the village likely to be his daughters. No, Charles, I am glad of your company, for I was never a great one for my own.'

'I shall endeavour to liven matters up,' Charles promised, 'but do you not admire my perch-high phaeton?'

'A splendid conveyance,' Henry admitted.

'Splendid indeed,' Charles added, then addressed the man who had been the other occupant of the phaeton. 'Run her round to the stables, Griggs, and roust out old man Catchpole. He's the steward.'

'Thinking of carriages, and so forth,' Henry said as they turned to walk into the house, 'there are a couple of light shooting gigs in the stable and an idea for a most amusing diversion occurred to me the other day.'

Henry stood back to admire his work. Beside him was the lake, with its surrounding path of pressed gravel. On the path stood two shooting gigs, light, two-wheeled vehicles designed to be drawn by a single pony. Both gigs were fully rigged, yet no pony was in evidence. Instead, a giggling girl stood harnessed between the shafts of each, naked but for her boots and an ingenious system of rope, chain and leather that acted as tack. The girls were Jane and Anne Silcott, local milkmaids.

'Jane is always game,' Henry remarked to Charles

Finch in an undertone, 'and can generally persuade her sister to dalliance. But a word of advice – by all means, press a hog into her cunny at the end, or bribe her for more speed, but do not make the offer plain. These are not London girls, and resent any implication that you might expect to pay entry to the buttock ball.'

'I see,' Charles replied. 'One could wish that all wenches were so.'

'To work, then,' Henry continued in a louder tone. 'First, I feel, we should test the mettle of our mounts and cast lots to see who gets whom – for the first run, at least.'

Jane Silcott smiled and lowered her eyes as the two men walked round to her front. Henry smiled back, pleased by her nervous excitement and ready acquiescence to his suggestion that she and her sister be harnessed to carts. As one of his earliest partners, she was a girl on whom he knew he could always rely for sport, yet in nearly ten years she had never lost the air of unwitting naughtiness that had so appealed to him as a lad.

Her figure was classic Devonshire – tall, well built with fleshy, cream-fed breasts and hips that supported a firm, meaty bottom. A tumble of brown curls surrounded a face that was both pretty and bold, with a smooth, pale complexion.

Henry reached out and took Jane's breasts in his hands, feeling their satisfying weight as she cast her eyes further down and gave a little moan of pleasure. Her large, pinkish-brown nipples were already erect, standing proud and resilient as he ran his thumbs over them. With her wrists strapped to the gig, Jane could do nothing but stand obediently still as her breasts were fondled. As his cock began to stir in his breeches, Henry stopped, standing back and making a gesture to Charles.

'Be my guest,' Henry offered, indicating Jane's breasts.

'Most kind,' Charles responded and stepped forward to take over the exploration of the girl's chest.

Henry moved to Anne, the elder sister and less familiar to him. She gave a shy giggle as he reached out and touched a nipple, tweaking the little bud of flesh quickly to erection. Her body closely resembled that of her younger sister, with just a touch less meat on her thighs and bottom. This was not true of her breasts, which were fat globes of pale flesh, surmounted by large nipples of a delicate rose-pink. Cupping one in each hand, Henry squeezed them together and buried his face in her soft cleavage, drawing a delighted giggle from her.

Satisfied for the time being with his exploration of her breasts, he moved round to take a handful of chubby bottom. She gave a pleased squeak as he squeezed, then a sigh as his smallest finger traced a line up the cleft of her cheeks. Leaning forward, he kissed her, first on the cheek and then on the lips. She responded, immediately eager, their tongues meeting as he reached up to touch her breasts. For a moment, he allowed a finger to stray between her legs, brushing against the silky fullness of her vulva. She shivered and her kisses became more urgent, to which Henry responded before pulling quickly back.

'Drive Anne, if you have no objections,' he addressed Charles. 'She's a game romp and has been chucking since I've been down, but Jane's been my bob-tail many a year. She'll not be wanting when the time comes to dance the gig.'

'Fair enough,' Charles responded from where he was still busy caressing Jane's breasts. 'Shall we say three laps of the lake at a bull a lap?'

'Be bold, Charles,' Henry responded. 'A guinea a lap, and a dozen of claret to the first to bedew his pony's rump after the finish.'

'Taken!' his friend answered joyfully, moving over to Anne.

78

'Fine,' Henry replied. 'We'll mount 'em kneeling, still in the shafts.'

Adjusting the leather straps that made up Jane's bridle, Henry readied his mount, finishing by slipping the improvised bit between her teeth and taking her reins in his hand. She knelt to allow him to mount, briefly presenting him with a yet finer view of her magnificent rear. She rose once more and, with a final pat to her bottom, he mounted the gig. Low-slung and designed for working the rough paths of the estate, it was the ideal vehicle to which to harness girls, a chance feature of design that had given him the idea in the first place.

Taking up his carriage whip, he gave Jane a playful cut across the buttocks, drawing a surprised squeak from her and leaving a long red line across the white flesh of her seat. He was enjoying himself immensely, and felt a fresh surge of excitement as he admired Jane's naked back, legs and bottom. To the side, Anne looked equally fine, harnessed and ready to run, with her plump bottom quivering slightly in her eagerness.

'D'you see the crow down over the village?' Henry called.

'Ah . . . no,' Charles replied. 'My eyesight's not what it might be.'

'No matter,' Henry replied. 'We start when it pulls level with the steeple. Anne can see it, I'm sure.'

A nod from Anne gave her agreement. Henry turned quickly, looking to where the crow could be seen flapping slowly towards where the church steeple rose above the trees of the valley. At that moment, Anne started forward, Jane following her sister's lead an instant later.

'Damn! Run, girl!' Henry exclaimed, seeing that Charles had taken an advantage at the start. 'Come on, dam't! A hog if you take the first lap!'

'A bull and a quart of cider if you do!' Charles yelled

to Anne in response, simultaneously using his whip on the girl's bottom.

The girls raced forward, both aiming for the narrow bridge that crossed the stream which fed the lake. Henry allowed Jane to do the work, holding her reins loosely and only occasionally applying his whip to her bottom. Charles, by contrast, was endeavouring to steer Anne as if she were a real horse and also using the whip with enough vigour to make her skip and falter.

Henry began to gain, Charles realising too late that his technique was inappropriate for a human pony. The bridge approached, the girls neck and neck, aiming straight at the impossibly narrow gap.

'My road!' Charles yelled.

'Damned if it is!' Henry called back.

Anne, faced with the immediate prospect of the lake, slowed, only for Jane – the younger and meeker of the two – to do the same. Charles immediately seized his advantage, turning Anne in and bumping the gig on to the bridge as Henry and Jane came to a stop.

Henry swore as he tried to back the gig up and his rival sped merrily away around the lake. Once back on the level, Jane began to gain, but too slowly, allowing Charles and Anne to take the first lap. Smarting under his friend's derisive hoots and demands for his money, Henry gave Jane a couple of firm cuts across the fullness of her bottom, then once more gave her her head. With her pride stung and her bottom smarting, she gained more ground, pulling up to Charles's rear as they reached the point where the lake bordered the lawn. She was running sweat, her hair a wet mane that hung halfway down her back, her buttocks glistening and damp, her thighs as red as the trio of welts that decorated her bottom. Her breath was also coming hard, although less so than that of her sister.

Sensing victory, Henry applied the whip once more to Jane's bottom, calling out encouragement and steering her on to the lawn. She obeyed the command, her muscles straining as she drew level and then ahead of Anne. Henry raised his hat to Charles and began to free the fastenings of his breeches as the gig bumped over the edge of the lawn and back on to the path.

They took the second lap and were still increasing their lead. Henry now had his cock free of his breeches and his attention focused firmly on Jane's bottom. It was a sight guaranteed to bring blood to the best-used penis. Her cheeks bounced and wobbled as she ran, the hard muscles of years of churn carrying showing beneath the softness of yet more years of feeding on the products of her labours. Four deep pink lines decorated the dancing, sweat-slick globes, evidence of the whipping she had received.

With his cock hard in his hand, Henry went into the third lap. Behind him, Charles was yelling encouragement to Anne and Henry turned to gauge his lead. The other gig was some twenty yards behind. For a moment, he watched Anne's heavy breasts bounce with the motion of her running, feeling his cock twitch in anticipation at the sight.

'A last round, then it's Moll Peatley's gig for you!' he called to Jane, who renewed her efforts at his words.

Laughing as he focused once more on his pony's beautiful rump, Henry sat back to complete the lap. Charles was working himself into a fury, but – as Henry had known from the start – Jane was the younger girl and so was made to do most of the work at the dairy. Triumphant, he crossed the line and quickly ordered her to her knees.

She sank down, kneeling with her bottom stuck out for entry, her head hung in exhaustion and her wet hair down around her face. Holding his cock in one hand, Henry jumped down from the gig and settled himself behind her. In front of him her bottom was a fat globe of wet, gleaming flesh, criss-crossed by welts and parted to show her anus, which pulsed with her deep, even breathing.

Resisting the temptation to force his cock up her bottom, Henry put it to her vagina, which proved every bit as wet and excited as he had hoped. He slid in easily, his balls bumping on her pussy even as Charles pulled Anne to a halt beside them.

'I'm not beat yet, Harry!' Charles declared as he dismounted hurriedly.

Henry turned, to find Charles flourishing a fully erect cock over Anne's naked buttocks. Yet, instead of sinking his penis into the glorious target beneath him, he kept it in his hand and began to masturbate furiously over Anne's upturned bottom. Ignoring his friend, Henry concentrated on the feel of his erection in Jane's vagina. Her flesh was tight around him, her big buttocks pressed warmly against his belly, wobbling like great, pink jellies with each of his thrusts. She was moaning loudly and clutching the shafts of the gig, clearly desperate to get her tied hands to her breasts and cunny but unable to do so.

At the thought of her helpless ecstasy, he started to come, jerking his cock free of her vagina at the last instant to spray come across her naked bottom, as the bet demanded. Sighing deeply, he drained himself over her, splashing her back and the cleft of her buttocks, before finishing by rubbing his cock against her wet, half-open bottom-hole.

'My game!' he gasped as the last of his sperm oozed out into the hair around her anus.

'Great heaven, Henry! Is there no depth of depravity to which you will not sink?'

Henry turned sharply at the words, Jane and Anne each giving a squeak of alarm as he did so. Behind him, standing on the path that led up to the house, was his brother Stephen. Further back, two other figures stood, a tall, black-visaged man and a small, curvaceous woman.

His witty retort to his brother died on his lips as he realised the identity of the other visitors. One was Captain Jinks, the man determined to call Charles out. The other was Peggy Wray, who he had last seen while he was being rolled naked into a gutter in a lane near Gray's Inn.

Henry took a swallow of claret and hunched forward over his plate. Dinner – which he had been looking forward to earlier that day – was proving anything but the jolly experience he had intended. The idea had been to invite Anne and Jane and take pot luck of the kitchens while making the best of the cellar. His father, he knew well, would have made no objection – he would have enjoyed the spectacle with what remained of his senses. It would have been a fine evening, and doubtless would have ended with the two milkmaids naked and game for whatever entertainment they might have devised between them.

As it was, the arrival of Stephen, Peggy Wray and Captain Jinks had put an entirely different complexion on things. Stephen's presence alone would have put a stop to any frolics, as he would have been shocked at the thought of even allowing two mere milkmaids to dine at the house, much less with the family. He had even had some pause before deciding that it was acceptable for Peggy to join them rather than eat in the pantry with the Catchpoles and Charles's man Griggs.

Each guest now added their own element of misery. His father sat at the head of the table, mumbling vaguely about a land dispute that had been settled shortly after Henry was born. Stephen was to the old man's right, attempting a ponderous analysis of the current political situation, to which nobody was paying more than cursory attention. Charles Finch, who might normally have been among the gayest of any company, sat picking morosely at his food with a look of both misery and terror on his face.

Peggy Wray was little better, evidently uncomfortable in the company and also sulking because of Henry's flat refusal to return to France with her. Once the reason for her appearance had been made clear, he had reacted with astonishment and then outrage. The idea that Peggy should expect him to risk life and limb to come to the rescue of Eloise de la Tour-Romain struck him as a piece of temerity so gross that, for some while, he had found himself bereft of speech. When he had finally managed to put his feelings into words, she had burst into tears, reacting as if Eloise had been his dearest friend rather than a woman who had not only utterly humiliated him but was also responsible for his indefinite confinement in Devon.

To make matters worse, both Stephen and Captain Jinks had taken Peggy's side, the one stating that the family honour demanded that Henry help, the other calling his courage into question in more general terms. The fact that Peggy had convinced them both that Eloise was actually enamoured of Henry had made matters worse, but he had stuck to his refusal to have anything whatever to do with the scheme. At the end, he had walked away in a blind rage, while Stephen stood looking noble and disapproving and Captain Jinks comforted a distraught Peggy.

It was Jinks who put the final touch to the sour atmosphere of the dinner table. Learning that Charles had made for the west, he had put two and two together and followed with Stephen, determined to pursue his argument. He was an arrogant, spiteful man who had already killed one opponent in a duel and severely wounded another. An excellent swordsman and a fine shot, he had little to fear from the languid and short-sighted Charles, who had been forced to accept the challenge but now stood in fear of his life. As a final

84

touch, Jinks's manner at the dinner table was anything but that expected of a man on the eve of a duel. Instead, he was the merriest of the company, cheerfully relating his deeds during the conflicts at the start of the decade. This boasting was evidently intended to awe Charles and impress Peggy, and Henry's sole crumb of satisfaction came from the failure of the latter intention.

Deprived of genial company and smarting from Stephen's remarks on his courage and morality, Henry was doing his best to punish the indifferent claret that Stephen had ordered up from the cellar. The drink, however, did little to soothe him, serving instead to inflame the lust that had been denied full expression by Stephen's untimely interruption of the pony-girl race, to stoke his sense of outrage at the sheer impudence of Eloise and Peggy and to increase his resentment of the insufferable Captain Jinks.

Claret passed on to Barsac, and Barsac to port, Henry becoming increasingly drunk, Stephen increasingly tedious, Charles increasingly white and Jinks increasingly loud. With Peggy's departure from the table, the Captain's boasts became less valorous and more bloodthirsty, also more evidently directed at Charles Finch.

'. . . always aim for the body,' Jinks was saying as Henry took the decanter of port from him. 'It takes longer for the wretch to die, but there's less chance of a miss, which is the important thing . . .'

'Damn you, Jinks!' Charles suddenly roared. 'Let's get this thing done then, now, outside!'

'Very well,' Jinks replied coolly. 'Barkers or cold steel?'

'Pistols,' Charles answered in a thin, tense voice.

'Generally quicker that way, I suppose,' Jinks responded. 'Who will act as my second, then?'

'Damned if I will,' Henry growled.

'Then it seems I must,' Stephen said quietly. 'Yet,

while I appreciate the demands of honour, you should know that I consider this behaviour both morally deplorable and uncivil, given that you are a guest in my house.'

'Well, needs must when the devil drives,' Jinks responded cheerfully. 'I've brought my irons down, so, when you are ready, gentlemen?'

Preparations were rapidly completed, with the men then assembling on the lawn. The clear, warm autumn day had given way to a cold night, and the grass was bright with frost reflecting the light of a moon that had just passed the full. Together, Stephen and Henry loaded the pistols, Henry's cold anger rising to hot fury as Jinks continued to brag and to torment Charles.

'. . . I suppose you imagine that the bad light will be to your advantage,' Jinks was saying as he sipped the glass of port he had brought out with him. 'You may be sure that the moon provides a sufficiency for my aim, yet it is a shame, in a way, for I do like to see the faces of the men I kill.'

Henry watched Charles take a swallow of brandy. His friend's face was deathly pale, taking on a spectral quality in the moonlight. Charles's hands were shaking too, spilling the brandy as he tried to return the stopper to the flask.

'Don't let him ruffle you,' Henry advised. 'You're shaking too hard to aim.'

'This . . . this isn't really my thing, Harry,' Charles stammered. 'Dam't, I mean, I'm no coward, you know that, Harry, but . . .'

'No coward? Ha! I've seen more courage in a bantling whore,' Jinks jeered from where he was standing some ten feet distant. 'You're nothing but a coxcomb, Finch, and not fit for the company of men.'

'Oh, the hell with this,' Henry retorted, cocked the pistol he had just finished loading, brought up his arm and depressed the trigger.

The roar and flash of the gun shattered the night, dying to leave a scene of absolute silence. Captain Jinks lay prone on the ground, his face still set in the malicious sneer he had worn at the instant of Henry's firing. Beside him, Stephen Truscott stood, his front blackened with powder and his mouth and eyes open in dumb shock. Charles Finch was likewise silent, staring wordlessly at the prostrate body of his tormentor. It was Stephen who finally broke the silence.

'My God, Henry, you've killed him!' he blurted out.

'Well, yes, dam't. I mean, what else was I supposed to do?' Henry retorted, immediately defensive now that the cause of his rage was gone.

'My God!' Stephen repeated.

'Besides,' Henry continued as he began to regain his wits, 'I couldn't let him shoot Charles. I'm still owed my dust from the pony-girl race.'

'For the sake of God, how can you joke at a time like this?' Stephen demanded. 'Don't you realise you could hang?'

'I doubt it,' Henry answered. 'Juries never convict in such cases, but I suppose it might be awkward.'[3]

'Awkward!' Stephen flared. 'What of me, then? What of my reputation? Dam't, man, they might even name me as an accessory!'

'No, they won't,' Henry replied coolly. 'Fellow was never here, was he? You dropped him outside Exeter, after you left the coach road. Nobody saw you, did they?'

'Yes, they did; Miss Wray, she was with us all the way,' Stephen answered hotly, 'and Father knows, and the Catchpoles and Charles's man!'

'All of whom may be relied upon for their silence,' Henry continued. 'Here's Father now, though, and Peggy.'

'What? What happened?' Henry's father demanded as he approached.

'Henry has shot Captain Jinks, Father,' Stephen replied in a hushed tone.

'Jinks? Shot him, you say?' the old man responded. 'Good, beastly fellow.'

'I was saying, Father,' Henry put in, 'that Captain Jinks never in fact arrived here.'

'Nonsense,' his father replied, 'there he is on the ground. You shot him yourself . . . Oh, I see; ah, yes.'

'Too many people know,' Stephen interjected miserably.

'I think not,' Henry retorted. 'We can rely on the Catchpoles and I imagine Griggs is sound; Charles pays him well enough, to be sure. What of you, Peggy?'

Peggy Wray turned to him, her face white and drawn but her voice betraying no more than a slight catch.

'I have no idea of what might have become of the gentleman,' she said softly, 'as at the time of his disappearance I was in Plymouth, escorted by Mr Henry Truscott, and on the way to France.'

Henry stood by the rail of the *Stewer's Hope*, a small, broad-beamed schooner carrying ingots of Cornish tin to the French port of St Nazaire. Luck had been with them, both during the frantic moonlit ride to Plymouth and the discovery that a ship which intended to touch in Biscay was due to leave within hours. Henry had used the time to visit the forge run by Todd Gurney and dragoon his friend into joining them. The big man had accepted, spurred by the prospect of pay and memories of Eloise's body.

Now the city was falling astern, showing as a cluster of grey houses slowly vanishing behind the flank of Mount Edgecombe as the ship veered to the west. At the horizon was the grey-green loom of Dartmoor, highlighted by the occasional reflection of the morning sun from water or damp rock.

Henry's feelings were mixed, his annoyance at being

88

dragooned into Eloise de la Tour-Romain's schemes tempered by a rising excitement at having escaped the monotony of the Torridge valley. He felt sure that the dangers of France were exaggerated, and probably had no more founding than previous rumours of revolution, in both that country and his own. What apprehension he did have was greatly allayed by the companionship of Todd Gurney rather than that of Charles Finch, whose offer of assistance Henry had politely, but firmly, declined.

For the death of the late Captain Jinks, he felt nothing but satisfaction, coupled with a mild unease that the story might somehow prove harder to cover than they had anticipated. Yet Jinks had left London on the spur of the moment, joining Stephen only when he discovered that Charles had fled for Devon. The last point at which strangers might be able to identify the missing man would be the coaching house outside Exeter in which they had spent the last night of their three-day journey. Even then, with the connivance of all concerned, it would be impossible to prove that Jinks had not died in a formal duel. With luck, all would be well, and without it Henry had at least escaped his immediate difficulties.

The feel of a hand closing softly on his arm broke his reverie. He turned to find Peggy smiling warmly up at him, her pretty, rounded face showing a look of happiness and sympathy that surprised him.

'You are gallant, Mr Truscott,' she said softly. 'For all your bombast and pretence of callousness, you are gallant at heart. How many men would have risked the gallows to save a friend?'

'Any decent ones, I would hope,' Henry replied. 'Charles and I have been friends since we were boys. What sort of a man would have stood by and done nothing? Jinks would have killed him, of that you may have no doubt.'

'I am sure of it,' Peggy replied, resting her head against his shoulder.

'You seem mighty friendly for a wench who sold me down the river,' Henry responded, still piqued by her behaviour but finding her physical presence hard to resist.

'I did only what I had to do,' she responded, 'and, should it please you . . .'

She broke off, leaving Henry to divine her meaning. A great weight of resentment still existed in his mind, yet everything about her stirred his lust. Besides, what better way was there to work out his ill-feeling than during sex with her? Finally, there was the matter of the half-crown he had paid her, for which he did not feel he had had full value.

'So, then, my cabin?' he said after a pause.

Several of the deck hands gave amused or jealous glances as he led her across the deck. The *Stewer's Hope* was moving slowly, with no more than a slight roll, making for light work and idle time. A good half of the crew was on deck, all of whom had been more or less attentive to Peggy. Henry favoured them with a smile and a polite inclination of his head as he ducked below.

Quartered in a tiny cabin towards the bow of the vessel, Henry had no illusions about the privacy of his situation. Indeed, the idea of the crew knowing that he was having sex with Peggy appealed to both his vanity and his sense of exhibitionism. That she was evidently either unaware or uncaring amused him, and added to his desire to make a show. How to do it was a more difficult problem, the tiny cabin offering none of the luxuries that made for enjoyable lovemaking.

'I don't fancy the floor,' he remarked as he closed the door behind them. 'Perhaps I should lie in the hammock and you may ride rantipole?'

'As you please,' Peggy deferred.

They moved together, Peggy returning his kisses with

a sensual eagerness that quickly banished the last of his resentment. With her soft body in his arms and her hand squeezing gently at his crotch, it was impossible to feel anything other than an overriding need for her. As his cock grew, he worked at the buttons of her dress, snipping them open with one expert hand while he kneaded a large breast with the other. A sudden lurch of the ship caught them unawares and Henry was forced to make a grab for a beam, successfully steadying himself as the giggling Peggy gripped on to him. Laughing, they climbed into the hammock, with Henry beneath and Peggy mounted astride him.

'Turn around and clutch the beam,' Henry suggested as another lurch almost unseated her.

Peggy obeyed, turning with some difficulty to present her rear to him. He swallowed, admiring the way her big bottom filled out her skirt, making a plump ball of blue cloth. With the hard bump of his cock pressed against her cunny, he could feel the heat from her and the urge to be inside her suddenly became overwhelming. Grabbing her bottom, he began to pull the material up, Peggy giving a squeak of alarm and then a delighted giggle at the passion of his assault.

Lifting her bottom, she allowed him to tug her skirt and petticoats out, leaving him with a fine view of her well-upholstered rear with the pouting lips of her cunny poised directly over the bump in his breeches. Working quickly on his buttons, he freed his cock, quickly tugged it to full erection and then placed the head against the wet opening of Peggy's sex. She lowered herself, sliding down his shaft so that he felt himself slowly engulfed in warm, moist flesh.

'Hold your dress up,' he groaned. 'I need to see your bottom.'

Peggy giggled and did as he had asked, using one hand to keep her skirts high and the other to steady herself against the rolling motion of the ship. Taking a fleshy bottom-cheek in either hand, Henry began to bounce her on his erection, watching his cock slide in and out of the taut pink entrance to her cunny with each push. Peggy moaned and stuck her bottom back, improving the angle of his cock inside her and also his view between her buttocks. With the two magnificent globes of flesh in his hands and the sight of her full vagina and stretched anus, he felt the first stirrings of orgasm inside him.

Her bottom-hole was stretched wide and slightly everted, a ring of damp pink flesh that invited a finger or even a cock. Tempted, he determined to bugger her, put the idea aside as being better for a more leisurely occasion and then once more changed his mind as he remembered that he had already paid for the privilege.

'Go up a bit,' he grunted and pushed to help lift her bottom clear of his penis.

It came out and he took hold of it, rubbing the head in the wet mush of her vulva and drawing a long moan of ecstasy from her.

'Oh, yes, Henry, like that, like that,' she sighed. 'Make it happen to me, Henry.'

He continued to rub, watching her buttocks and anus for the tell-tale contractions that would signal the onset of orgasm. Sure enough, as her moans rose to panting squeals, her muscles started to spasm, including her bum-hole, which opened like a little pink flower to show a dark centre. Henry waited until the very peak of her climax and then pulled his cock abruptly back, pressing it to her anus as the tight hole once more opened in involuntary response to her orgasm. The head of his cock popped inside, drawing a squeak of alarm from Peggy.

'Henry!' she managed in breathless protest, but it was too late; the head of his penis was past her ring and locked in place up her bottom.

Catching her quickly by her hips, he prevented her

from lifting herself, instead easing himself a little deeper up her bottom.

'Oh, Henry, must you?' she sighed.

'Yes, I must,' he answered, 'there's something about a big bottomed girl that just cries out for sodomy, and they don't come much bigger bottomed than you, my dear.'

Her only answer was a resigned groan, which he took for acceptance if not necessarily agreement. Tightening his grip on her hips, he pulled down on her, watching his cock force an entry to her back passage. Several times he was obliged to lift a little to lubricate the next section of his shaft. Each push drew a little grunt from Peggy, and he noticed that she had hung her head, presumably in shame. He also noticed that she kept her skirts high, ensuring that he was rewarded with the best possible view of the cause of that shame. Without lubricant it took a lot of pushing, but finally his erection was wedged fully up her behind, straining the anus out into a tight circlet of taut pink flesh around the very base of his shaft.

'God but that feels good,' he panted and began to bugger her.

Peggy's noises became louder and more urgent as she was bounced up and down on his cock, an abandoned, dirty show of helpless response to what was being done to her. It was also a response that delighted Henry, especially at the thought that her coarse, animal grunting might be heard by the sailors above the creak of planking and cordage. Several knot-holes studded the crude walls of the cabin and, as he quickened his pace inside her, he looked back, thinking to sense a sudden movement by at least one of the holes. Delighting in the thought of the crew watching him bugger Peggy, he let go of her hips and pulled her plump cheeks wide apart, providing the hidden onlookers with a prime view of her anus straining around his intruding cock.

93

For a long while, he kept his pushes short and regular, delighting in the feel of having his cock squeezed in the velvet soft flesh of her rectum. Peggy continued to respond with grunts, which then became joined by little whimpering noises. Finally, she let go of her skirt and put her hand down between her thighs to masturbate.

'Wanton trollop!' Henry laughed, drawing a sob from Peggy that combined both pleasure and misery.

He began to pace himself, concentrating on the sight of her naked bottom and the way her anal ring was alternately sunk in and drawn out by his cock. His orgasm began and he slowed, breathing evenly as her masturbation became more urgent and she began to bounce herself on the rigid pole of flesh in her rectum. She began to sob, then pant, little urgent noises of total surrender to the pleasure of being buggered. Then her anus tensed around his shaft and he knew she was coming. With a flurry of frantic pushes, he took himself to his own orgasm, feeling his sperm erupt inside her as the powerful pulsing of her bottom-hole drew it out of his cock. She screamed his name, loud and urgent, then slowly began to sink down as he too finished his orgasm in her bowels.

'You bastard!' she managed weakly as she slumped back on to his body.

He made no response, despite several more or less witty rejoinders that came to mind. Instead he cuddled her to him, allowing his cock to slip slowly from the sticky embrace of her anus. Her mind, he knew, would be a flood of emotions, centring on shame, not for allowing him to sodomise her, but for taking so much enjoyment in the dirtiest of acts. Yet the ease of entry made him certain that he had not been the first to bugger her and he was confident of her ability to come to terms with her own wantonness. For a long time he held her, only kissing her and pushing gently at her shoulders when having her weight on top of him began

94

to get uncomfortable, due to the string of the hammock cutting into his flesh.

'That was a great treat,' he said evenly as she dismounted. 'May I assume that such delights will be a regular feature of our coming journey?'

'You may,' she responded very quietly.

'Splendid,' he answered, 'but you should have said so in the first place, then I'd have come along happily.'

'Until we reach St Romain, I want you to be mine,' she said, suddenly passionate.

'Why not after?' Henry queried.

'Eloise will want you,' Peggy informed him resignedly. 'She is in love with you.'

'Well, she's got a damned funny way of showing it!' Henry exclaimed.

'She is; she calls your name in her sleep, and sometimes when . . . when . . .'

'When she plays with herself, you mean. Don't worry, I know just what you girls are like. I'll grant she fancies me, then, but love? Hardly, I think; else why leave me boot-blacked in a freezing alley? Mark you, I've known women with some damn peculiar tastes in my time – the piece Charles had, for instance, apparently she likes a lighted candle stuck up her arse, or so he said.'

'You don't understand. Eloise hates herself for loving you. She is too proud to admit to loving any man, least of all you, after the way you treated her.'

'Teasing little baggage deserved it, have no doubt. Anyway, who's to say I'd rather have her than you?'

Peggy responded with a weak smile, as if to imply that he was only humouring her. Dipping a cloth into a half-full bucket of water on the floor, she pulled it up and lifted her skirts to dab between her legs. Henry watched, fascinated by the process and entirely indifferent to the slight blush on her face. When she had dropped her skirts back into place, she took a fresh rag and wetted it before giving him an enquiring glance.

'Going back to your earlier remarks on my character,' Henry remarked as he lay back in the hammock. 'It is true that I am fond of Charles, and I'd not like to see him put below ground by Jinks, nor any other. Yet I cannot lay claim to absolute altruism. The late Captain Jinks, you see, was one of those unpleasant types who actually enjoy killing their fellow men. So I had to do it, or sooner or later he'd have got to me, probably when —'

'Do not so deprecate yourself, Henry,' Peggy interrupted softly as she applied the wet rag to his genitals. 'You need not hide your true nature from me.'

'Oh, I have no illusions as to my qualities,' Henry continued casually, 'nor as to my failings – or what society deems failings. I am every bit the rake and ne'er-do-well my brother paints me but, for all that, I'll not desert a friend. No, the thing with Jinks – as I was about to say – is that eventually he'd have been bound to discover that I'd bedded his little sister.'

Five

Henry Truscott, Peggy Wray and Todd Gurney came to a stop and peered out from among the scrub at the edge of the cliff they had reached. Below was the bowl of green that surrounded the village of St Romain, with the Château perched on its crag at the far side. If the disaster which Peggy had feared had happened, then no sign was evident. Indeed, the scene appeared to Henry to be one of rustic calm. Briefly, he wondered if the whole trip was not in fact some fantastic wild goose chase dreamt up by Eloise de la Tour-Romain.

Yet the turmoil of the French countryside had been fully evident during their long journey.[4] Docking at St Nazaire, they had taken passage on a barge as far as Tours and then hired a skiff. At first the countryside had been quiet and Henry had wondered what all the fuss was about. Then, as they left the Vendée for Anjou and then Touraine, they had come across increasing signs of unrest. Twice they had seen the burnt ruins of châteaux and, of those that remained, many were evidently deserted. The attitude of the people was also very different from what Henry had been used to on his previous visits to France. Fawning, indifference and miserable sulking had been replaced with disrespect, suspicion and surly antagonism, none of which had made the journey any easier. Nevertheless, by carefully avoiding trouble, they had arrived at Cosne unmolested.

Travelling east across the Bazois, they had found the land emptier and its people increasingly bucolic, to the point where once more it seemed as if nothing was amiss. On arriving at the small town of Châtillon, they had even taken rooms at an inn, spending their first night in real comfort since leaving St Nazaire. Throughout the journey, Henry had been sleeping with Peggy and also taking whatever other opportunities for sex with her were offered. Being of a generous nature and keen not to cause bad feeling among the party, he had also persuaded her to give Todd Gurney the pleasure of her mouth and breasts each evening. In their room at Châtillon, this took on a new dimension, with the two men sharing her eager cunt, once her excitement had broken down her reserve.

From there, they had struck out across country, keen to avoid Autun, which Peggy held to be a hotbed of insurrection. After three days of tramping through the dank black woods and precipitous valleys of the Morvan, they had arrived at the cliff above St Romain, wet, footsore and exhausted, but filled with elation at having made the journey. Now they watched the Château, each seeking evidence of Eloise's presence.

'No pennons fly from the Château,' Peggy said in a small voice. 'Perhaps we are too late.'

At her words, Henry realised that what he had taken for an air of peace was in fact one of desertion. Not only were there no pennons flying from the towers and spires of the Château, but no smoke rose from its chimneys and no movement whatever could be seen in its environs. Feeling something of a heel, he placed his arm around Peggy's shoulders.

'Nonsense, nonsense,' he assured her, with a good deal more confidence than he felt. 'She'll be there, slinging chamber pots and bullying the menials with all her normal fire.'

'See, sir,' Gurney spoke up, 'two men in brown

lounge by the gate to the left of the castle. They've no soldierly look to them, neither.'

'There you are, you see,' Henry addressed Peggy. 'Why bother with a guard if nobody is within?'

Her only response was a faint sniff, which Henry chose to take for agreement.

'So we need to get in,' he continued. 'Any ideas?'

'Walk round the cliff top, knack their jolly knobs together and take the dells while they're not in their senses,' Gurney suggested.

'A plan that has the merits of simplicity and practicality,' Henry replied, 'but falls short on two counts. Firstly, they might resent the treatment and they appear to have muskets. Secondly, I would speculate that the approach to the Château is visible from at least part of the village. No, we need to get close without being recognised for who we are.'

'A priest might pass,' Peggy suggested.

'I didn't think the church was any too popular,' Henry objected.

'Only for their greed and ungodliness,' she answered, 'the faith of the peasants is strong and a simple priest would still command respect.'

'Perhaps,' Henry admitted reluctantly, 'but could I pass? What do I know of papist mummery? Where would we get a cassock or whatever it is they wear?'

'You could pass in a cowled habit, such as friars wear,' she insisted, 'and as for their ways, simply walk slowly with your head bowed, play with your rosary and mutter in Latin.'

'I know only dog Latin,' he answered, 'and besides, where would I get the habit?'

'Simply mutter words,' she said.

'As to the friar,' Gurney cut in, 'we find one, knack his jolly knob on a tree and pinch his habit.'

'And how many friars have we seen since leaving Châtillon?' Henry demanded.

'Two, maybe three,' Gurney admitted.

'To our right is the hamlet of Orches,' Peggy put in. 'In the rocks above lives a hermit.'

'For every objection you have an answer,' Henry sighed. 'So be it, then; let us accost this hermit and hope that he is not unduly lousy.'

Henry's confidence waned as he approached the Château. After visiting the hermit of Orches and divesting the unfortunate man of his habit, they had returned to the top of the cliff. Henry had taken his leave of the others with a sense of bravado and mischief that at the time had been in keeping with his real feelings. Indeed, the venture seemed no more dangerous than had his youthful forays to seduce the village girls. The guards, he was sure, would prove to be merely local bumpkins, no more capable of distinguishing him from a real priest than of telling his English accent from a regional French one, and probably drunk at that.

On closer approach, they proved to be large, active-looking men with unpleasantly intelligent expressions, for all their evident boredom. Suddenly it seemed inevitable that they would penetrate his disguise, yet both were looking at him and it was too late to back out. Mumbling vaguely under his breath and toying nervously with his rosary, he came closer, hoping vainly that they might simply allow him to walk past.

'What are you about, Father?' the larger of the two enquired as Henry drew level.

The deference in the man's voice immediately boosted Henry's confidence. For all his presumed revolutionary ambitions, here was evidently a man who retained a life-time's respect for the cloth. His sense of his own innate worth returned as quickly as it had fled.

'I come to take the confession of the wicked hoyden de la Tour-Romain,' he answered boldly. 'I have travelled far, from the city of Nantes, at tales of her depravity. I understand that she is within.'

'That she is,' the guard replied, 'and as to her wickedness, you may expect to be some hours inside.'

The other guard laughed, Henry giving a muttered blessing in dog Latin and continuing on his way, buoyed by the ease with which he had passed.

'And don't forget to ask her about the pool in Chaume woods,' the second guard called after him, showing less reverence but no more suspicion than the first.

No challenge followed him as he crossed the space between gates and the door of the Château, nor was there any resistance as he pushed it open and stepped within. Looking from side to side, he wondered where Eloise would be, and wished he had thought to ask Peggy for a description of the interior of the Château. One route seemed as good as another, and he crossed the hall to a tall doorway.

This proved to enter on to the chapel, a grand, ornate structure that seemed to him entirely in keeping with his preconceptions of both Eloise's family and of the Roman Catholic church. Glancing around, he wondered whether any of the smaller ornaments might serve a more useful purpose transferred to his purse. They would, after all, undoubtedly be looted by the local populace if he did not rescue them first. Just as he was about to examine a promising-looking chalice, he caught the sound of a footstep, turning to find Eloise herself coming into the chapel.

'Father?' she queried.

Henry turned, intent on making a dramatic revelation of himself as her saviour, then stopped abruptly.

'My child,' he said gruffly. 'I have come to take your confession.'

Without a word, Eloise stepped towards a double chamber of dark, intricately carved wood, entering it and closing the tall, narrow door behind her. Henry followed suit, entering the other half of the confessional and seating himself on the bench within, entirely at a loss for the orthodox form of the Roman Catholic confession, yet still full of the sense of mischief that had brought him so far. Also, a number of suspicious-looking stains within the confessional hinted at a somewhat dilute reverence among its usual occupants.

'Speak, my child,' he ventured, still talking in a low, guttural voice to disguise his accent.

'Forgive me, Father, for I have sinned,' Eloise's voice came quietly from beyond the screen.

'Confess your sin, my child,' Henry continued.

Eloise paused and Henry realised that he had said the wrong thing, but then her voice started once more, quiet and urgent.

'It has been a month since my last confession, Father,' she said.

'That is a long time, my child,' Henry replied, taking a guess that such a break would be unusual.

'Life has not been as it might, Father,' Eloise answered, the apology evident in her voice raising Henry's confidence.

'What then of your sin?' he enquired.

'I have had many wicked and unworthy thoughts . . .' she began.

'Carnal thoughts, my child?' Henry interrupted, keen not to get into the minor and undoubtedly extensive details of Eloise's sins.

'Some . . . yes . . . many,' she admitted.

'And have you acted upon these?'

'Yes.'

'In what way, my child?'

'I . . . I . . .'

'You may speak freely. God, remember, already knows what is in your heart.'

'I . . . I have had carnal knowledge of my maidservants,' Eloise answered in a tiny, quite voice.

'Indeed?' Henry replied. 'And what form did this take?'

'I . . . I am shamed to say, Father,' Eloise replied.

'You must do so,' Henry responded firmly.

'It has happened many times since my last confession,' she stammered. 'Once, I became aroused while beating my lady in waiting and commanded her to . . . to perform an act upon my person with her tongue. The night my father left, I took her into my bed, for comfort, but that night and each night since we have had knowledge of each other's bodies.'

'This is a most grievous sin, my child,' he replied in the most dolorous tones he could manage. 'Confess the full depth of your shame, that your soul may be relieved of its burden. I fear you must be specific.'

'I . . . I have taken her in my arms and had carnal thoughts while kissing her full on the mouth,' Eloise continued haltingly. 'I have kissed her breasts and known pleasure in the act, to which she has also responded in a like manner. She has kissed me in that most intimate of places and I have done likewise, both in the hours of night and in the light. We have even come together head to toe, with our lips pressed to the private persons of one another . . .'

Henry swallowed. His cock was a hard lump within the confines of his breeches, straining for release and the satisfaction of Eloise's body.

'. . . and a yet darker sin have I committed,' she continued from behind the carved screen. Following the beating I mentioned, I had her kiss my posteriors, and . . . and between them . . .'

'You made her lick your breech?' Henry gurgled.

'No, Father,' Eloise responded hastily. 'She did it willingly, for pleasure . . .'

'That is worse!' Henry exclaimed. 'Filthy, lascivious harlot! Worse still, if it was done without darkness to cover your shame, was it?'

'Yes, Father,' Eloise replied as Henry gave in to his lust and lifted his habit.

'How so?' he demanded as he pulled his penis free of his breeches.

'I . . . I bade her lie on the floor,' she went on, 'and I made to curtsey over her face, settling myself upon her so that she might kiss my posteriors. She put her lips to one and then the other, and so great was my pleasure that I could not resist settling myself full upon her mouth, and . . . and . . .'

'And she kissed your fundament?' Henry asked weakly, his head swimming with the image of Eloise sat proudly on Natalie's face, the maid's tongue pushed well into her mistress's anus. 'For how long?'

'Many minutes,' Eloise admitted. 'I could not stop myself for the pleasure of it, and . . . and . . . touched myself as she did it . . .'

'Enough,' Henry gasped, unable to hold himself any longer. 'There is only one remedy for this . . . this abhorrence. You must be beaten, and immediately. Now step outside and kneel before the statue of the Sainted Denis with your skirts lifted high enough to screen your head, that you may absolve your sins.'

'Beaten, Father?' Eloise quaked.

'Beaten!' Henry responded firmly, only with an effort maintaining his mode of speech.

'But, Father,' Eloise wheedled, 'might I not redeem myself in some more seemly manner? Perchance I would benefit from a penance more suited to my sin?'

'No!' Henry stated flatly. 'You are to be beaten, and beaten as God intended, with your posteriors naked!'

'But, Father!' Eloise pleaded. 'I would be willing to give much, even the comfort of my mouth, even . . .'

'Silence!' Henry thundered.

'Yes, Father,' Eloise squeaked and an instant later Henry heard her rise.

Holding his furiously erect cock in one hand, he forced himself to count to fifty, then rose and pushed open the door of his side of the confessional. Eloise, as ordered, was facing towards a niche in which stood the statue of the patron saint of France, the only one he had been able to remember on the spur of the moment. She was kneeling, face down, with her head and body entirely concealed beneath a sea of cloth. Skirt, petticoat and no less than three underpetticoats had all been thrown up, leaving her lower body naked except for her stockings, garters and slippers.

Henry swallowed, his eyes locked on the enchanting sight, taking in her dainty feet and slender calves, her well-formed thighs, the flare of her hips from her tiny waist, the full bulge of her pear-shaped bottom, the rich growth of red-gold curls between her legs, the puckered brown ring of her anus and, best of all, the juicy, swollen lips of her cunny. She was shivering slightly, and waiting so obediently in her exposed position that Henry wondered if her real priest wasn't in the habit of taking advantage of her. Indeed, both the stains in the confessional and her responses suggested that he was.

Transferring his cock to his left hand, he pulled his belt from his breeches. Flipped over and doubled up, its weight felt satisfying in his hand, the buckle providing a convenient grip while the remainder formed a thick strap some two feet in length – ideal for taking to a girl's bottom. Standing somewhat to the side, but not far enough to deprive himself of the full view of Eloise's charms, he hefted the belt and brought it down hard across her quivering buttocks.

She jumped and squeaked as her bottom bounced under the belt, then began to mumble something in Latin, her words tumbling out with an urgent haste. A broad red stripe now decorated the whiteness of her bottom, running down at a low angle over the fleshiest part of her cheeks. Henry licked the dryness from his lips and again lifted the doubled belt, then brought it down with a ringing smack across Eloise's behind. Again she bucked and squeaked, then went back to her prayer with even greater fervour.

Resisting the urge to plunge his cock into her clearly receptive vagina, Henry went to work on her rear, taking out all the discomfort and alarm of the long journey to Burgundy on the shivering, excited girl who had been the cause of it all. Ten more times he brought the belt down across her bottom, leaving the cheeks criss-crossed with red welts. She was shaking hard, and still praying, while the pleasure of beating her had in no way diminished. Yet as the strokes had fallen and as the sharp cracks of leather on girl-skin had rung out around the little chapel, the visible signs of her arousal had increased dramatically. Her cunny was a soaking, swollen hole, its juices running down into the hair of her mound. At the heart of her vulva, her clitoris stood proud from its hood, like the head of a minute cock. The brown ring of her anus showed clearly in its nest of hair, swollen and puffy with the blood that her confession and the beating had brought to her hindquarters.

'By God, I've got to fuck you, you wanton little baggage,' Henry swore, hurling the belt to the floor and dropping quickly to his knees, 'and now, or I'll spend in my hand!'

He had spoken in English, and loudly, yet Eloise showed no signs of alarm, merely raising her posterior in mute acceptance of penetration. Henry put the head of his cock to her vagina and pushed himself in with a grunt, feeling her wet flesh engulf his length as it slid inside her.

'Oh, yes, Father,' Eloise groaned. 'Enter me, do it in me, deep in me!'

Henry came, feeling his sperm flood into Eloise's vagina as the blissful sensation of orgasm swept over him. She moaned, pushing herself back on to him as he drained his cock into her, then started to mumble broken thanks into the floor beneath her face.

'A pleasure, my dirty little puppy, any time it pleases

you,' Henry puffed in response as he pulled his cock slowly from her vagina.

Eloise froze, then suddenly threw herself to the side and grabbed for the folds of cloth that hid her head. An instant later, her face appeared, the eyes and mouth open wide in amazement amid flushed cheeks and dishevelled hair.

'At your service, mademoiselle,' Henry said, inclining his upper body in a slight bow.

'You . . . you . . .' she managed weakly, then groaned, rolled on to her back and spread her thighs.

'One is obliged, I suppose,' Henry remarked to the detached head of Saint Denis and then leant forward to bury his face in the moist openness of Eloise's vulva.

She came quickly, holding Henry's head and moaning out her passion as she climaxed under his tongue. Even as he was wiping the stickiness from around his mouth, she had jumped up and demanded to know how and why he had arrived.

'How, you know,' Henry responded, 'and I'll not bore you with the details of the long and tedious trip from St Nazaire to here. As to why, I would have thought that would be evident; I am here to rescue you.'

'I do not require rescue,' Eloise replied stiffly.

'What?' Henry demanded, immediately piqued that, instead of being grateful for his presence, she seemed to regard it as a nuisance.

'I mean to stay here, in my home,' she went on. 'These peasants have no right to treat me so, and presently all this will blow over and justice will be visited on the whole treacherous bunch of them!'

'I wouldn't count on that,' Henry replied warmly. 'Indeed, some of the things we saw on the way here suggest precisely the opposite.'

'Ha!' she retorted. 'They can do nothing; they wouldn't dare!'

'Wouldn't they, by God?' he answered. 'Let me tell you something, my girl. In Gien, we heard of an infernal

107

device that lops men's heads off at a single blow. It resembles the old Scottish maidens, yet is said to be the invention of one Dr Guillotine.'[5]

'I know,' she snapped, 'and I also know that he will rot in the lowest pit of hell, along with the rest of them!'

'For God's sake, girl, have some sense!' Henry snapped back. 'Do you want to die? I mean, how old are you – twenty, twenty-one?'

'I am nineteen,' Eloise told him, 'but I am the daughter of a count, and I would rather die the daughter of a count than live in exile!'

'Dam't, it's not worth it!' Henry blustered.

'What do you know of such things?' she sneered back.

'What?' he growled. 'Who in hell's name do you think you are? My family hold land, too, you know – have done since the middle ages, 1209, in fact – so I do know how you feel, but I tell you, it's not worth letting some bastard of a peasant lop your knob off!'

'Ha!' she yelled. 'You have no pride, no feeling! I do, and I'll not leave!'

'By God, but you will!' Henry swore as his temper finally snapped. 'I've not tramped the breadth of this rotten country to go home empty-handed!'

'Never!' Eloise spat. 'Never! This is my home! My land! My people! I'll not leave, not if a thousand spade-faced peasants come to my door! Not if ten thousand!'

'You'll come willingly or you'll come across my shoulder like a sack of potatoes!' Henry shouted back. 'Look, you fool woman, they'll kill you! Don't you understand? They're not your people; they never were! They're a bunch of down-trodden brutes who've finally plucked up the spunk to fight!'

'No!' Eloise screamed. 'It's not so! Not here!'

'Why are there two village men at the gates with muskets, then?' Henry sneered. 'I suppose they're there to protect you, eh? Let me tell you, your lot are no better than the rest: worse than many.'

'No,' Eloise retorted, but more quietly. 'It is not so. They are simple peasants, fired to hatred by bourgeois agitators. Presently all will be calm and my life will begin again, with rides and balls and friends and . . .'

She broke off, sniffed and then suddenly burst into tears, flinging herself on to Henry's chest as her inner terror and hurt broke through her rage. Henry's own anger dissolved on the instant and he put his arms across her back, patting her head and hugging her as she screamed out her pent-up emotion into his chest. For a long time he held her, saying nothing, until her cries faded to broken sobs and finally stilled altogether.

'We had best hasten,' he said gently. 'Does the boy who brings you bread at midday also come in the evenings?'

'Yes, but what are you going to do?' Eloise asked uncertainly.

'Leave everything to me,' Henry replied cheerfully, finding his confidence unexpectedly high from the experience of holding the trembling Eloise in his arms. 'Peggy Wray is here on the cliff top, and my man Gurney. We'll have you out and away to England in a trice.'

'How?' Eloise demanded. 'And what of Natalie, my maid?'

'Essentially the plan is this,' Henry explained, 'a fine compound of my spirit, Peggy's imagination and Gurney's practicality. First we use a rope to lower Natalie from the eastern battlement, also as many supplies as she can carry. She is slight and it should be no great feat. Then, when the boy arrives, I lump his head with a bottle, or some such convenient implement. We unrig him, bind and gag him and dress you in his clothes. I then leave with you close behind, passing the guards, and so away. By the time the guards get suspicious, we'll be well gone.'

'The boy is a surly brute who only dumps his basket

at the door and turns back,' Eloise objected. 'He is tall and lank besides.'

'You must call him inside on some pretext or other. He'd not believe it of you, perhaps, but should Natalie flash her tits for him, I'll be bound he'd come in fast enough.'

'You are mad,' Eloise answered him. 'It's a stupid scheme, bound to failure.'

'Trust to luck,' Henry answered, 'or I could lower you and Natalie both; yet, with all that fine flesh you carry, I'd not trust to the strength of my arms.'

Eloise threw him a dirty look but made no further objection, instead leading the way from the chapel towards the upper storeys of the Château. Natalie was in the bedroom that Eloise and she had taken to sharing, working nervously on a piece of embroidery. On seeing Henry, she was as surprised as Eloise had been, but expressed none of her mistress's doubts or determination to stay. Instead, she threw herself wholeheartedly into the preparations for their escape, frantically gathering supplies while Eloise and Henry argued as to what was and was not a necessity.

Finally, her assertion that she could not possibly travel with less than six dresses came up against her equally blunt refusal to actually carry anything herself. Henry, likewise, was forced to reduce the number of bottles of fine old Burgundy he considered appropriate for the journey by Natalie's physical inability to pick up the bundle they had prepared. Finally, they reached a compromise, with their stores wrapped in two of Eloise's dresses while Natalie wore a third, and the portable wealth of the Château was piled in a heap on Eloise's bed.

As dusk deepened to the point where the east face of the Château was cast into black shadow, Henry and Natalie climbed to the battlements. Soothing her with hearty reassurances of his strength, he pulled what had recently been in service as a bell rope around her chest, looping the end back through the eye. Then, with Natalie tight lipped and trembling, he picked her up and began to lower her down the side of the wall. As his arms took the strain, he found himself profoundly grateful that he was not going to attempt the feat with Eloise, and by the time the maid touched the ground, his muscles were burning with pain and his hands sore and red. The bundle followed, lowered with the same care as the girl to avoid the risk of breaking any of the three precious bottles packed within.

No sooner had Natalie given the gentle tug that signalled that all was well than he saw the light from the supper boy's lantern coming slowly up the road from the village, as he had been told to expect. Pulling the bell rope quickly up, he ran for the stair that led down into the Château.

In the great hall, he met Eloise, dressed in only a diaphanous shift that displayed more of her breasts than it concealed. His smile of appreciation was met with a black look and a gesture at the open doorway, through which the boy's lantern could be seen approaching. Energised by both the tension of the situation and the sight of Eloise *déshabillée*, Henry found himself grinning as he took his station just inside the doorway. The boy would come in, he was sure of it, but there would be only one chance to land a telling blow.

He watched as Eloise stepped forward, her body back-lit by the torch in the hall to show her gentle curves through the shift. It was a sight that Henry knew he would have been quite unable to resist, and, as he had guessed, the boy was no less subject to his natural urges. At Eloise's soft request to enter he came boldly forward, giving a snort of lust and perhaps contempt as he crossed the threshold.

The candlestick in Henry's hand caught the back of the boy's head, sending him sprawling on the floor.

111

Instantly Henry was on top of him, ramming a wad of cotton into his mouth as he set his knee into the centre of his victim's back. Eloise shut the door and no challenge came from the guards at the gate, Henry's elation growing yet stronger at their success.

Dragging their captive down to the cellar, Henry made short work of stripping and then binding him. Just as the work was being completed, the boy groaned and opened his eyes, his expression turning to terror as he saw his assailant.

'Don't worry, boy,' Henry assured him. 'Lie quiet and you'll come to no harm. Eloise, get his farting crackers on, and the coat and boots; with the hat, that should suffice.'

Eloise made no response, but quickly peeled the shift up over her head. Henry chuckled as the boy's eyes grew round at the sight of Eloise in her glorious nudity, then swallowed himself as her breasts lolled forward with the motion of picking up the boy's breeches from the floor.

'You need not watch quite so avidly,' she chided him as she slid a foot into one leghole.

Blowing his breath out, Henry turned to make an inspection of the ranked bottles in the bin closest to him. The slate at the front bore the legend 'Corton – les Languettes 1771', which quickened Henry's interest. However, with the edge of his vision including the entrancing sight of Eloise struggling to pull the boy's breeches up over her thighs, it was hard to concentrate. For a moment, he was torn between the urge to find a corkscrew and that to watch Eloise, but finally lust won out.

He paused from his inspection of the bottles to watch, chuckling at Eloise's efforts to pull the leather breeches up over her well-fleshed bottom. The belt had caught beneath her buttocks, lifting them into chubby prominence and for an instant parting them enough to afford Henry a teasing glimpse of the hair in between.

112

She turned at the sound of his laughter, threw him a burning look and, with renewed force, managed to tug the breeches up over her bottom. With a final wiggle, she succeeded in pulling them up to her waist.

As she fastened them, Henry found himself licking suddenly dry lips. The display of her nudity while she stripped and dressed had been enticing, yet the humour of watching her attempt to put a thoroughly feminine figure into clothing cut for a boy had been sufficient to delay his lust. Now it was different. Eloise's bottom resembled a pear wrapped in leather, the twin spheres beneath stretching the hide out to glossy balls. The breeches were also tight around her thighs, with little ridges of tension showing where the fullness of her bottom tucked down between them, as if they were about to burst. By contrast they were slack at the waist, serving to increase the impression of a leather sack with two heavy spheres inside.

His cock was a rigid pole within his own breeches. With no more than a glance to the cellar stair he had reached forward and seized the twin leather-clad balls in his hands, drawing a yelp of surprise from Eloise. Staggering from the unexpected assault on her rear, she went forward over a barrel. For a moment Henry was presented with a yet more magnificent display of her bottom, with the seat of the breeches stretched taut across it.

A ripping noise signalled the end of the garment's unequal struggle to accommodate Eloise's bottom, the rear seam bursting to show slices of buttock, thigh and the plump lips of her vulva. Henry came forward with an oath, tearing at the buttons of his breeches, and reached Eloise before she could recover her balance.

'Imbecile!' she squeaked as his cock bumped against the soft flesh that was bulging from the rip in her breeches. 'Stop! This is not the time!'

She made a half-hearted effort to get up and then

moaned as his erection found the moist hole of her vagina.

'Idiot!' she managed weakly as her vagina filled with penis.

His only response was a grunt as he began to hump her over the barrel. Each push made her bottom-cheeks bulge and increased the size of the rent in her breeches, until the full length of her cleft was naked and a good six inches of creamy cheek was spilling out to each side. Delighted by the view, he took hold of her buttocks and pulled them open, exposing the well-furred depths between, the dull brown dimple of her bum-hole and the pink ring of flesh where his cock disappeared into her vagina.

'God, but you've a fine arse!' he grunted.

Eloise responded with a resigned sob and lifted her bottom to make it easier for Henry to move inside her. He increased his pace, making her grunt and pant in reaction as his belly slammed into her buttocks. The faint sound of a bell reached them, forcibly reminding them of the need for haste.

'Be quick, you English lunatic!' Eloise panted.

Henry gave a frantic flurry of shoves, forcing his cock to the very hilt with each one. Eloise gasped as the breath was knocked from her body and sprawled across the barrel, losing her balance from the force of his thrusts. She swore incoherently and then he was coming, deep inside her without thought for the consequences.

'We had better get on with it,' he puffed as he pulled out of her. 'You can come to climax later, if you've a need.'

'You are a maniac, an idiot!' Eloise gasped. 'How can you think of sex at a time like this?'

'Presented with your bottom, mam'selle,' Henry replied, 'I would think of sex on the very steps of the gallows.'

'You are like a wilful child!' she stormed. 'You cannot

contain your beastly lust for five minutes! And you are obsessed with my bottom!'

'Only a corpse would not be, and perhaps a backgammon player,' he replied smoothly as he fastened his breeches. 'But come, there's not time for petty quarrels.'

Eloise responded with a snort of utter contempt but grabbed the supper boy's coat from the floor and made for the cellar stairs. Pausing only to gather up a trio of bottles of *les Languettes*, Henry followed. Despite having just had her, the sight of her bare bottom pushing out from the torn breeches as she climbed the stair sent a hot flush to his loins, especially when she stumbled and thrust it to within inches of his face.

In her room, Henry replaced his habit and began to load himself with the treasure of the Château. Finally, so hung about with purses of gold, silver, coins and jewels that he could barely stagger, he was ready. Eloise was likewise heavily laden, the boy's long coat at least partially hiding both her voluptuous figure and her burdens. Yet even with her hair pinned up under his hat, she looked not only distinctly feminine but very unlike the supper boy.

'You need more height,' Henry declared critically, 'and less hip. Also, he moves as if his legs were made of sticks, while your walk has always reminded me of a Covent Garden nun I know by the name of Becky.'

'You know a nun?' Eloise queried.

'Hardly that,' Henry laughed, 'unless a nun might be had against a wall for a threepenny. Becky's a doxy, *putain* to you.'

Eloise opened her mouth to speak but closed it, instead adjusting the hat to hide more of her face.

'It must pass,' Henry continued. 'Merely keep to my right and out of the light. I shall exchange a quip with the guards and will wager that the two mumpheads won't spare you a glance. If they do, then we must trust to my barkers and the speed of our legs.'

115

'I can barely walk, let alone run,' Eloise complained.
'Then let us hope that the need never arises,' Henry replied and stepped towards the door.

Jean Faugres watched the last trace of light fade over the St Romain cliffs. He was in an ill temper, the general unrest and a poor vintage having reduced the demand for his professional services, while the constant presence of his wife and children had made it impossible for him to pay his long-overdue visit to Eloise de la Tour-Romain. This, however, was the night. Marie and the children were with a cousin in Chassagne, a sufficient distance to ensure that he would remain undisturbed. With the old order gone and the fiery Emile Boillot laid up with a cracked skull, his dominance in the village was undisputed. Certainly none would dare dispute his right to visit the Château, nor to question his reasons for the visit.

Pulling on his finest coat and clapping his hat on to his head, he made for the door. The village was gloomy in the last of the dusk, the houses showing as black shapes against a background only fractionally less dull, the occasional candlelit window providing the sole illumination where a householder had failed to close their shutters. Using his stick to guide himself, he set off along streets that had been familiar to him since his family had moved to St Romain. Briefly he moved downhill, and then turned along the base of the spur on which the Château stood, looking up to the outline of its turrets and battlements. Passing the church, he struck up the road to the cliffs, all the while thinking of how he would enjoy Eloise once he had persuaded her that she had no option but to surrender.

For him, her attraction lay not so much in her bounteous curves, nor in her pretty face. Rather it was her very arrogance that attracted him, her automatic assumption of absolute, unquestioning superiority over

116

all not of the nobility and especially, it had always seemed, to him. He knew full well that she would no more consider him as a lover than she would one of her horses or dogs – less so, if some of the nastier rumours that had been circulating were true. To even have suggested dalliance would have resulted in a flogging at the least, and he had never dared do more than steal covetous, lust-filled glances at her when she rode through the village.

Now, things were very different. Her power was gone while, if he so chose, he might be the one ordering her flogged. Indeed, he decided, that was a good idea. Yes, he would have her stripped and tied to the back of a cart by her hands, the local dung cart perhaps. Then she would be whipped through the streets of the village, naked, with not so much as shoes on her feet. She would look a great deal less haughty with her lush buttocks, belly and breasts criss-crossed with welts from hazel wands and plaited apple shoots. Then, when she was a sweaty, dishevelled mess, with her red-gold hair bedraggled and her face streaked with tears, he would have her thrown in the pond by the Auxey road, or perhaps placed in a pillory for public ridicule. The shaving of her head would make a final, degrading touch, and one he felt sure she would appreciate to the full.

His cock was growing stiff in his breeches as he thought of the state she would be in and, at the idea that at the end of it he could make her beg for her life, it grew stiffer still. He hastened on, wondering whether it would be safe to force Eloise to suck his cock or if the risk of her fiery temper and sharp teeth exceeded the gain. Perhaps it would be best to explain her options to her first, pointing out that only by absolute surrender to him did she stand a chance of leniency. Then again it might prove more enjoyable simply to force the little minx down on the floor and fuck her were she lay with

117

her skirts turned up, her fat boobs pushed out of her bodice and her thighs well parted to accommodate his body.

As he turned the corner where the road reached the flat top of the spur, he noticed two figures coming towards him, one of fair size and hunched into a cloak or cassock, one smaller and moving with a peculiar gait.

'Good evening, my friends,' he ventured uncertainly, assuming them to be villagers but curious as to their reason for being on the spur.

Neither answered.

'Michel? Hubert?' he queried, using the names of the two men set to guard the Château.

The larger of the two gave an odd grunting sound as the smaller stepped to the side.

'Who are you?' Faugres demanded and grabbed at the hat of the smaller figure.

The hat came away in his hand and for an instant he was looking into the faint, yet unmistakable face of Eloise de la Tour-Romain. He grasped at her clothing even as he was opening his mouth to shout for the guards. Something heavy struck his forehead, sending the world spinning around him, then it struck again and his senses slipped away.

'Damn!' Henry swore under his breath. 'Of all the luck!'

'It is Jean Faugres!' Eloise hissed from where she was examining the prone man. 'Give me your knife, Henry.'

'What for?' Henry demanded.

'I'm going to slit his throat!' Eloise hissed.

'You can't do that,' Henry objected, shocked at the sheer bloodthirstiness of his companion.

'What else are we to do?' she questioned. 'Besides, he was coming up to ravish me!'

'You don't know that,' Henry objected. 'Look, leave him. Come on!'

'I am sure of it. Give me the knife!'

'No. Look, leave him, will you, you bloodthirsty bitch? As it is, they may not even bother to look for us. Kill their upright man and they'll be after us like a pack of hounds!'

Grabbing her arm he pulled Eloise up and dragged her, still protesting, into the screen of undergrowth that they had so nearly reached when accosted by Faugres.

For the next hour they groped their way through the dark, following the line of the cliff and finally locating Peggy and Todd. Natalie was already in the camp, and threw herself sobbing into Eloise's arms as soon as they arrived, with Peggy quickly joining her.

'Bene darkmans, sir,' Gurney greeted Henry, with greater restraint. 'Evening, Miss Eloise.'

Six

All morning they had been climbing into the Morvan, with the woods becoming denser and the ground more uneven, while what few tracks existed became increasingly rough. For Eloise, the extent of her loss was simply too great to take in and she walked in a daze, her mind balking at the acceptance of reality. Her rank was to her a certainty, a God-given right, which could no more be taken away than her heart. With that rank came the right to her land, to her privileges and to a superiority as unquestionable as it was natural.

Disbelief quickly gave way to self-delusion, with her old arrogance reasserting itself. The events that were shaking her world, she concluded, were no more than a brief disturbance. Shortly the trouble-makers would be put down and everything restored to its rightful order.

'We should have taken horses!' Eloise stormed as they reached the crest of another hill to find yet more dark, tree-shrouded upland before them.

'And how, pray, was I supposed to do that?' Henry demanded. 'Lower them from the battlements? Perhaps while playing the pianoforte and dancing a cotillion? Or perhaps we should simply have rode out of the Château gates, passing the guards with a disdainful sniff?'

'Idiot,' Eloise replied and turned her back on him to look out across the gloomy hills of the Morvan.

Henry drew a long sigh. The return journey had so far

been altogether harder than the one out. Gurney was tough, while Peggy had proved remarkably game and never complained of hardship. Natalie was not only tiny but soft from years of light domestic work, yet at least tried to put a brave on things. Eloise, however, was a very different matter. Not only had she wanted to wear a gown of brilliant yellow silk that was as impractical as it was conspicuous, but she had also proved much the slowest of them, while constantly reviling Henry for what she evidently saw as a lack of foresight and finally demanding that she be made a litter.

He had been forced to give in on the dress because the other one she had chosen was a vermilion brighter even than the yellow, while his suggestion that she wear what remained of the supper boy's apparel had resulted in her sitting on the ground and refusing to move at all. On the matter of the litter, he had finally put his foot down, resulting in a shouting match that had ended only when he and Gurney had flatly refused to construct the thing.

'A clever man would have purchased a wagon and horses in Cosne or Châtillon,' Eloise now said, apparently musing and keeping her eyes directed out over the Morvan but clearly intending her words for Henry. 'No, not even a clever man, any man with a whit of sense. He would also have purchased a light carriage, or perhaps a gig. Thus I might have travelled in the comfort and style suited to my station in life. The wagon would have allowed us to bring an adequate quantity of provisions and at least the bare necessities of my wardrobe.'

'And attracted every bloodthirsty peasant for a score of miles!' Henry retorted, merely drawing a haughty sniff from Eloise.

For a moment there was silence, Henry struggling to hold his temper, Eloise standing still with her upturned nose pointed disdainfully skyward. Everything about her projected her high self-opinion, a superiority so assured, so prideful that it made Henry's blood boil with resentment. Not only was Eloise profoundly ungrateful for her rescue, but she also seemed to feel that those who had done it were now obliged to act as her servants. Henry had expected gratitude, or at least a sense of obligation to her rescuers, rather than the sulky, resentful attitude she seemed to be displaying.

'Why,' she said suddenly and aloud, 'is it my misfortune to always be served by such lackwits and buffoons? My . . .'

Her sentence was never finished, for Henry had made two fast steps and taken a firm grip on her arm. Eloise's poise vanished in a squeal of alarm as she was pulled off balance. An instant later, he had sat back on to a decaying stump and thrown her across his knee. Her flailing arms and furious protests were ignored as he pulled up her dress and petticoats with one brisk motion, as was the scream of indignation at the exposure of her bottom.

'No!' she yelled. 'Not that, you bastard!'

'Yes, that,' Henry replied. 'A spanking, Eloise, a spanking to hue your big arse and leave you blubbering.'

He twisted her arm hard into the small of her back, cocked his knee up to project the chubby pear of her bottom further into the air, and planted a hard slap full across the cheeks. Eloise squealed in pain and outrage, only to receive a yet harder slap that sent a wave of flesh over her bottom and thighs and set her legs kicking. Soon she was howling, with her buttocks red and sore as slap after slap was applied to their quivering surfaces. Henry's expression of grim determination faded as the spanking progressed, to be replaced by a happy, satisfied grin.

As Eloise's buttocks danced in the soft forest light, the villagers of St Romain were being exhorted to inflict a far sterner punishment on her. Emile Boillot, his head still wrapped in bandages, was attempting to raise enthusiasm for her pursuit. Jean Faugres stood by his side, occasionally adding a bellowed comment on Eloise's depravity and the need for her to be brought to justice.

Despite the general dislike of Eloise's family among the villagers, the efforts of the two agitators were coming to very little. The vintage was in, and the wine fermenting, allowing little spare time for the workforce. Moreover, despite the doubtful quality of the crop, it was, for the first time, entirely theirs. Few indeed wished to waste such good fortune for the sake of returning Eloise to St Romain, and the great majority were simply content to enjoy not only her absence, but that of the entire de la Tour-Romain family.

Boillot brought his speech to its climax, ending with an exhortation to follow Eloise and her rescuers and bring them back to St Romain. A ragged cheer greeted his demands, but only two voices were raised in agreement, those of Michel Brochon and Hubert Magnien, the two guards who had allowed her to slip past.

Eloise lay over Henry's lap with her burning bottom thrust high and her thighs cocked apart in what she was faintly aware was a thoroughly lewd display of her sex. It was immaterial, though, the pain of her spanking having driven all thoughts of self-respect from her head and taken her to the point where she no longer had control of her own body.

She knew vaguely that her two maids had watched her beaten in mingled horror and delight, horror that their mistress should have such indignity visited upon her, delight that the woman who had made their own bottoms dance to the tune of physical punishment so often was now howling and blubbering over a man's knee with no more self-restraint than they themselves had shown. Suddenly it stopped, just at the point when her pain and misery were giving way to the inevitable sexual response.

'Are you sorry?' Henry demanded, giving her bottom a gentle pat that made it very clear what was going to happen if she said no.

'Yes,' she sighed.

'And will you be good from now on?' he continued.

'Yes,' she responded glumly.

'I don't believe you,' Henry answered and laid another hard smack across her seat.

Eloise squeaked, then gave a louder cry as her spanking started again, as hard as before. Soon she was mewling and beating her free hand in the leaf mould of the forest floor. Her bottom felt huge and swollen, also desperately in need of a cock between the warm, roughened cheeks, then in her cunt, perhaps even in her anus, yet a spanking was a spanking, and it still hurt. Finally it stopped, leaving her breathing hard and uneven.

'Now, will you be good?' Henry demanded.

'I'll be good, I promise,' she snivelled.

He made no response, but slid a hand between her thighs. She could only moan in pleasure as a finger found her vagina and slid in easily. Indifferent to the audience, she stuck her bottom up, hoping to be masturbated. Henry merely laughed and called her a slut, then let go of her wrist and pushed her to the ground. She knelt, hot bottom thrust out to the forest, as Henry fumbled with his breeches and freed his erection.

Still sobbing bitterly, Eloise opened her mouth for Henry's cock. Her need for sex had been rising steadily since midway through the spanking, until she knew that, should the proposal be made, she would accept whatever the men considered proper for her. Half of her had been hoping that the spanking would be purely admonitory; the other half had known full well that the sight and feel of her naked, throbbing bottom would leave Henry with a raging erection that he was bound to want to quench in the damp hole of her cunt.

'In it goes, little one,' Henry said happily and fed his erection into her waiting mouth.

Both hating herself and exalting in the sensation, she started to suck his cock. Henry gave a knowing chuckle and began to fuck her mouth, holding her by the hair as he slid his penis in and out.

'I must spank you more often,' he remarked. 'You're ever so much the better for it.'

Eloise felt a new flush of shame and resentment at his words, but carried on sucking, unable to resist the feelings that the spanking had started – and, more importantly, the fact that it was Henry who had spanked her.

Following Eloise's spanking, things began to go more smoothly. Taking advantage of her submissive state, Henry had cut her dress to a more practical length, leaving her legs showing but disposing of the ribbon bows that had constantly caught in vegetation earlier in the day. She now walked at the back with Natalie, still sulking but making considerably better time than before, especially as each time she lagged too far behind Henry had only to threaten her with a repeat of the morning's performance.

Finally, as dusk began to fall, they reached the ridge above the priory of St Peter, which appeared as orderly as it was remote. After a cautious approach, they knocked at the portal to what Eloise declared to be the wing for lay guests and were admitted. To Henry's relief, they proved entirely welcome, Eloise being known to the abbess, who was full of sympathy and concern. Unfortunately, this extended only partway to himself and Gurney, who were shown rather brusquely to the stables and told to make themselves comfortable in the straw while the girls were taken off to enjoy the amenities of the guest wing.

Henry dropped to the straw beside his bundle with a sigh of resignation. His entire body ached, he was hungry and his throat was dry. Given that no mention had been made of supper, he began to dig into a bundle for some of the provisions they had taken and also one of the precious bottles of Corton.

'No bloody gratitude,' he complained as he worked on the cork of the bottle with his knife. 'You'd have thought Eloise could have found us a room of some sort. I mean, they could even have locked the door if they really think we're not to be trusted.'

'Very precious with their wares, these nuns are,' Gurney concurred.

'Pretty little things, mark you,' Henry continued. 'Did you see the little novice peeping out from behind the mother hen's skirts? Damn, I'm going to have to push this thing in.'

'Let me try, sir,' Gurney answered.

'It's all right, I've got it,' Henry said as the cork slid down into the neck of the bottle. 'Pretty as a picture, she was. I wonder if there are any more like her in there?'

'Stands to reason, sir; it's a nunnery,' Gurney replied. 'Dozens, I'd think.'

'Good God,' Henry muttered, and took a pull at the bottle as he tried to imagine even a single dozen girls like the novice nun who had chanced to be in the guest house when they had arrived at the Priory St Pierre. Just the sight of Gurney and himself had flustered her to such an extent that she had hidden, blushing, behind the senior nun responsible for the house. She had been strikingly pretty, delicate and somehow fey, with big liquid eyes, yet it had been her shy response to his mere presence that had excited him. Shaking his head to try

126

and rid himself of the disturbing thoughts, he passed the bottle to Gurney.

The big man put it to his lips and took a deep draught, then passed it back.

'Eighteen-year-old Corton,' Henry informed his friend, 'from one of the best vintages. What do you think?'

'Tastes like pig-dung in blackberry juice,' Gurney remarked.

'I shall remember that tasting note, next time Christie's auction some fine Burgundy,' Henry answered.[6]

For a long while they were silent, passing the bottle back and forth and each thinking their own thoughts, also taking bites of the bread and rich cheese that had been dug out of the provisions. Henry, despite his best efforts, found his mind drifting back to the little nun. The priory loomed above them, visible through the half-doors of the stable in which they had been quartered. Centred on the chapel, it was a maze of quadrangles, colonnades and towers, apparently tacked on to one another as circumstances dictated, presumably across centuries. Several windows showed light and Henry found himself wondering which belonged to the novice – or any other novice, for that matter. Taking the bottle from Gurney, he put it to his lips, only to find that it contained nothing but dregs.

'Damn!' he spluttered. 'You've given it a black eye, Gurney. No matter, I'll open another.'

As he struggled with the cork, he began to wonder about the possibilities of doing something about his rapidly increasingly sense of sexual frustration. The half-bottle of wine he had drunk was beginning to have an effect, setting his tiredness aside and making him feel increasingly bold. Surely, he surmised, it should be possible to seduce a young girl, nun or otherwise, who had obviously been so affected by his presence? Then again, somewhere within the priory were Eloise, Peggy and Natalie, whose willingness could more or less be taken for granted.

'I tumbled Eloise in the Château,' he remarked to Gurney, 'but I could well do with another. I dare say you'd not turn down a chance to tup Peggy, either?'

'I rather fancied a go at that little Natalie, as it is, sir,' Gurney replied.

'Fine, isn't she?' Henry replied. 'Although I like a little more meat, as a whole.'

'She's not much stock in the apple dumpling shop, it's true,' Gurney said, 'but I'll wager she has a sweet little arse.'

'She does,' Henry assured him, 'she does. Do you think we could find them?'

'They might be in the wing we arrived at, sir,' Gurney suggested. 'Then again, they might not. Still, there's no shortage of flash-tail elsewhere. The nuns, I mean: think of 'em, dozens of 'em, and every one a white ewe and maiden to boot.'

'I am thinking of them,' Henry answered as the cork finally gave way. 'I wish I wasn't.'

'The little one was built a bit on the lines of Natalie,' Gurney continued meditatively, 'only paler of skin.'

'The novice?' Henry asked.

'Ay,' his friend confirmed.

'I wonder where she is?' Henry sighed as he once again looked up to the dim maze of roofs.

Henry paused as a nearby window sprang into light, the flickering, orange-yellow quality of which indicated that someone was a carrying a candle. For a moment he wondered if he might have been heard, but no challenge came and no window opened. Moving cautiously forward once more, he signalled Gurney with a gentle tug to his sleeve. The illuminated window was three along from where they were crouched, and they quickly reached it. Peering inquisitively within, Henry discovered that the expedition was about to pay off, at least partially.

The room into which he was looking was a cell, a dull, cheerless place devoid of any ornamentation other than that which Henry considered most important – the occupant. This was a young, delicate woman with long black hair and a face both beautiful and innocent. Normally, innocence in women was a virtue for which he had little time, preferring willing, wanton girls who knew what they were doing. This occasion was different, the nun's innocence adding spice to what was a purely voyeuristic thrill.

Rapt in his attention, he watched the young woman pull up her shift of plain wool and present her pert and naked bottom over a chamber-pot. His view was excellent, including the lightly furred crevice of her bottom, her pouted anus and then, as she began to relieve herself, a stream of golden fluid running from her cunny. He watched her pee in delight, half-hoping she would do something ruder still or maybe play with herself when she had finished. As she wiggled her bottom to shake loose the last drops of pee, Henry found himself with his cock a hard and uncomfortable bar of rigid flesh within his breeches. Yet, for all his lust, there was a coldness about the nun's beauty that made him hesitate, and instead of accosting her he waited until she had extinguished her light and then moved on, crawling carefully below her open window.

For all the ethereal, icy aspect of the nun, Henry was by no means disheartened. One, he reasoned, might hold herself remote from worldly cares. Others, equally, were bound to have joined the priory for less spiritual reasons, possibly having dallied with the wrong man at the wrong time. The absence of any interesting sights in the next three lighted windows did little to dent his optimism, and on the fourth it was borne out. Two girls occupied a cell, one petite, one tall, but both slender and dark haired. Their age suggested them to be novices, although as they wore nothing but plain woollen shifts, it was difficult to be certain.

The smaller girl was kneeling at the foot of her pallet, head down and hands clasped in prayer. Beside her stood her companion, holding up the girl's shift to expose a small, round bottom from between the cheeks of which peeped the brownish dimple of her anus and the taut, pink lips of her cunny. Why her friend was holding up her shift was not apparent, although Henry guessed that it was somehow intended to magnify the girl's sense of shame or humility to have her bottom showing as she prayed. Henry swallowed, wondering how it would feel to immerse his cock in the silky purse of the girl's vagina as she knelt in prayer. He could almost feel the firm little buttocks pressed into his lap and hear her cry as her virginity was taken.

'Strange doings, these brisket-beaters,' Gurney remarked.

'Damn fine, though,' Henry whispered back.

The kneeling girl stopped praying and turned her head up to speak to her companion. As she moved, her face became visible, with a rapt expression that Henry was sure came only from lust – and a powerful lust at that.

'What's she saying, sir?' Gurney asked.

'She's begging to be made penitent,' Henry explained. 'Hold hard . . . splendid! She's asking to be beaten.'

Gurney made no reply, but watched intently as the two novices continued their ritual. Having been asked to beat her companion, the tall girl stepped to the side. The small girl's shift was left stranded halfway up her back, leaving the full moon of her pretty bottom naked for the men's inspection. Henry made the best of the view, squeezing his cock and balls through his breeches as he admired the girl's rear.

'I'll swear her cunt's a touch dewy,' Henry stated quietly.

'I reckon so,' Gurney replied, 'with the thought of a whacking, I dare say.'

The tall girl had been searching beneath the pallet and drew out an evidently well-concealed switch of plaited withies. The implicit guilt of concealing the thing increased Henry's optimism further, as what the girls were doing was clearly not with official permission. The smaller girl shivered at the sight of the switch, looked up into her friends eyes, then bowed her head and raised her hindquarters.

'By God, I'd like to sink my cock in that!' Henry exclaimed as the girl thrust her cunny up into a yet more provocative position.

The tall girl raised her switch, then brought it down across her companion's bottom, drawing a sharp cry of pain and leaving a thin red line across the pale skin of the pert buttocks. There had been an ecstatic quality to the small girl's yelp, and Henry found his cock harder still. Another stroke of the switch left a second red line on the girl's bottom, this on one cheek and terminating within a inch of the pouting anus. The beaten girl's vulva had continued to moisten, with a bead of white fluid showing over the vaginal opening, while her anus pulsed sullenly with the expectant clenching of her buttocks.

Twelve times the vicious little switch was applied to the girl's quivering bottom, leaving it criss-crossed with red stripes. She was sobbing, yet had her bottom thrust out in a pose that suggested anything but reluctance. Further testimony was given to her sexual excitement by the swollen, glistening wetness of her vulva and her heavy, urgent breathing. After the twelfth stroke, the tall girl knelt to kiss her shivering, chastened friend, first on the lips, then the nape of her neck, and then on the fiery globes of her bottom. The response was for the

131

small girl's thighs to part, offering her cunny in a yet more blatant display. Henry, imagining the feel of his cock in the girl's virgin quim or even the tight rose-bud of her anus, decided that he could wait no longer.

'These two are, I think, more to our taste,' he remarked as the tall girl's fingers slid between her companion's reddened buttocks, 'and, by God, if I don't have them now, I'll burst!'

'Best not to be hasty, sir,' Gurney answered doubtfully. 'They might not be ready for what you and I've got to give.'

'Nonsense,' Henry retorted. 'Look, the little one's cunt is running like a burst pump.'

Rising, he pushed open the casement, favouring the girls with a polite bow as they turned at the sound.

Eloise heaved a deep sigh. Across the table at which she was seated, the prioress, Reverend Mother Anna Danne, had been listening to an abridged version of her story with a sympathy that contained a hint of self-righteousness.

'So I am bereft,' Eloise continued, 'and thrown into the company of an insane Englishman who regards life as a jape set up solely for his amusement. I will return, though, once all this foolishness is over, and reclaim my lands – with or without my father.'

'I have no doubt that you will come through your trials a wiser and more devout woman,' the prioress answered.

'So I may hope,' Eloise responded, ignoring the thinly veiled dig at her reputation, which both women knew was far from that of a devout Catholic.

'I must retire,' the prioress announced. 'I will have a prayer said for you at matins.'

'Thank you, Reverend Mother,' Eloise replied, only to be cut off by a piercing scream from high among the priory roofs.

Seven

'Idiot!' Eloise raged. 'Do you think of nothing but bedding women?'

'How the hell was I to know?' Henry blustered.

'They're nuns, you imbecile!' she stormed. 'What did you expect them to do when two great hairy barbarians come crashing through the window in the middle of the night?'

'As a whole, such trespasses have received a warm welcome,' Henry said defensively.

Eloise snorted and turned her back on him, her mind seething with fury at his lust and stupidity – also with jealousy, although this was not something she would have admitted.

They stood on a track some way from the priory, surrounded on all sides by the black woods of the Morvan. Feeble moonlight illuminated the area, making ghostly shapes of the trees. Peggy and Natalie stood to one side, accepting their expulsion from the priory with stoicism if not grace. Of Gurney there was no sign, although she was sure he had been present when her anger at Henry had broken to the surface.

A sound among the trees made her start, provoking a quickly suppressed need for masculine comfort. Again it came, now distinct as the clip of horses' hooves.

'Henry,' she said querulously, her night fears abruptly overriding her anger as visions of a vengeful Jean Faugres crowded into her mind.

'Just Gurney, I expect,' Henry replied. 'He went back to steal some horses.'

Natalie Moreau looked up at the night sky through the bare tree branches high above. Her ears were straining, but not for the eerie night sounds that occasionally came from far off in the forest. Rather, she was intent on the tone of Eloise's breathing. Only when she was sure that her mistress was asleep did she rise slowly into a crawling position and start off across the carpet of leaves and fern towards the dark bulk of Todd Gurney.

Despite their inability to communicate in more than monosyllables, she had found herself drawn closer to the big Englishman throughout the day. His bulk and power seemed to offer protection, for which she felt a strong need; and, while she knew that the end result of her actions would almost certainly be a well-whipped bottom from Eloise, she was determined to at least offer him the chance of sleeping with her.

She found him, and tentatively reached out a small hand, only to have a massive one lock on her wrist. A little shock of surprise and pleasure went through her and then she was being drawn in towards him. Their mouths met and his hand moved from her wrist to her bottom, cupping the whole of one tiny cheek through her dress. His other arm went around her back and strong fingers began to stroke the nape of her neck. Natalie melted into his arms, making no protest when her own hand was placed on his cock, nor later when he mounted her and slid his full length into her juice-sodden cunny.

Henry awoke damp, cold and in a foul temper. A night spent in a hollow in the woods had left him with a number of aches, while his head throbbed with a pain that he was sure came from Eloise's constant nagging before they had made camp. A combination of darkness and his own sense of guilt had dissuaded him from giving her the spanking he felt she deserved. Neither she, nor Peggy, had been game for the erotic play he so desperately needed after peeping at the nuns. To make matters worse, he had spent much of the night listening to sounds of passion from Gurney and Natalie.

He stretched, wishing for coffee, and ham and perhaps kippers with a liberal portion of Devon butter. None of it appeared: only the dank trees, the huddled forms of his companions and their newly acquired horses, which stood nearby looking as dispirited as their masters. Eloise had been furious at Gurney's theft of the three horses from the priory stable, but had been quick to accept their boon, selecting a filly which Henry now noticed was roan.

After walking across to where Gurney lay – snoring with Natalie in his arms and apparently oblivious to the conditions – Henry poised his foot for a hearty kick, only to think better of it and give Natalie's out-thrust bottom a gentle prod with his toe.

'Up, the lot of you!' he called; then, on a sudden, mischievous impulse, 'To arms! Peasants in the camp! It's Jean Faugres and the devil himself behind!'

Eloise's immediate scream of alarm and frantic scramble returned the smile to Henry's face, as did the succeeding expression of indignant fury when she realised that they were alone.

Henry's mood continued to improve as the morning went on. The clammy autumn night had given way to a day even warmer than the last, and riding not only allowed him to ease his legs but to offload the various coins and trinkets they had carried away from the Château de St Romain. Better still was the fact that he had Peggy riding before him, with her magnificent bottom pressed hard to his crotch. The jogging motion of the horse and his frustration of the night before had combined with the feel of soft female buttocks to give him a raging erection, which was now so prominent that Peggy had began to giggle and throw him bright-eyed glances.

His mount was a grey gelding of moderate stature, while Gurney and Natalie rode a great dun carthorse with white on its forehead and legs. The third horse was little more than a pony. Eloise had speculated that it was the personal mount of the prioress, yet that had not prevented her from commandeering the animal. She now rode it like a man, with her gown of bright vermilion velvet spread across its back and, Henry conjectured, her cunny pressed to its spine with no more than a layer of folded petticoat between, if that.

Shortly before noon, the woods and hills gave way to a valley, across which further hills could be seen. Eloise declared this to be the head of the Yonne river and suggested that it might be followed to the north and west to save time. Henry agreed, and soon found his spirits rising yet further as they moved out on to flatter land and broke first into a trot and then a canter. Peggy shrieked at the increased pace, laughing yet clearly nervous, and her bottom began to bump firmly against Henry's front. Suddenly, the temptation to indulge himself between her ripe cheeks became overwhelming, along with a joyous delight in the possibilities offered by being on horseback.

'Ho, Todd Gurney!' he called. 'Have you ever taken the double ride?'

'Betimes,' his companion called back.

'Then a quid says I'll finish in mine before you!' Henry yelled.

'Taken!' Gurney shouted, his call immediately followed by a squeal from Natalie as he began to pull at her skirts.

'What? Henry!' Peggy squealed as her skirts were tugged sharply out from under her thighs.

136

'Lift up!' Henry responded.

'What! You're not . . .' she answered. 'Henry! We'll take a fall!'

'Damned if we will!' he answered. 'Hold hard to the beast's neck. It'll be done in a trice.'

She bent forward, obeying more from terror than her desire. The rubbing of Henry's cock between her bottom cheeks had been exciting her, yet she had expected him either to slake his lust with Eloise – or, more hopefully, to pause by some dense copse and tumble her quickly down among the leaves. Instead it was to be both dangerous and distinctly public, as more than one cottage looked down on the long, flat water-meadow along which they were travelling.

'Henry!' She tried a last, feeble protest against the inevitable as her skirts were tugged out from beneath her and her bottom exposed to the air.

Sure that a dozen French peasants would be watching her intercourse, she buried her face in the horse's mane, her cheeks hot with shame, fright and not a little lust. Gripping the mane beneath her chest, Henry was trying to mount her, whooping and calling out to Gurney as he struggled with his breeches.

'Got him!' she heard him call and the next instant something turgid prodded at her vulva.

It missed, rubbing against her clitoris to send a series of pangs of exquisite pleasure through her. Henry cursed, his knuckles brushing the soft underside of her bottom as he tried to reposition himself. His cock prodded at her bottom-hole and she responded with a frantic wriggle, determined that if she were to be treated so rudely she would at least avoid the pain and indignity of buggery. A cry of feminine surprise and delight indicated that Natalie had been entered and then, suddenly, Henry's cock found its target.

Peggy gasped as her vagina filled with penis, a movement of the horse ramming it home with

137

unexpected force. A similar sound from Henry showed that the sudden penetration had not been quite what he intended, and then he had began to hump her, bouncing against her bottom with the animal's motion as she clung desperately to its mane.

Maddened by the unaccustomed goings-on, the horse increased its speed, changing gait to a full gallop that had Henry whooping with joy. Peggy shut her eyes, concentrating on the frantic and delicious bobbing of the cock inside her and trying not to think about the ground rushing by below. Henry's position changed, half his length slipping from her vagina so that the swell of his knob was rubbing in the sensitive entrance while his body weight came down on top of hers. A hand groped under her chest. Her neckerchief was pulled loose, then her breasts popped from her bodice. Henry laughed as he took a full globe in his free hand, kneading it, pinching the nipple to quick erection and then settling down to concentrate on fucking her.

Peggy groaned deeply as her naked breasts began to slap on either side of the horses neck. She was pushed well down, her vulva rubbing on the beast's spine, the rough hair of its back directly on her clitoris. Henry's cock was pumping inside her, adding to her ecstasy. Her initial shame at being exposed and ridden in public gave way to pure, helpless ecstasy as she started to come and then she was screaming out her lust into the coarse hair of the horse's mane. At the very peak of her orgasm she opened her eyes, to find herself looking directly into the astonished face of a squat man who stood among a group of pigs.

Then the vision was past and her orgasm was dying, only to rise again at the erotic shame of having been seen in so rude a position. Even as she cried out once more Henry started to come, his cock pushing hard into her and then jerking as he gave a grunt of pleasure. She felt the wet of his come at the mouth of her vagina, then slick and slippery between her vulva and the horse's back, giving a final, lesser peak to her orgasm.

'Mine, by God!' she heard Henry call, only then realising that her grip had started to loosen in the aftermath of her ecstasy.

Scrabbling desperately for a hold, she heard Henry's yell of triumph turn to alarm and then the whole world turned upside down. The sky spun by over her head. For an instant her foot was silhouetted against blue and then her bottom struck something, knocking the breath from her body.

The next thing she was conscious of was Henry's laughter. Pulling herself into a sitting position, she found that she was on a bank, the soft earth of which had cushioned her fall. Henry lay nearby, on his back in the grass, laughing incontinently with his erection sticking up into the air like a flagpole. Of Gurney and Natalie there was no sign, but Eloise was approaching, her face set in an expression that conveyed more amusement than concern, but which also showed more than a hint of jealousy.

Some way down the track, Todd Gurney had managed to rein his horse in. He was still inside Natalie, her trim, pale-brown bottom spread in front of him with his penis disappearing into her gaping cunny. She had responded to the sudden stripping of her bottom and to entry with enthusiasm, clinging to the horse's neck and squealing with fright and pleasure as he had fucked her. Unfortunately he had found himself unable to get the rhythm needed for orgasm and so had lost the bet.

Now, however, was different. Spreading Natalie's pert cheeks fully apart with his hands, he began to move into her with short, hard pushes, all the while admiring the spread of her bottom, the tight dimple of her anus and the junction between her well-furred cunny and his cock. It was not just a beautiful sight to him, but exotic,

Natalie's pale-brown skin providing a striking contrast to the creamy-white bottoms of the Devon girls he was used to. He came with a grunt, keeping himself well in her until he was fully drained. She was moaning softly and making little rubbing motions with her bottom to show her own need. Keen to oblige, he withdrew his cock, took her slender thighs in his hands and began to rub her naked cunny against the horse's back. She came in moments, squealing out her pleasure and thrusting her bottom up and down in a display of abandoned lust that left a deep impression on him.

Jean Faugres reined his horse in beside that of Emile Boillot on the slope overlooking the Priory of St Peter. His humour was less than good as, for the entire morning, Boillot had either been pontificating on the rights of man or explaining his reasoning for searching in the direction they had taken. Magnien and Brochon, impressed by the young man's fire and certainty, had hung on to his words and so Jean's suggestion that the fugitives were more likely to have headed north for Dijon and the main road to Paris had been put down.

Eloise, he was sure – along with the bastard who had struck him down with some metal object – would now be well to the north. The demoiselle, he knew, set a high value on her comfort, and would never stoop to travelling on foot, let alone trudge through the damp autumnal woods of the Morvan. Indeed, had it not been for the one thing, he would have abandoned the chase altogether. That one thing was the man who had attacked him near the Château de St Romain. His forehead now carried a dark, longitudinal bruise, and if there was one thing he wanted more than to bring Eloise de la Tour-Romain to broke, it was revenge on that man.

Riders sent to Orches and Auxey had reported no sightings of Eloise and so he had been forced to accept

Boillot's theory and tag along, moving ever higher into the Morvan.

'Here is the place that logic dictates she took sanctuary for the night,' Boillot was saying. 'We shall . . .'

'Or any other nest of blackfly for miles!' Faugres retorted.

'Not so, Citizen Faugres,' Boillot replied, 'for here alone comes within the radius possible to them after a day's travel on foot. No, rest assured that Eloise Delatour came here, and with luck is still in residence.'

Faugres answered with a snort of contempt, but the others were already edging their beasts down the track. He followed, half hoping that Boillot would be proved wrong and half hoping the opposite.

At the priory gates Boillot demanded an audience with the prioress, using an arrogance that impressed even Faugres. Rather than respond with a curt refusal, as Faugres had been expecting, the elderly nun at the lodge quickly arranged a meeting with the prioress. This proved to be a tall, stern-faced woman who Faugres frankly expected to deny Boillot's demands for information and attempt to send them back to the road empty-handed. Anticipating the prospect of searching the nunnery by force with considerable relish, his temper began to improve, only for the prioress to respond to Boillot not with antagonism but with something close to friendliness.

He watched in mounting irritation as the two of them spoke. Despite their differences of background, Boillot and the Reverend Mother Anna Danne proved to share a high moral tone and a conviction that Eloise de la Tour-Romain represented a nadir of virtue transcended only by her companions. Faugres, who considered Boillot a prig and a bore, for all their shared political convictions, took a different view, finding the prioress's outrage the sole ameliorating factor to his chagrin.

They left the Priory with all the information the Reverend Mother had been able to supply, including descriptions of the fugitives' clothing and of the three stolen horses. In return, Boillot had promised to return the horses and add their theft to the long list of enormities he considered Eloise to have committed. Faugres remained silent as they rode away, unable to concede that Boillot had been right all along.

Henry smiled happily to himself as they walked the horses up the steep incline that led out of the Yonne valley. They had been riding for some hours by the river, directed by Eloise in the direction of a Château at which she hoped to gain aid. Henry was sceptical of this but, as the route lay in a generally westerly direction, he had made no complaint. Despite a few bruises, he was also pleased with himself for what he considered a particularly fine feat of erotic equestrianism. Not only had he managed to come before he fell off and win his guinea from Gurney, but both Eloise and Peggy had become notably more attentive since the event. This was entirely contrary to his expectations and reinforced his long-held belief that women were, at heart, incomprehensible. He had expected a fit of jealous sulking from Eloise, but instead she had become flirtatious, even possessive. Peggy, who he had expected to be furious, had been in a remarkably gay mood ever since and had even dared to flirt a little, in spite of the presence of Eloise.

They breasted the rise, finding themselves looking down into a valley smaller than that of the Yonne. At the base, among woods but surrounded by a large and formal garden, stood a Château of four towers, each topped with the conical roof and patterned tiles that he had come to recognise as typical of the region.

'Château de la Roche Luzieres,' Eloise declared. 'Seat of the family of that name and old friends of my own family. Here we may be assured of shelter.'

'If there's anyone there,' Henry replied sceptically.

'They will be there,' Eloise replied confidently. 'Unlike my father, the Seigneur de Luzieres is no coward.'

Henry gave a doubtful snort and angled his horse down the track that appeared to lead in the direction of the Château. As they approached, it quickly became clear that Eloise's optimism was unfounded. The Château showed no signs of life whatever, and as they rode through the wide open gates even she had to admit that the Luzieres had fled.

'Try the stables, Gurney,' Henry ordered, 'and you girls, see if you can't get some food.'

Gurney and the two maids did as they were told, Eloise alone ignoring his order and trotting her horse forward towards the main door of the Château. With a resigned shrug, Henry followed her, tethering his horse to the balustrade.

The inside of the Château was quiet, a place of awesome solitude, the magnificent hall as bereft of cheer as some vast sepulchre. Standing in the doorway, Henry felt suddenly cold, as if the ghosts of generations of Luzieres were demanding his right to step within. As Gurney came up behind him, the big man's footsteps echoed loud in the empty hall, a noise that seemed as inappropriate as laughter in a cathedral.

'There's a landau in the stable yard, sir,' Gurney announced cheerfully, instantly shattering the eerie atmosphere.

'Eh?' Henry queried. 'Oh, yes.'

'She's old but looks sound,' Gurney continued.

'Any tack?' Henry enquired, turning once more to the welcome light of the courtyard.

'Plenty, sir,' Gurney answered.

'Well, rig her up, then, and we'll travel in style,' Henry responded. 'Where are the girls?'

'Round in the kitchen gardens, gathering apples,' he answered.

'At least they've got some sense,' Henry responded. 'Eloise is away upstairs, after ribands and a new gown, no doubt. Do you think I should spank her again tonight? She could still do with some starch taking out of her.'

'Might do her some good,' Gurney agreed. 'Then again, there's a lot of starch in that one to take out.'

'Very true,' he agreed. 'She's been better today, but I might do it anyway, just for the hell of it. Besides, she does react so well.'

Gurney responded with a curt laugh and walked off in the direction of the stables.

With the landau rigged to an improvised three in hand and Gurney riding postillion on the massive cart-horse, they struck out due west, along a track notably better than those in the high Morvan. Eloise found herself more relaxed than she had been since leaving St Romain. Not only were they travelling in reasonable comfort, but the bulk of the wealth they had salvaged from the Château de St Romain was artfully concealed beneath the seats of the landau. Also, they had apples and wine to supplement the hard cheese and spiced sausage they had brought away for provisions.

Slowly, the countryside around them became less harsh, the high, wooded hills giving way to gentler more open land and small villages and peasant farmsteads becoming frequent once more. They stopped at one of these towards noon, purchasing bread, cheese and cured ham. Despite their caution in sending the harmless and definitely unaristocratic Natalie to fetch these provisions, they drew curious stares from the squat, rude-looking locals. Eloise looked disdainfully away, yet not without a prickle of fear very different from her normal reaction to peasants.

They moved on, eating as they went and washing the food down with bottles of a rich white Meursault that

Henry had unearthed in the cellar at Château de la Roche Luzieres. This cheered her further, even reviving a measure of mischief in her character. Opposite her, Henry was draining the last few inches of the third bottle. His legs were well apart, providing her with a fine view of the not unimpressive bulge in his breeches. Thinking of the thick, eager cock the leather concealed, she began to wonder if he might not once more be goaded into taking her with the rough forcefulness she so enjoyed. She was also beginning to feel the need to pee, and wondered if she should not use the fact as an excuse to stop.

They had reached a place were the fields and cottages of peasant land abruptly gave way to solid forest. Passing by an untenanted lodge, they came into this. Before them, the long ride of the Forest of Premery opened up, a flat, straight cut between stands of oak and chestnut that vanished over a low brim at the limit of vision. Gurney increased the speed of the landau as Eloise considered how well suited the thick woods would be to her being laid naked on the ground and mounted. Again she glanced at Henry's crotch, imagining how his cock had felt in her mouth after her impromptu spanking of the previous day. The thought of her undignified exposure, the pain of the spanking and how he'd then made her suck him increased her lust. As he turned towards her, she favoured him with a flirtatious glance and moved the hem of her gown to display an ankle. He returned a lustful grin, only for his expression to alter abruptly to one of concern.

Eloise turned, her dirty thoughts dying on the instant as she saw what had alarmed him. Pushing between the high limestone pillars that marked the start of the estate, now some quarter mile to the rear, came four horsemen. They were moving at a canter but, as she watched, they urged their horses into a full gallop and the leader among them looked up, revealing the dark, bearded countenance of Jean Faugres.

'Faugres!' she exclaimed. 'How?'

'By asking after a chit with red-gold hair and a vermilion velvet gown,' Henry answered sternly. 'They'll be tired though, I'll warrant. Ride hard, Gurney!'

The landau surged forward, with panic and fear welling up in Eloise's breast as Faugres yelled out at them.

'It's Emile Boillot, Michel Brochon and Hubert Magnien with him,' Natalie declared, peering over the rear of the landau from beside Eloise. 'They'll kill you, and rape us for sure!'

'Damned if they will!' Henry cursed, fumbling shot from his pouch. 'Gurney, drive like Jehu!'

Despite their efforts, the horsemen continued to gain, while Henry tried desperately to load his pistols. Eloise's fear rose as she recalled Faugres' surly, malicious manner and the hatred and lust that had always been in his eyes. Before he had been powerless, but now all too little stood between her and him. For all Henry's devil-may-care courage and Gurney's strength and size, she felt sure that they would be able to do little against the monstrous Faugres, especially with three others to aid him.

With her heart in her mouth, she stared back over the rear of the landau. Boillot was in the lead, coming up like a zephyr with the heavier men strung out behind him. Faugres came last, yet it was his massive figure that struck terror into Eloise.

'Got the buggers!' Henry finally declared. 'Move aside, girl.'

Eloise hastened to obey, allowing Henry to kneel on the rear seat and aim his pistols. Boillot saw what was happening and ducked down even as the pistols roared and spat fire. For a flicker of time, nothing happened and then Eloise saw a puff of something explode from the shoulder of Michel Brochon's coat.

'Winged the bastard!' Henry declared. 'Come on, Todd, ride!'

With a new horror, Eloise realised that Henry was not merely fighting back because he had to, but was actively enjoying himself, an attitude that struck her as verging on lunacy. He had also used his man's first name, something she had never heard him do before, and in general he seemed happier than at any time except on those occasions he had had his cock immersed in one or another of her bodily orifices.

'We're taking them!' he now shouted, following the remark with an insulting gesture to the pursuing horsemen. 'We've got the legs on them, Todd; keep riding!'

Eloise saw that it was true. With a vast surge of relief, she realised that they had began to gain, despite the load in the landau and their ill-assorted team. Even with their every effort, the heavy loads and long forced ride of their pursuers were telling on their mounts.

For another quarter mile, they rode pell-mell down the ride, their lead increasing at first gradually and then more rapidly as Faugres and then Brochon were forced to drop out of the chase. Seeing his companions halt, Magnien reined in too and thus Boillot was forced to do likewise.

Henry laughed and yelled back a few choice curses, his face glowing with triumph and excitement. Finally Eloise allowed herself to relax, her fear flowing away to leave her trembling with reaction and overcome by a renewed need to pee, now desperate. Stopping, she realised, was hardly practical, yet she was by no means certain how long she could hold herself.

Her despair grew as they crossed a brow to reveal an equally straight and even longer section of ride ahead. Hoping to wait until Gurney was forced to rest the horses, and so avoid the embarrassment of having to ask for a halt to relieve herself, she hung on, gritting her teeth at each jolt of the landau. As they raced down the long ride, the four horsemen appeared behind, now moving at a purposeful trot. Clearly there was going to be no rest, yet their lead seemed sufficient to allow her the brief moment of privacy that was all she needed.

'Henry,' she whispered, placing her lips close to his ear, 'I need to pee; could we stop?'

'Stop?' Henry swore. 'We can't stop now! Do it on the floor, for God's sake! Or stick your arse over the edge of the carriage.'

'I will not!' Eloise snapped back as the blushes on her face rose to a heat not far less than that between her thighs.

'Well, wet your dress, then!' Henry answered. 'I'm damned if I'll risk a musket ball for the sake of your modesty.'

Eloise gave him a look that had been known to reduce maids to tears, but Henry took no notice whatever. Instead, he continued to work on loading his pistols while the pain in her bladder rose to a new peak of urgency. With her thighs clamped hard together, she struggled to hold herself. Her bladder was agony, a hard, swollen ball of pain in her belly that begged for release. All she need to do was relax and to let the pee gush out freely from her cunny to bring the blessed relief – and with it unendurable shame.

The landau bumped on, Gurney taking the ground at a breakneck speed that sent shock after agonising shock through Eloise's bladder. She held on, sitting bolt upright with her thighs clamped tight together and her toes wriggling in her desperation, only for each fresh jolt of the landau to break her concentration.

Despite her best efforts, it began to come, erupting out in little spurts as her pee-hole spasmed in the agony of trying to retain her load. She felt a wet feeling between her thighs and under the tuck of her bottom, and with it came the unbearable shame of knowing that she was wetting herself. At that realisation, her resolve broke, and she let go with a last, miserable whimper.

Her pee-hole opened and the urine she had tried so desperately to hold in exploded from her cunny with a hissing, bubbling noise that she knew the others could not fail to hear.

She gave a groan of utter despair and embarrassment as a pool began to form around her feet. Still the pee gushed out, freely now that she had abandoned herself to the inevitable. Soon her stockings were soaking, her boots full and her dress drenched, while the pool beneath her had spread and run with the bouncing of the landau, revealing her shame to the others. Henry merely laughed and continued to load up. Peggy paid no attention, being too rapt in the progress of the distant horses. Natalie alone gave a sympathetic response to her mistress's plight, a wan smile and the offer of an empty Meursault bottle in a somewhat belated gesture of assistance.

'Right, Gurney,' Henry called suddenly as he rammed the charge home in the second pistol. 'Bring her round and we'll stand the bastards off among those big beeches.'

'You bastard!' Eloise swore as the last of her pee dribbled into the now substantial puddle on the floor.

Emile Boillot watched as the distant landau slowed, slued around and stopped beside a stand of great beeches. A lump formed in his throat and he steeled himself for the coming confrontation, determined not to show fear in front of his companions.

'We've winded them!' Jean Faugres voice came from behind him, a triumphant bellow that showed nothing of fear.

Magnien and Brochon joined into the cry, spurring their horses into a canter on either side. Boillot followed suit, ducking down low to his horse's mane and keeping his eye ahead. Figures were jumping down from the landau, a man, then Eloise, recognisable by her red-gold hair and sumptuous gown. The two maids followed and lastly the large man who had been astride the carthorse. All ran in among the beeches, disappearing from view.

'We've got them now!' Faugres called. 'Ride low and fast. Michel, Hubert, ready your muskets.'

To Emile's left, Brochon hefted his musket and swung it round with one hand to ready the iron-shod butt. Riding fast towards their adversaries, Boillot knew that one shot would come, maybe two, then no more. The giant cooper and the two ex-soldiers could, he decided, take care of the men, leaving him to secure Eloise. If the maids ran, then it was no great loss, the capture of Eloise was all that mattered. Fired by new determination, he rode on. The trees were rushing to either side, the stalled landau growing larger and clearer.

A glimmer of bright vermilion showed among the beech trunks – Eloise's dress. Another figure showed and Boillot crouched lower, expecting the flash and whine of a pistol shot. Nothing came, then a sudden crack and a panic-stricken whinny to his side. Another crack followed and something whistled by his head. Someone cursed and his horse shied, stumbled and then he was flying through the air.

Pain shot through his shoulder as he struck the ground. His brain was telling him to rise even as his body curled tight by instinct. He heard a grim laugh and Faugres' furious bellow. Magnien's voice sounded nearby, angry and followed by a thump and a curse in English. A hoof passed perilously close to his head and he rolled to the side.

Scrambling to his feet in panic and confusion, he found Michel Brochon only feet away, striking down from his horse at the big Englishman. Beyond, Magnien had been unseated and was staggering back in front of an assailant who wielded his pistols like clubs. Further, well down the ride, Jean Faugres was desperately trying to control his bolted horse. Brochon's musket came down, only for his fierce glare to turn to surprise and then pain as the big Englishman ducked, rose and drove a massive fist into his opponent's side. The horse snickered and kicked out in fear, then pranced suddenly to the side. Brochon's balance went, the musket flying from his hands even as the Englishman leapt clear.

Regaining his wits, Boillot leapt forward, grappling the Englishman's arm, only to be flung aside as if he were no more than a child. Brochon was half-up, then down again as a heavy fist struck his jaw. Beyond, Magnien was reeling and clutching his head, then raising his hand in a gesture for quarter that was answered with a derisive laugh.

'Run, then,' the smaller Englishman said, in clear French, 'and mind you don't come back, or you'll get a proper drubbing.'

Magnien staggered away, Brochon also starting to retreat as the big Englishman drew back. Boillot backed away, his hand raised defensively even as shame and anger welled up inside him.

'Kill them, you idiots!' came a female voice that he knew well as belonging to Eloise de la Tour-Romain.

Boillot turned, real fear rising inside him as he saw the demoiselle, some hundred yards away, her face red and her hands raised in fury.

He ran, following the already retreating Brochon and Magnien back the way they had come, abandoning their horses and muskets. Eloise's furious demands and threats followed him as he fled, accompanied by the derisive laughter of the two Englishmen.

Eloise de la Tour-Romain stood in the centre of the great ride of Premery Forest. Her brain boiled with fury, indignation and frustration, yet all this could do nothing to quell her triumph as she watched her persecutors put to flight. Even the humiliation of wetting herself had been put aside in the terror and excitement. As Henry and Gurney had disappeared into the forest to take the attackers in the flank, Natalie and Peggy had done as they were told and fled for cover in the depths of the woods. She had stayed, at first crouched behind a beech tree and poised to run, and then out in the open when it had become apparent that her side would be victorious.

Fury at Henry's refusal to obey her orders and the villagers' sheer arrogance in assailing her in the first place now gave way to jubilation. She joined in the men's scornful laughter and then opened her arms for Henry as he walked back. Her kiss was returned with a fervour that matched her own and, as his hands locked on the flesh of her bottom and lifted her from the ground, she abandoned herself to him. Quickly, she was pulled into the forest, her breasts were popped out from her bodice and her soiled skirt turned up. A moment later, she was kneeling as Henry fed her his cock and fondled a naked breast. Then she was on the ground, skirts and petticoats in disarray and thighs pulled apart as he mounted her. His cock found her vagina and slid in, her passage made easy by copious lubrication. They made love with urgency and passion, Eloise's pleasure rising close to orgasm as his cock pushed deep into her again and again. As she was ridden, her thoughts turned to the way the two men had beaten off the villagers and she hoped that Gurney was also taking his reward with his cock sheathed in Natalie's tight purse. Then, as Henry began to grunt with the passion of approaching orgasm, she found her mind turning to the way she had wet herself in front of them all and the depth of humiliation she has felt as her pee had run down her legs to pool on the floor. It was still in her boots, and her belly was wet with it, feelings that now inspired her with a sense of absolute wantonness.

She cried out as Henry came, then put her fingers to her cunny as soon as he had pulled out. He watched her masturbate with his handsome face set in a pleased smirk, then slid a hand under her buttocks. Eloise grunted as his thumb found her anus and pushed inside, then began to come as two fingers slid into her sopping vagina.

'I've wet myself Henry, look at me,' she gasped as her climax rose. 'Look at me, Henry, I'm going to do it again. I'm going to do it again!'

As she reached orgasm, her bladder squeezed tight and a spurt of pee erupted from her cunny, spraying out around her rubbing fingers and splashing on his hand. A stab of ecstatic shame went through her as she screamed out her lust. She felt her semen-slick vagina and anus clamp on his intruding digits as a second peak hit her. For an instant, she was in a sate of perfect wanton bliss, and then her orgasm was subsiding to leave her limp and groaning on the damp leaves with the last of her pee still trickling down between her vaginal lips.

Eight

Henry drew the landau to a stop. He had taken Gurney's place as postillion and, with Magnien's grey added to their team, they had made good time. Ahead was a view very different from the gentle swells of the Bazois. The land ahead dipped, falling gradually to form a great valley at the bottom of which ran a band of silver-grey – the Loire. Beyond the land rose to bold, open hills with a plateau at the horizon, showing dull mauve in the haze of distance. Some way to the south, a fortified town stood out on a spur, appearing to hang directly above the river.

'Sancerre,' Eloise stated, following the direction of his gaze. 'Ahead is Cosne, where you left the river before.'

'Where I suggest we sell the horses and this old bishop to purchase a boat,' Henry put in.

'The plain we see,' Eloise continued, 'is the Sologne, mostly swamp and forest with few roads or villages.'

'Sounds an infernal place,' Henry remarked.

'But a safe place,' Eloise retorted. 'What we should do is drive on to Cosne and make a great show of buying a boat. You can then sail some little way up river while your man crosses the river. The landau can collect us on the far bank, from which we vanish into the heart of the Sologne while the bastard Faugres and his mob continue up the Loire.'

'Deuced expensive scheme just to elude some peasant,' Henry objected. 'Don't tell me you're scared

154

of the fellow? Not the Demoiselle de la Tour-Romain, scared of a peasant?'

'He is an artisan, a cooper,' Eloise replied, 'and if the Demoiselle might not be scared of the cooper, then the woman is scared of the giant, as you would do well to be yourself.'

'Ha!' Henry laughed. 'Let him come; I'll show him a trick or two. Besides, I'll wager we put the wind up the fellow back there and that he'll have slunk back to St Romain with his breeches bewrayed!'

'Bombast is easy now, when he is not here,' Eloise stated. 'As to the expense – you seem to forget that the wealth we carry is mine.'

Nettled, Henry gave what he hoped was a derisive snort, yet found the image of the massive Jean Faugres looming up unpleasantly in his mind. Turning briefly for a reassuring look at the only slightly less impressive bulk of Todd Gurney, he considered the merits of Eloise's plan. The Sologne sounded a dismal place, with little opportunity for exploiting the erotic opportunities offered by the presence of the three girls. A boat on the Loire was only marginally better, yet at least had the merit of towns at which worthwhile provisions might be purchased. The nights in the Morvan had sated his taste for outdoor living, while along the river it might be possible to risk an inn and take the comfort of a bed. At the thought of Eloise in a feather bed, his mind became set.

'Five times we've danced Moll Peatley's gig,' he said aloud, 'or perhaps six, and not once in comfort. We risk the river, and to the devil with Faugres and every damn peasant in France besides.'

Eloise opened her mouth to protest, but Henry merely lifted his hand and tapped the palm, a gesture that had an immediate calming effect.

Four men sat before the church in the tiny village of St Laurant. Emile Boillot, with a map spread before him, showed restrained anger and a grim determination. Jean Faugres showed only rage, with his great hands opening and closing as he reflected on the undignified retreat that had been forced upon them. The other two showed less forceful emotions, Michel Brochon picking thoughtfully at the ragged hole at the top of his coat sleeve while Hubert Magnien studied a group of sparrows with feigned interest and nursed his bruises.

'Only a fool would cross the Sologne at this time of year,' Jean Faugres objected. 'They will use the river.'

'They would be at risk from the people in Orleans, Blois, and half the towns along the Loire,' Boillot objected. 'In their place, I would try the Sologne. Safety, after all, must be their prime concern.'

'Ha!' Faugres snorted. 'After the way that English pig winkled his strumpet out of St Romain, do you think he cares for safety? Not a wit, nor his companion.'

Grunts of heartfelt agreement sounded from both Brochon and Magnien.

'Besides,' Faugres continued, 'remember that I am a Touranjou. I learnt my trade in Romorantin-Lathenay, on the far side of the Sologne. I have seen it in autumn, a swamp fit only for duck.'

'It has not rained for close on two weeks,' Boillot objected.

'And solidly for the four before that,' Faugres answered him. 'No, if they try it they'll turn back. We follow along the river and hope to overtake them. Once my hands are on that fop's neck, we'll see how loud he laughs.'

'No,' Boillot countered. 'It is wiser to ride hard for Tours, through which they must surely pass. We can have a mob roused against them and provide as warm a welcome as they could wish for.'

'And have them strike north for Rouen or south to Bordeaux?' Faugres answered. 'We must follow them close, it is the only sure way.'

'I disagree,' Boillot stated. 'What of you, Hubert? Michel?'

Hubert Magnien answered with an embarrassed grunt.

'I have a wife and child in St Romain,' Brochon replied diffidently, 'and, to be frank, I do not want to spar with those two Englishmen again. The demoiselle can go for all of me, for her punishment shall surely come in hell.'

'What?' Faugres roared. 'Coward! Are you a man? What of revenge for her wrongs? What of returning some blows to the Englishman who blacked your eye?'

'I am man enough to know where my duty lies,' Brochon replied with a touch of heat, 'and that is with my family, not with a pistol-ball in my guts in some mud-pool in the Sologne.'

Faugres answered with a snort of contempt. Brochon rose and began to walk off, Magnien throwing his erstwhile companions an apologetic look and hastening to follow.

'And now?' Faugres demanded.

'I ride for Tours,' Boillot replied. 'You follow the river and seek them out. If you succeed, raise a mob against them.'

'I have no such need,' Faugres spat. 'I'll pull them apart with my hands!'

'What luck?' Henry asked as Gurney and Peggy pushed into the room from the dank November night.

'Plenty enough boats,' Gurney answered, 'but we saw that bell swagger Faugres down along the quay, in an inn.'

'Faugres!' Eloise exclaimed. 'Could you be sure?'

'Certain sure, miss,' Gurney answered.

'The damned fellow's a zealot!' Henry declared. 'Doesn't he ever give up?'

'He has always hated me,' Eloise replied. 'Why, I don't know, but I fear he also lusts after me.'

'We'll have to get rid of the fellow,' Henry declared. 'Any suggestions?'

'Kill him,' Eloise said flatly.

'And have the traps after us for murder?' Henry replied. 'A truly profound scheme.'

'Back in Plymouth, we'd have 'im pressed,' Gurney put in.

'Sadly, we are not in Plymouth but Cosne,' Henry answered. 'Yet still . . .'

Eloise walked along the quay, shivering both with cold and fear. Ahead were the lights of the shabby waterside inn in which Faugres was lodged. In the warmth and companionship of their hired room, it had been easy to be proud and brave, declining the offers of both Peggy and Natalie to act as bait. Now, among the flickering orange shadows of the quayside, her fear and uncertainty had begun to rise.

Her hand was shaking as she pushed at the rough door of the inn. Every face turned to her as she entered, their expressions showing belligerence, lust, amusement. Faugres was immediately obvious, standing at an upright barrel with a mug in one hand, his great shaggy head rising its full height above those around him. His back was to her, making her task that much more difficult. Moving forward through the press, she made for the opposite side of the room, her eyes constantly on the giant cooper. His put his mug to his face as she drew level, downed the contents and wiped his mouth on his sleeve, turning a little as he did so.

Instantly – or so it seemed to Eloise – he gave a great roar and shot out a massive hand. Eloise screamed and leapt back, despite him being all of twelve feet away. A man blocked Faugres's path, making a remark in admonition, only to be swept aside. With a frantic lunge, Eloise pushed between a group of men, drawing a curse and a laugh as she scrambled for the door. It opened under her hand and then she was running, her steps pounding loud in her ears as she sped for the pile of bales among which Henry and Todd Gurney were concealed.

Behind her, she heard Faugres's roar and the slam of the inn door, raising stark terror in her breast. Suddenly the bales seemed impossibly distant, the whole idea completely insane. Faugres would catch her. He would beat both her companions aside, treating them with the same contempt as he had the man who had blocked his path. She would be thrown down among the bales, her skirts wrenched up, her legs spread open . . .

Eloise tripped, half righted herself then stumbled again, to fall among a stack of bales well short of those she had been aiming for. A roar of triumph sounded behind her and she rolled to see Faugres thudding towards her. Scrambling desperately to her feet, she dashed for the open quay, calling out in desperation. A massive hand snatched out, gripping her bodice and tearing downward. She screamed as her breasts burst free of their constraint; then she stumbled back to fall full length among the bales behind her.

Faugres loomed over her, his face a demonic red in the distant torchlight, scarlet eyes staring and teeth set in a triumphant grin. Frozen, she saw his hands go to his belt and pull the buckle loose, then move to the pegs that held in the terrifying bulge in the leather of his breeches.

'This is for your cunt, whore,' he snarled.

Eloise shrank back, unable to speak or move, yet painfully aware of the cold night air on her naked breasts. Her eyes were riveted to the pegs of Faugres's breeches, watching them pop open one by one, each movement bringing the moment of her violation closer.

'Best do as you're ordered,' he growled. 'Now spread those soft white thighs and show me your cunt.'

Terrified, Eloise moved to obey, watching Faugres's

expression of vicious lust build as she edged up her skirts and opened her legs to display herself. For a moment, his grin broke apart, displaying a thick red tongue-tip. His fingers opened the last catch, his breeches came open and his grossly erect penis broke out as he began to sink down towards her. She gave a broken sob as his hip touched between her open thighs, only dimly registering the sound of pounding boots on stone as she braced herself for rape.

Gurney swung his hand around and brought it down on the back of Faugres's skull with all his force, a blow that would have rendered most men senseless. The giant roared in pain and turned, hurling a great arm out in a wild swing. Gurney jumped back and swung in again as Faugres fought for balance. The blow impacted the giant's forehead, forcing another bellow of rage from him. For an instant, Gurney caught a glimpse of Eloise's face, wide-eyed in more than simple terror. Then the massive body of the Frenchman had come between them, Faugres aiming another vicious swipe even as he struggled to rise. Gurney caught the blow on his arm, driving his fist in as he lurched to the side under the sheer weight of the giant's swing.

As Faugres staggered upright, Gurney realised that his two blows had been more telling than they had seemed. The huge man was clearly dizzy and, as he swung his arms out in an effort to come to grips with his opponent, Gurney jumped easily away. Faugres gave a furious roar, swinging out blindly. Gurney ducked the blow, darted a jab to his opponent's stomach and jumped back. Once more Faugres came forward, roaring wildly and swinging punches that met empty air.

Henry's voice called out from behind and Gurney ducked and turned, leaving the raging giant faced with the barrels of both the late Captain Jinks's pistols. For a moment, it seemed as if Faugres would charge in regardless, but he slowed and stood back, glaring wordlessly at his antagonists. Beyond Faugres, Eloise appeared, limping slightly and with her breasts hanging free of her bodice.

'Idiot!' she managed, addressing Henry. 'Why weren't you quicker?'

Faugres looked round, throwing a glare of utter hatred at Eloise, then turned back to Gurney and Henry.

'Who are you?' he demanded.

'Henry Truscott, a friend of the demoiselle,' Henry replied, 'who I see is in as charming a temper as ever. The fellow with the dowsers is Todd Gurney, a man you would do well to avoid, despite your size. Now, as your breeches are already halfway to the ground, I suggest you pull them off.'

'What?' Faugres growled.

'Undress,' Henry ordered. 'You're going on a boat trip.'

For a moment, Faugres seemed to once more consider the advisability of a renewed assault, then reluctantly began to remove his clothes. They made swift work of tying him, using his clothes and a length of cord to bind his wrists and ankles before gagging him with a cloth. Finding a sack that seemed by the smell to have been used for carrying fish, Gurney pulled it down around the big Frenchman's shoulders and tied it firmly in place.

Choosing a skiff from among the boats moored below the quay, Gurney and Henry rolled Faugres into it and untied the painter, ignoring the big man's increasingly furious struggles as he realised what was happening.

'*Bon voyage*' Henry quipped as they pushed the skiff out on to the dark waters of the Loire, 'and may we sincerely hope it's a long one.'

The skiff drifted out into the current, spinning slowly. The low black shape became a shadow amongst other shadows, then disappeared entirely, with only the occasional muffled curse providing evidence of Faugres' continued resistance.

'Shouldn't you put your tits back in?' Henry remarked to Eloise, in an attempt at suavity.

Henry stood up, surveying the landscape from the landau which Gurney had pulled to a stop. They had reached a junction, with tracks leading south and north but a wide lake to the west.

'North or south?' he asked Eloise.

'Am I a Tourangelle peasant girl, that I should know every track in the Sologne?' Eloise answered with a drunken laugh.

Henry sighed. The previous night, after disposing of Faugres, they had agreed to attempt to cross the Sologne after all. Not only did it seem probable that Faugres' companions were searching for them, but the ease with which they had been followed suggested that they were simply too conspicuous. Not only might they be caught by their pursuers, but there seemed a high chance of running foul of revolutionary mobs. Recalling the burning *seigneuries* seen on his journey to Burgundy, Henry had finally given in to the majority.

Eloise had began the day morose and fearful, but drink and the memory of what they had done to Jean Faugres had cheered her, until by noon she was boasting of how she had lured him from the tavern and trying to goad Henry into sex. He had ignored her, despite the temptation, determined to push on and thus ensure that they reached the far side of the great bend of the Loire long before any pursuit that remained. Now they seemed stuck, faced with another of the interminable Sologne tracks, all of which looked the same and none of which appeared willing to take them west. The flat land of the plateau made matters worse, with an apparently endless succession of bogs, ponds and forest making navigation difficult in the extreme.

'Let us eat, then,' he sighed. 'I will scout a little way to south and north to see if this lake is easily rounded.'

'As you like sir,' Gurney responded.

'I shall come with you,' Eloise said merrily. 'I am a little stiff from sitting in one place all morning.'

Henry glanced at her, meaning to suggest that she would only hinder him but finding his eyes locked to the deep, creamy white division of her breasts, across which a curl of red-gold hair lay in artless display. Suddenly, the need for haste seemed less important. Their discussion the previous night had been pessimistic, he reasoned. When he was eventually extricated from the skiff, Faugres would have little choice but to turn back for St Romain, while there had been no sign of their other pursuers at Cosne.

'A pleasure,' he said instead. 'To the south first, I think.'

Peggy threw him a curious look as he climbed down from the landau, half amused, half jealous. Henry returned his brightest smile and pondered asking her to join them, only to abandon the idea. Eloise was plainly drunk and had relaxed the aloof air she still tried to maintain, except when terrified or in the throes of passion. Clearly she was game for dalliance, but Henry was unsure whether the game could be pushed to the point where both women might surrender themselves with equal abandon.

Eloise spun, making the truncated yellow dress rise to show off yet more of her legs. Already dizzy with wine, she slipped and sat down hard on the springy turf, giving a squeak and then a giggle. Henry, she was sure, could not fail to respond to her open flirting, and she was looking forward to the moment when he took her in his arms.

Yet, despite the opportunity presented by her fall, he remained calm, his real feelings betrayed only by the

163

conspicuous bulge in his breeches. She pouted, wondering if his interest was moving towards Peggy and whether he had visited the plump English girl during the night. Anger and determination flared up in her at the thought that he might prefer her maid over her. Turning and pretending to slip once more, she artfully allowed him a glimpse of the red-gold curls between her thighs, then giggled, closed her legs and looked up at him from beneath long eyelashes.

Henry returned a polite smile and glanced away over the lake. Piqued, Eloise followed his gaze, finding only a broad stretch of dark brown mud and then the ruffled surface of the water. Turning back to him, she found him idly scratching the back of his neck.

Torn between the urge to jump to her feet and storm away and the desire to turn on her front and present him with her naked bottom, she did neither, instead giving him a resentful, sulky pout. As his hands went to the buttons of his breeches, her moue turned to a smile. Clearly he had simply been preoccupied, and was now ready to give her what she needed.

She watched as he undressed, admiring his muscular body. Feeling deliciously wanton, she spread her legs apart and put a hand to her cunny, masturbating shamelessly as he stripped. She was wet and quickly becoming wetter as he removed the last of his garments and placed them to the side. His cock was half-erect, jutting from his body with the head already protruding from the foreskin.

'Take me, Henry,' she sighed. 'Take me now.'

He bent, scooping her up so that her thighs spread across his trunk and his cock pressed on her vulva. She groaned and wiggled her bottom to rub herself against the firm shaft, only wishing that it had been hard enough to slide straight into her. Not that it would be long, she realised, as it began to harden against her wriggling cunt. He slid a hand under her bottom, pressing his cock into the groove between her buttocks. It rubbed, and then the head was against her vagina and suddenly she was full of thick, hard penis and groaning out her pleasure to the empty woods.

With her hands around his neck, she began to bounce, laughing and crying out at the blissful sensation of the cock inside her. Henry responded to her movements briefly, then began to walk, quite casually, with her still riding his cock.

'What are you doing?' she asked as he moved on to the fringe of grass by the lake. 'Not on the ground; I like it this way!'

He made no response, but pulled her up from his cock and stood her down on the spongy turf.

'Hey!' Eloise protested as firm hands turned her to face the lake. 'Oh, so be it, then, but there are other parts of me besides my bottom!'

She began to bend, expecting entry from the rear. Henry's hand went to her bottom, spreading the cheeks. She wondered if she was to be buggered, then squealed with alarm as he gave a sudden and unexpected thrust of his hands.

Henry laughed as Eloise pitched forward to fall face down into the lakeside mud. Her scream of outrage was abruptly cut short as she landed with not only her chest and arms but also her face in the thick brown goo. He was still laughing as she came up spluttering, then cursing after blowing out a mouthful of thick brown-black mud. Trying to stand, she raised herself halfway, only to slip once more and land with a meaty splat, sitting in the glutinous brown mess with her skirts up and the red-gold tangles of her cunny on plain view. One breast had also popped out, peeping over the top of her filthy bodice like a small pink pig looking out of a mud wallow.

'Will you help me?' she snapped as she endeavoured

165

to cover her shame with the tattered remains of her dress.

'Certainly,' Henry chuckled, and stepped forward carefully, bracing one foot against a decaying branch as he extended a hand.

She gripped it and pulled, her bottom pulling from the mud with a sticky sucking noise. For a moment she hung poised, Henry leaning back to pull her slowly upright. With a soggy crack the branch he was on broke, sending Eloise flying back into the mud while he was forced to flail his arms desperately in order to effect a recovery. Regaining his balance, he found Eloise once more sitting down in the mud, only this time with her legs splayed out at right angles to each other and what remained of her skirt spread like a flower on the mud. The expression of absolute disgust on her face told what had happened as eloquently as did her somewhat pathetic position.

'I am soiled!' she groaned. 'Soiled everywhere!'

'Which is how I want you,' Henry assured her. 'Come on, spread those pretty thighs for me.'

'Just get me out, you childish idiot!' she spat.

Henry laughed and knelt down, his bare knees sinking into the goo, and leant forward. Ignoring her protests, he pushed her back and mounted her, feeling the mud squelch between their bodies as he settled himself between her thighs. Her legs were splayed under him, one of them cocked out at an angle, leaving his crotch in contact with the soft mound of her cunny. Her flesh was slippery with mud and, as she wriggled to free herself from beneath him, her other breast came free.

'Hold still,' he ordered, reaching for his still half-stiff penis.

'What are you doing?' she demanded. 'Get off, you imbecile!'

He fumbled at his crotch, his knuckles knocking on her mud-smeared pudenda as he began to pull at his cock.

'Henry!' Eloise exclaimed in alarm as he put the tip of his half-stiff penis to the slimy inlet of her vagina.

Ignoring her, he tugged hard at his shaft and buried his face in the plump softness of her exposed breasts. Eloise gave a sharp little gasp as the stubble of his cheek brushed a nipple.

'No! Henry! Not in me . . .' she faltered even as she abandoned her attempts to escape his hold. 'I am soiled, really soiled!'

Erect, he pushed his cock at her vagina, finding it cool, slimy, open – yet oddly resistant.

'Henry, no!' she squealed, even as his cock began to squash into her vagina.

'Ah! That is cold,' he breathed, 'but good. Your cunt must be full of mud.'

Eloise responded with a noise expressing utter disgust, only for it to change into a low moan as Henry pushed his cock into her. He could feel the mud, firm and heavy against his penis, squeezing out around the sides as he entered her and folding his cock in a clammy embrace.

The sensation of cold mud in her vagina was as exquisite as it was unfamiliar. Drawing in his breath, he began to fuck, pushing Eloise down into the soft mud so that it rose to squash around his balls and at the juncture of his cock and her already filthy vagina. At first she maintained an angry silence but, as he continued to hump merrily away, she began to moan softly and finally to grunt as her arms went around his back and she hugged him to her filthy body.

'That's my Eloise,' Henry gasped as he mired his penis to the very hilt in her mud-filled vagina. 'Good, isn't it, my little puppy?'

Her answering sigh signalled agreement and he began to speed up, intent on reaching his orgasm while the mud enveloping his cock was still cool. Even as his pleasure rose towards orgasm, his mind filled with the thought of how her luscious bottom would look smeared with mud and he realised that he had to make use of it before he came. Checking himself, he pulled back, Eloise giving a disappointed moan as his cock pulled free of her vagina.

'Turn over, trollop,' he ordered.

'Oh, yes, see my bottom; it must be filthy,' she moaned. 'Slap it, then put your cock in it.'

Henry had intended to slap a fresh handful of mud into her vagina and then finish himself off in that orifice. The idea still appealed, yet the invitation to sodomise her was too good to pass up.

Her buttocks were covered in mud, a filthy brown mess that clung to the skin and matted her hair. Taking his cock in one hand, he nursed his erection as he scooped up a big handful of thick, sticky mud and slapped it on to Eloise's genitals. She gave a little gasp, then a deep sigh as he used his palm to press a good volume of the muck actually into her vagina.

'You bastard!' she moaned. 'Go on, fill my cunt, then do it in my bottom. Oh, it's going to come out, Henry; look, look.'

As he watched, her vagina closed, exuding a thick worm of mud that stood out for a moment and then fell into her ruined petticoats.

'By God, you're a dirty bitch, Eloise,' he laughed. 'So you want it in your breech, do you?'

'Yes,' she breathed. 'Sodomise me, Henry. Do it in my bottom, Henry: deep, deep in my bottom, while I touch myself.'

Her anus pouted as she spoke, bulging out under its coating of mud to show a pink centre as she offered it. As he readied his cock, she slid a hand back between her thighs and began to rub the slime into the area around her clitoris.

Henry edged forward, slipping once, then pressing his mud-slicked cock to the proffered bum-hole. Eloise groaned loudly as her anus stretched out around the head of his cock, then began to grunt as he started to force himself up her back passage. He drew in his breath as the soft, warm flesh of her rectum enfolded his cock. The cooling effect of the mud made her body heat seem unnaturally high, almost scalding. Always sensitive, the tip of his penis felt as if it was being pushed into a pat of hot lard. Even as the hilt of his erection wedged up against the straining ring of her anus, he came, spurt after spurt of boiling come erupting into her bowels. At the very peak of his ecstasy, he felt her sphincter clamp on the base of his cock and she too started to come, her screams of desire blending with his grunted oaths as they climaxed together.

Some miles to the north, on a river bank near the town of Gien, Jean Faugres was undergoing an equally muddy but less pleasant experience. Morning had found his skiff on a sandbank in the middle of the Loire. He had still been securely bound and unable to do more than squirm and rage in the evil-smelling sack. So conditions had remained until finally a fisherman had noticed that something was amiss and released him.

Covered in insect bites and wearing only his shirt, he now sat on the quay at Gien, munching a generously donated sausage and thinking black thoughts of Eloise, Gurney and, in particular, Henry. There had been something about the Englishman's manner that was particularly irritating. Gurney, with his ready fists and rough manner, he felt he could tolerate, even respect, as few men indeed had had the courage to challenge him since he had grown to his full height. Henry was different, combining all the features that Faugres most despised – wealth, breeding, looks and the smug arrogance that went with them. Worse still, he strongly suspected that the preening, self-satisfied Englishman was Eloise's lover.

* * *

Natalie Moreau twisted the hank of sodden yellow silk in her hands, spraying drops of water across the lush grass of the bank. A stinging sensation in her bottom bore testimony to Eloise's rancour at having been used by Henry in so humiliating a fashion. Or rather, as Natalie knew, to having taken so much pleasure in being so used.

She had been birched, yet even while she had writhed naked under the blows of a hastily assembled bunch of twigs, she had been aware of a difference in Eloise's manner. There had always been an intimacy to her beatings, and both women accepted that the normal end to such a punishment would be cuddles and the fervent licking of each other's genitals. This occasion was no different, with Natalie being told to strip and wash her mistress, then made to kneel on the damp grass and wait while Eloise selected twigs. The beating had been brisk and hard, leaving Natalie trembling with pain and need. Eloise had then ordered her to masturbate and watched with a smile of quiet satisfaction on her face as her red bottomed maid brought herself to a climax.

The difference had been that, while Eloise was normally indifferent to who saw or heard Natalie's degradation, she had been very careful to ensure that the beating took place well out of Todd Gurney's hearing. Even in the extreme of her pain, Natalie had felt a quiet comfort in the knowledge that her mistress evidently respected the big man who had become her lover. Then, when bringing herself to orgasm under Eloise's gaze, she had thought not of the anguish of her punishment, but of how her mistress would look kicking and thrashing over Todd Gurney's knee in the course of a bare-bottomed spanking.

As the shadows began to lengthen across the western Sologne, the landau reached more broken land, with small valleys cutting down through the clay. Henry's mind began to turn towards the prospect of another night in the open, which, with the evening chill already beginning to bite, was a less than pleasant prospect. Glancing at Eloise and Peggy, he wondered if the cold of the coming night might not provide the excuse he needed to further his desire to bed them simultaneously. Peggy returned his smile, but he found Eloise frowning and looking into the sunset.

'Is something wrong?' he asked, turning on his bench.

'The light, it seems . . . strange,' Eloise replied.

'Fire,' Gurney answered from the carthorse. 'Some way ahead and down to the south.'

'Best avoid it,' Henry replied.

'True, sir,' Gurney answered, 'only the track seems to run true and there hasn't been a turning for a way.'

'Then we'll pull the landau in among the trees,' Henry stated. 'Make yourselves comfortable, girls, but don't start a fire. I've a mind to see what's afoot.'

With the landau unrigged and hidden well in among a copse of young willows, Henry and Gurney saddled the two greys. Ignoring Eloise's protests that they would be better employed guarding the camp, they set off in the direction of the fire, now a clear orange patch against the evening sky.

The fire became audible as they approached, the crackle of flames punctuated by the occasional crash and also by human voices raised in glee. With great caution they approached, until the lane turned sharply and brought them out over a nightmare scene.

Below them stood a Château, the windows of its splendid façade and high turrets red with fire. Part of the roof had already collapsed, creating a fiery maw from which great red embers rose into the cold air. Black and orange shadows danced a wild jig on the formal lawn, where peasants in looted finery cavorted in patterns no less savage. Among them, up on a chair and with his neck in a noose suspended from the bough of an ornamental cherry, stood a man. His hands were tied and he had little option but to watch the conflagration in front of him, yet he remained straight and proud, while his face carried no fear but only an expression of haughty distaste. His fine clothes and powdered wig proclaimed him a noble and perhaps even the master of the Château.

'He holds himself well,' Gurney remarked.

'Indeed,' Henry replied. 'Damn few at Tyburn or Newgate ever wore a face like that.'[7]

'Proud buggers, these French lords,' Gurney stated.

Henry grunted his assent and took a pull from the bottle of Méursault he had brought to sustain himself.

'Cowardly mob, as a whole, the French,' he went on as he passed the bottle to Gurney. 'I mean to say, take these revolutionary fellows. They used to bow and scrape and fairly grovel, but give 'em the whip hand and look at them. Now talk down to an Englishman and he'll likely black your eye, but he won't burn your house around your ears, nor yet hang you. Cowards, as I say.'

'That's nothing but a parcel of old crams, begging your pardon sir,' Gurney answered. 'When they were with the rebels to America, I've seen 'em stand to the last man.'

'But those were soldiers and veterans to boot,' Henry answered. 'This crew would scatter if a party of your brothers so much as said "boh".'

A fresh section of roof collapsed, sending a spray of sparks high into the night sky. The crash of timbers and tile came to Henry with a gust of laughter and cheering from the peasants. One, a lanky man with a straggling beard, thrust his torch close to the helpless noble, forcing him to move. The chair rocked and for a moment hung on one leg as the man struggled to retain his balance. By a desperate effort he succeeded, returning to his stony immobility as the mob laughed at his plight.

'Wicked bastards, cowards or no,' Gurney spat.

'Don't tell me you're squeamish?' Henry responded. 'You must have seen enough men meet their end, surely?'

'Not like this, sir,' Gurney growled. 'A fair fight's one thing, but . . .'

'D'you say we run him off then?' Henry asked. 'It shouldn't be hard. Ride in like fury. I slash the rope, you pinch the fellow and away before they can raise a belch.'

'Could be done, sir,' Gurney answered thoughtfully, 'but what of the wenches?'

'I wasn't suggesting they came,' Henry laughed. 'Lend me your knife, would you? My own lacks weight.'

'I don't know about this, sir,' Gurney objected, but still drew the wicked foot-long knife from the sheath at his belt.

'Nonsense,' Henry laughed, 'they're paying no mind to the road and drunk besides. Come, let's take the fellow, it'll make a fine tale in the Five Shillings of a winter's evening.'

'And after?' Gurney asked.

'The devil with after,' Henry replied and clapped his heels into the flanks of his horse.

'Sir!' Gurney's voice sounded after him, but an instant later the clatter of hooves signalled that he was not alone.

A wild surge of exhilaration welled up inside him as the grey tore between the banks of the track. For a moment, only the burning turrets of the Château were visible. Then the peasants were ahead, leaping and swinging torches and farm tools, laughing and calling out to one another. One turned, his expression of drunken pleasure turning to horror as the grey crashed over a low hedge and burst on to the lawn.

Henry gave an exultant shout as the man fell away beneath his horse's hooves. More heads were turning,

173

faces stupefied with drink and destruction registering terror as they found themselves in the path of the two horses. The nobleman turned, his impassive face briefly showing terror as Henry slashed out with the knife. The blade caught the rope, cut, slipped free and Henry was past, leaving the nobleman kicking frantically at the air as the chair fell from beneath him. Henry wheeled, slashing at an adze-wielding peasant even as he struggled to bring the frightened grey about. Briefly, he saw Gurney grappling the nobleman and then a foot caught at his stirrup. As he brought the knife hilt down in a hard arc, his fist hit something hard. Someone screamed and the pressure on his foot vanished, leaving him to complete his turn.

'Done, sir!' Gurney called, and Henry shouted to his mount.

The grey accelerated, swerving to avoid a knot of men and breaking for the hedge as Henry wrenched hard at the reins. An instant later, he was through, the grey hard on the hooves of Gurney's horse, across the neck of which lay the nobleman, his face purple and his tongue protruding.

'Loosen the bloody rope, man!' Henry called as they made the mouth of the lane.

The darkness of the track closed on them like a trap as they left the area lit by the fire. Screams of rage sounded behind them, bearing a demented quality that gave Henry his first pang of fear. Praying that the horse would not stumble, he urged it on, his vision slowly adjusting as they clattered up the track. Finally they stopped, turning back to find the peasants milling about on the lawn with a great deal of shouting and cursing but no evidence whatever of organisation.

'Best get back to the landau and under cover,' Henry panted, 'before one of them decides to search out some horses. How is he?'

'Live enough, sir,' Gurney answered, 'but there's

another thing. I'll swear I saw that mop-stick Boillot down among the mob.'

'Boillot?' Henry demanded. 'Here, ahead of us?'

Emile Boillot stared out into the blackness of the hillside, trying to discern detail where none existed. The attack had come so swiftly, the horses appearing from nowhere and retreating as fast, taking the Vicomte d'Arche with them. Yet one of the men had spoken in English, and their horses had been greys. It could only have been the two who had taken Eloise de la Tour-Romain.

Seething with outrage, he began to call out, trying to put some order into the rabble of drunken peasants before the burning Château.

'Henry Truscott, at your service,' Henry introduced himself.

'Donatien, Vicomte d'Arche,' the nobleman replied, taking care to address his remark solely to Henry, 'and be assured that your singular service to my person shall not go unrewarded.'

'Think nothing of it,' Henry replied, brindling slightly at the implications of the other's response.

'Best keep it down, sir, there's torches down along the lane,' Gurney put in.

Henry put his hand to his horse's muzzle, and began to stroke soothingly. They had dismounted and pulled the horses well in among the woods in order to release the noose from around the neck of the nobleman.

'Let us hope the girls have the sense to stay quiet,' he whispered.

'Reckon they will, sir,' Gurney replied.

'You have others with you?' the vicomte asked. 'Women?'

'The Demoiselle Eloise de la Tour-Romain,' Henry answered casually. 'She's a friend of mine, don't you know? A brace of maids as well.'

175

'The daughter of the Comte Saônois?' the vicomte asked in apparent amazement.

'The very same,' Henry replied.

'Death of my life! And what does she do here? In . . . in such company?'

'Oh, this and that. We're on our way to England.'

'England? The poor demoiselle. These are terrible times indeed.'

'England, sir,' Henry retorted, 'has the advantage that one is neither likely to be roasted nor decapitated at a moment's notice.'

'Quiet, sir; they're coming,' Gurney hissed.

The vicomte choked off whatever he had been about to say and ducked down. Together they watched, first hearing the clatter of hooves as three horsemen passed, then watching silently as a large group with torches walked no more than fifty yards from their place of concealment. While the horsemen had been silent, the others were not, but called out angry boasts and drunken threats aimed at their unseen watchers.

Finally they passed and Henry, Gurney and the Vicomte d'Arche began to move cautiously towards where they hoped to find the landau. Despite the dim moonlight Todd Gurney managed to locate the copse of willow and was presently rousing the frightened girls. The vicomte greeted Eloise with obsequious enthusiasm, ignoring the others with the same total disregard that he had shown Gurney.

'It is clear that I owe my very life to you, Demoiselle,' he finished. 'From now on I am your most humble servant, and swear to give you my protection, be it even at the expense of my life.'

'You are kind,' Eloise replied smoothly, 'yet it was no more than courtesy. Observing the flames, and fearing for your safety, I prevailed upon my companions to effect a rescue.'

Henry swallowed his response at Eloise's outright lie,

contenting himself with an internal promise that, at some more convenient moment, she would pay for her coquetry with a sore bottom.

The night passed with the group huddled shivering around the landau, through cold and in some cases through fear. Several times, groups of torch-bearing peasants passed along the track, and the moon had covered a quarter of the sky before the three horsemen, who had been first to pass, returned. Finally all became quiet, and even the dull red light in the western sky faded as the Château was consumed.

Nine

Henry awoke to the plaintive tones of the Vicomte d'Arche bewailing his loss to Eloise. An immediate pang of irritation faded as he rolled and bumped against Peggy's ample bottom. At some point during the night, she had come to him for comfort and warmth, which he had provided by having her curl into his lap and entering her from the rear. The memory of his cock inside her and her full bottom squashing against his front went some way to relieving his annoyance at the newcomer's monopolisation of Eloise, but no more than that. Promising himself to think twice before rescuing anybody else, particularly men, he sat up and yawned widely.

'Wealth and beauty such as may only be found in our dear land,' d'Arche was saying. 'The finest expressions of French art – Le Nain, Boucher, Clouet – burnt to ashes. Tapestries dating back to the fourteenth century, destroyed in flames – marbles, silks, jade, alabaster! My horses! My dogs!'

'Oh, I doubt they'll have burnt the horses and dogs,' Henry quipped. 'Deuced useful things, horses and dogs.'

D'Arche turned him a look that was both puzzled and annoyed, clearly failing to find amusement in the remark.

'Where are Gurney and Natalie?' Henry enquired.

'Your servant is on watch,' Eloise replied. 'I have sent my maid to fetch water.'

'Hm, right,' Henry answered, ignoring the temptation to respond to Eloise's sudden formality with a reminder of how she had allowed Gurney to come between her breasts. 'So, then, the country is up. How do we make past?'

Henry reined in his grey with a sigh. The day had been trying, although less dangerous that he had expected. Guided by the expert local knowledge of the Vicomte d'Arche, they had crossed the plateau of the Touraine by moving between areas of hunting preserve and avoiding the more populous riverside areas to the north and south.

Also, as d'Arche explained in a voice heavy with regret, the majority of the Touranjou nobility had signed a declaration expressing sympathy with the revolutionary ideals of liberty, brotherhood and equality. He was among the few who had refused to join what he saw as a treacherous and cowardly cabal, but it did mean that the area was quieter than it might have been. Indeed, the vicomte maintained that even he would have been spared, had it not been for the inflammatory rhetoric of a lank stranger who had appeared in the district on the very day his Château was attacked.

This was clearly Emile Boillot, who had evidently ridden hard across the Sologne while Henry's party had been either lost or indulging their lust. Both Henry and Eloise tactfully forbore to point this out to the vicomte.

While d'Arche had proved a useful guide, his presence had otherwise proved an irritation. Not only had he monopolised Eloise's company and conversation, but he seemed to regard this as his natural right. He also assumed that the maids, Gurney and even to some extent Henry were automatically subject to his orders. After a while, Henry had abandoned the landau and joined Gurney as postillion, sharing a sympathetic glance with the man who to him was as much friend as servant.

At length they had crossed the great Ambois Forest and arrived on the bank of the Loire at an area of crumbling cliff, ragged forest and vineyard, above which stood a Château which bore every sign of desertion.

'L'Husseau,' d'Arche explained, pointing up to the Château. 'Seat of the Borillon family, who, like myself, refused to countenance the concept of equality with base artisans and soil-turners . . .'

'A good place for the night, perhaps?' Henry asked before d'Arche could start once more on his favourite theme. 'The horses could do with rest and fodder and it seems secluded.'

'Perhaps,' d'Arche agreed, 'but let us make an inspection. Man, pull the carriage in among the trees.'

Gurney gave a muttered oath but obeyed, pulling his horse round to draw the landau in among a thick stand of oak and thorn. Henry dismounted and, together with the vicomte, ascended the broad yellow-stone steps that led from the river bank up to the Château.

A narrow courtyard fronted the Château, a structure which Henry now realised was not merely built into the face of the cliff, but to a certain extent actually carved from the cliff. Commenting on what seemed to him a curious practice, he was informed by the vicomte that such construction was commonplace in the Touraine, with everything from the meanest hovels to churches and fine houses carved direct from the rock.

The brief but amicable conversation had the effect of breaking something of a barrier between the two men. They spoke for a moment more, discussing neutral topics until the vicomte went quiet and Henry sensed that something of greater moment was about to be said.

'Today has not been easy for me,' the vicomte began as he turned to look out over the Loire. 'I have lost everything I held dear, save for one.'

180

'Think nothing of it,' Henry replied airily, guessing that the vicomte was about to make an emotional thank you for his life.

'You are a gentleman, of sorts,' d'Arche sighed, ignoring Henry's remark completely, 'and I must tell someone. I am in love with the demoiselle: desperately, agonisingly in love, in love with a passion you could not begin to understand!'

'Something of a swift decision, I might think,' Henry replied after a moment of uncertainty as to a suitable response to a revelation that was not only embarrassingly intimate but somewhat awkward, in the circumstances.

'Not at all,' the vicomte replied. 'Not at all. I fell in love with her at the seat of the Seigneur de Fourchaume. She was radiant, in blue silk, a vision I will never forget . . .'

'Did you, er . . .?' Henry enquired, thinking of Eloise's wanton, if scarcely straightforward, response to his own advances.

'Did we consummate our love?' d'Arche finished for him. 'No, we did not, for she is a delicate, innocent creature – shy and modest. Beneath, there is passion; it could not be otherwise.'

'I see,' Henry replied diffidently as it became plain that the vicomte, in fact, hardly knew Eloise at all.

'Yet you must know something of this, for all your cold English blood?' d'Arche enquired.

'A little, perhaps,' Henry responded.

'To woo her, I needed time, and solitude,' the vicomte continued. 'Alas, it never came.'

'Yes, I know,' Henry replied, with feeling. 'Many's the fine wench I'd have tupped, given half an hour alone with her.'

D'Arche shot him a sudden, sharp look, but an impatient call from Eloise herself cut off whatever he had intended to say. Henry walked to the balustrade

181

and signalled for the landau to come round to the drive. As he looked down, he saw that Gurney was reprimanding Eloise for having called out and, to his amusement, that her response was more apologetic than haughty.

Little more than a mile distant, in the village of St Martin-le-Beau, Emile Boillot sat in the common room of an inn. A map was spread out before him and a cup of pale wine clasped in his hand while he studied the routes his quarry might have taken. The rescue of the Vicomte d'Arche had added new resolve to his quest, while the failure of his search parties on the Sologne had added a further note of frustration.

Looking at the map, and assuming that the group were intent on making for England without delay, few routes seemed open to them. Their presence in the southern Sologne argued against their making for the ports of Normandy, which meant that they would be hard put to avoid passing through the cities of Tours and Angers. Of the two, Angers was nearer the sea, and seemed the most likely place to head off his quarry.

Briefly, he wondered what had become of Jean Faugres. While a fine ally, the giant's irascibility was a hindrance, as was his refusal to do anything other than that which he himself decided. Putting the thought aside, he returned to the map, stabbing his finger down on the city of Angers as he decided on his course of action.

Having made a brief exploration of the Château while the landau and horses were being stabled, Henry found Gurney in the courtyard. Leaving the Vicomte d'Arche to join Eloise at the balustrade, he made his way over.

'I've put her well under cover, sir,' his companion announced as he approached, 'and sent Natalie and Peggy to gather fodder.'

'Good,' Henry replied. 'The house has been looted to the last pisspot, or else smashed. It's not likely any'll come by here tonight.'

'Still, sir,' Gurney answered, 'we'd best sleep in the cellars.'

'I,' d'Arche stated coldly from behind them, 'shall sleep in a bedroom. No d'Arche yet hid from a rabble of peasants.'

'Well, they'd best learn,' Gurney retorted.

'And you had best learn to curb your tongue!' d'Arche answered.

'Care to try?' Gurney growled.

'By God, I'll teach you to be insolent!' d'Arche exclaimed.

'Donatien, please!' Eloise interrupted. 'He understands nothing of noble pride and seeks only to guard us from harm.'

For a moment d'Arche remained silent, his face red and his lips tight. Todd Gurney returned the angry stare with a look of contempt and calmly folded his heavily muscled arms across his chest.

'So be it.' D'Arche spoke coldly. 'For your sake, Demoiselle, I will refrain from giving the insolent lout the thrashing he so richly deserves. Perhaps if you would be so kind as to send your maids to make two bedrooms as comfortable as is possible amidst this wreckage.'

Henry let his breath out slowly, half glad that Eloise had managed to defuse the situation, but half wishing that Gurney had laid the arrogant vicomte out with a few well-placed punches. Harmony of sorts had existed before their rescue of d'Arche, and it was largely the nobleman's superior airs that had caused this to deteriorate.

'There seem to be plenty of vineyards in the district,' he stated in a bluff attempt to rescue what remained of the party's comradeship. 'Perhaps there are some bottles in the cellar. This is partridge eye country, isn't it?'

'Not at all,' d'Arche drawled. 'We are close to the towns of Vouvray and Montlouis. The wine is fine, white and sweet at its best, with scents of apples and honey – a true elixir.'

'Hm,' Henry answered. 'We've no more than a half-dozen of the Méursault left; let us make a brief foray to the cellars.'

'Undoubtedly it will have been looted,' d'Arche stated.

'Who can say,' Henry responded, 'without at least making a search? Gurney?'

Together, he and Todd Gurney quickly located a route to the cellar, a narrow stairway which spiralled down to a door that bore signs of having been forced, and recently. Henry pushed in, refusing to allow the fact to overcome his optimism.

The cellar was a great room divided by numerous squat arches. Marks on the floor and walls showed where barrels had stood and a litter of broken glass carpeted the place, with a few half-dried puddles of wine lying in depressions. Narrow windows provided light, but at the back – where the building met the cliff – patches of black gloom showed. They crossed towards these, finding them to be tunnels carved from the native rock and, as Henry's eyes adjusted to the dim light, he caught the dull yellow-brown gleam of stacked bottles. He chuckled to himself as he moved forward, then called to Gurney to come and inspect his discovery.

'Plenty enough there, sir,' Gurney remarked as he came up with Henry, 'but I'd give the lot for a peck of good cider or ale.'

'Wine must suffice,' Henry replied cheerfully. 'Now, let us see if we can find something in which to carry it.'

As they pulled bottles from the grime-encrusted stack and transferred them to a broken wooden case, they fell to discussing the Vicomte d'Arche.

'The fellow's a burden,' Henry stated. 'I say we leave him to go his own way.'

'I'd not be sorry to see the back of him,' Gurney agreed, 'but he knows the country, and that could count.'

'True enough,' Henry responded, 'but there's another trouble, the nincompoop is smitten with Eloise! Not that he's come in for more than a dog's portion, by his own account, yet still.'

'More than likely that's true of half the nobs in France, sir,' Gurney responded. 'She's a rum piece and a biter, too, when all's said.'

'That she is,' Henry agreed, 'and I'll be damned if I'll miss out on my share tonight, moon-struck vicomte or none.'

Donatien, Vicomte d'Arche, adjusted the cuffs of his somewhat soiled coat of heavy lavender cloth. The shattered remains of a once beautiful mirror showed his reflection, which remained that of a poised young nobleman, despite his various deprivations. Eloise de la Tour-Romain would be unable to resist him, of that he was certain. After days spent in the company of the coarse Englishman and his yet coarser servant, she would undoubtedly be grateful for his company. Moreover, while the collapse of the *ancien régime* might have torn his world apart, it also meant that the codes and restraints that might previously have prevented him from applying sufficient duress to overcome her natural maidenly resistance no longer applied.

With his cock stiffening in his breeches, he made a final adjustment to his coat and left the room. A gay greeting answered his knock and increased his confidence of an easy seduction. Within the room, Eloise stood over her bustling maid, watching the girl's efforts to make a comfortable bed from the torn remains of cushions, curtains and a blanket from the landau. At his entrance, Eloise looked round, expressing exactly the measure of ingenuous surprise he had anticipated. The

185

game, he knew well, would involve her feigned reluctance to his advances, gradually giving way to passion as her feelings overwhelmed her. The sole remaining question was how much force he would have to apply in order to overcome that pretence of unwillingness demanded by her station.

'Vicomte,' she greeted him. 'I had thought you retired.'

'With the fairest rose in all France so close?' he answered. 'Am I made of stone, to resist such temptation?'

'Yet to enter my room can serve only to increase that temptation,' she replied, placing a delicate hand to the swell of her breasts and glancing at him from beneath lowered eyelashes.

D'Arche's pulse began to hammer at her response, which represented a level of flirtation far more open than he had expected. Clearly, the beauty was as eager for his embraces as he for hers.

'Come,' he breathed, 'enough of this. We both know our needs. Send your maid away.'

'Sir, you mistake me!' Eloise answered, backing away giggling.

'Come,' d'Arche answered in passion, 'do not be coy! All around us our world is in flames. We few are left who truly appreciate what it means to be French and noble. Come, Eloise, let us console ourselves in each other's arms! Let us make love with the true fire and passion of our souls!'

'Sir!' Eloise giggled, her hand going to her mouth in mock alarm at his passion.

He came forward, reaching out for her bodice as the maid squeaked and scurried to the side. Eloise gave a gasp of shock as her breasts tumbled out of the torn bodice and then she was in his arms, the last shred of her resistance fading as he crushed his lips to hers.

A cough sounded from the direction of the door,

d'Arche turning to find Henry Truscott standing in the portal.

Henry watched with a cool smile as the vicomte stood back and Eloise hastily returned her breasts to her bodice.

'You, sir, are intruding,' the vicomte said in a cold voice.

'To the contrary,' Henry answered. 'It is you who intrude, and I must ask you to go, immediately.'

'What?' d'Arche demanded. 'By what right?'

'By the trust placed in me by the Comte Saônois,' Henry lied. 'To whom I swore to allow no man to lay hands on his daughter. Now go.'

D'Arche hesitated and Henry raised his chin in an effort to look as noble and determined as was possible. Eloise glanced at him, then at the vicomte, apparently in the throes of a difficult decision. For a moment Henry thought she was going to give him the lie, and then she hung her head and gently bit her lower lip.

'Very well,' the vicomte answered at last and, with a stiff bow, left the room.

As the door shut, Henry walked forward, half angry, half inflamed by Eloise's obvious state of arousal. She gave him a worried look that quickly turned to a nervous smile.

'Thank you, Henry, for your timely arrival,' she stammered as he came close. 'I was in fear of my virtue.'

'Virtue!' Henry retorted. 'You were going to tup, by God! Weren't you, you little bob-tail?'

'And if I was?' Eloise retorted, suddenly changing tack. 'When you've been mounting my maid?'

'A maid you had seduce me, so don't play that game!' Henry snapped. 'Besides, I haven't risked my neck in your country of murderous peasants without some reward.'

'Ha!' Eloise snorted. 'You'd not have come at all if

you'd not killed a man in a drunken rage! Do you think I don't know that?'

'Well, I did come, didn't I?' Henry answered. 'I'll get you clear yet, as well; you'll see.'

'Maybe,' she snapped back, 'but if we make England, it'll be by luck alone. God, why of all the men in the world do I get a drunken, brawling, lecherous, childish ape?'

'By God, I'll give you the spanking you deserve!' Henry roared. 'Here and now!'

'I feel sure you will, you wicked brute,' Eloise retorted, 'and use me most brutally afterwards!'

'Just as you please,' Henry answered, his anger fading as he realised that, since the onset of their argument, Eloise had been angling for exactly the response he was now giving.

'Do it, then, you big, strong man,' she continued hotly. 'Show how strong you are. Strip me bare and beat my bottom, then use my cunt while I'm blubbering on the floor!'

Henry darted forward and grabbed her by the arm, throwing her off balance so that she sprawled on the pile of ruined upholstery from which Natalie had been preparing a bed. In an instant, he was on her back and had pinned her down. In the corner of the room, Natalie looked on, her mouth open in surprise and not a little pleasure as Henry began to strip her mistress.

Eloise struggled, kicking her legs and beating her fists on the floor as Henry undid the buttons of her dress one by one. He simply laughed and continued his work, finishing the buttons and then opening her chemise and tugging her upper clothing down so that her breasts popped out to squash against the floor. Moving down, but keeping his weight firmly on top of her, he tugged her dress over her hips to expose the plump swell of her bottom beneath her petticoats. Her breathing was coming deep and hard as he fiddled with her draw-strings and she gave a sigh of resignation as the bulk of her petticoats were pulled down to expose her magnificent bottom.

Chuckling, Henry slapped a plump cheek, then quickly turned to straddle her back once more. Her struggles had reached a crescendo at the moment her bottom was bared, and she now lay almost still, with no more than an occasional feeble kick to make a show of resistance. Henry peeled away her skirts and petticoats, then removed her boots to leave her entirely naked but for her garters and stockings.

'Bastard!' she swore breathlessly as he laid his cock between her naked buttocks.

He merely laughed and began to rub his penis in the soft cleft of her bottom as he wondered whether to carry out his threat of spanking her, or simply to mount her from the rear and slip his cock into what he had no doubt would prove a well-lubricated vagina. Her bottom was tempting, a bare, pink peach with the cheeks moving sluggishly in her anticipation of punishment, clenching and then opening to reveal a puff of deep red hair. He put a hand to one cheek and wobbled it, drawing an impassioned sob from Eloise. As he did so, his cock slipped a little deeper into her crease, which then closed to fold the shaft in hot, female flesh.

'By God, but I've got to fuck you, you ripe little baggage,' he growled as he began to rise. 'Get on your knees.'

'No! Henry!' she protested, making no move to obey his order.

'Come on,' he urged, 'get that big arse in the air!' He slid an arm under her stomach and began to lift, forcing her to raise her bottom.

'Henry! No, please!' she protested as he pushed her legs apart with his knee to expose the swollen rear of her vulva.

189

'Why not?' he demanded. 'God knows but your cunt's ripe enough. I'll warrant you could take a horse!'

'I want to be spanked!' she wailed.

Eloise lay across Henry's lap, hot-bottomed and whimpering, with her need for sex an urge that pushed all else from her mind. Lost in the delicious ignominy of being spanked bare-bottomed across a man's legs, her most earnest hope was that Henry would spare nothing in bringing her degradation to a peak.

Having been pushed to the point where she had begged for punishment, she felt no more need for reticence. Nor had Henry given her any opportunity to display any. The spanking had commenced with Henry making himself comfortable in one of the window seats and dragging her across his lap with an arm twisted firmly into the small of her back. He had then cocked a knee up between her thighs so that her cunny was spread over the hard muscle of his leg and started to spank her. Each slap had pressed the heart of her vulva on to his leg, applying a merciless friction to her clitoris. At first, the stinging slaps had made her squeal and writhe, but the sensation of clitoris on cloth had quickly had her beyond pain. Using an obscene bucking motion in time to the slaps of Henry's hand, she had began to masturbate herself on his leg. She knew how wanton was her behaviour; she could hear Natalie giggling at her arousal and distress; she knew that every wretched squirm of her body provided a fine show of both cunt and anus. None of it mattered, indeed; as her bottom danced and wiggled in pain and ecstasy, the knowledge of the display she was making only added to her pleasure.

Grinning, Henry raised his hand for another smack. Eloise's buttocks were a deep pink and speckled with red-topped goose pimples, while plenty of her deep-red anal hair was visible in the cleft between them. He cocked his knee up, lifting and spreading her bottom to fully expose her anus and reward him with a tang of female scent that showed her arousal as much as her frantic rubbing. She would come soon, he knew it, and the idea of her masturbating helplessly on his leg while he beat her made him feel both excited and powerful.

He shook his hand, which was stinging slightly, then once more began to spank her. Immediately she began to rub again, her bare belly juddering against his cock with each slap. Soon she would come and, from the way her fleshy midriff was rubbing on his cock he was far from sure that he would not do the same. Her squeals of pain had long since turned to moans, and now became gasps. Her anus began to pulse and juice squeezed from her vagina with each of her bucks, a filthy sight that he watched in fascination. She called his name, begging to be beaten yet harder, then crying out loud as he responded with a volley of furious slaps at the point where her buttocks met her legs. His hand came away sticky from her pussy as she screamed a drawn-out howl of ecstasy.

Henry's cock felt as if it was about to explode. The shaft was embedded in the soft flesh of Eloise's belly, the glans half into her belly button. Her orgasm had brought him to the edge and he could wait no longer. Even as he decided to make her take it in her mouth, the door flew open to reveal the Vicomte d'Arche with a broken chair leg in his hand.

'Someone screamed . . .' d'Arche said and then stopped, staring open-mouthed at the sight of Eloise's near-naked body, with her red bottom and sodden, gaping vagina.

For a moment, the scene held, then d'Arche raised his improvised weapon.

'By God, how dare you!' the furious man spat. 'You need a sharp lesson in manners, you cur!'

191

'Don't be a fool!' Henry answered. 'We're lovers, don't you see it?'

'Lovers? Ha!' d'Arche snapped.

Eloise rolled off Henry's knee and sat down hard on her freshly spanked bottom. Her face was flushed with pleasure, her eyes bright and her mouth slightly parted – an expression Henry realised might be misread for shock, even as he rose to his feet.

'Eloise, tell this idiot!' he demanded.

'It is true, Donatien,' Eloise managed. 'Henry and I, we are lovers.'

'There we are,' Henry added, 'it was just a playful spanking you see, nothing –'

'Dog!' d'Arche roared. 'You've soiled her, by God! I'll kill you!'

'Calm yourself, man!' Henry retorted. 'Damn you, you'll raise the whole district!'

'You talk of calm?' the vicomte roared. 'When you've soiled my Eloise? I –'

'I'll do as I please, damn you!' Henry answered him. 'And besides, I wasn't the first – nor, I believe, among the first dozen!'

D'Arche produced an incoherent spate of words, his face puce and his fists clenched in fury. For a moment, it seemed that he would lash out blindly, only for the crash of the door being flung open once more to distract him. Todd Gurney stood in the doorway, his shoulders filling the frame, save for a slim gap through which Peggy's face could be seen.

'Temper, temper, Donatien, old fellow,' Henry managed as the vicomte's expression changed from fury to frustration.

Gurney stepped into the room, great fists held ready and eyes fixed on the vicomte. D'Arche returned a wary look, hurled the chair leg to one side and then turned on his heel and stormed from the room without another word.

'Sensitive fellows, these French,' Henry quipped, 'but

192

the demoiselle and I were having a merry time before we were so rudely interrupted. I'm sure she can accommodate you, should you care to join us?'

'With him around?' Gurney asked.

'I'm damned if I can see why that pompous ass should spoil our pleasure,' Henry retorted. 'Come, Natalie, Peggy; your mistress is in fine fettle.'

Eloise smiled and blushed, a shy gesture that did nothing to suggest she was other than willing.

'Tell you what,' Henry continued. 'She's got a thing about rank and what not; put her across your knee and spank her pretty arse for her.'

Gurney responded with a knowing smile, Eloise with a squeal that may have been intended to sound like outrage but fell well short of the mark. Nevertheless, when Gurney stepped forward, she made a dart to the side and it was some moments before he could catch her and lead her to a window seat by the hand.

'There's no getting out of it, my pretty,' he announced as he patted his lap and began to pull her down by the wrist. 'This has been coming to you for a fair while.'

As Eloise was turned over Gurney's knee, her face took on a wonderful expression of consternation. Half-willing, the knowledge that she was about to be spanked by a servant was clearly getting to her, yet she made no move to resist, merely setting her lower lip in a sulky pout as the big man's hand came to rest on her out-thrust behind.

Despite the magnificent view of chubby buttocks, pouting cunny and wrinkled bum-hole that Eloise was presenting to him, Henry felt that a better purpose could be served from the other end of her. Raising a finger to tell Gurney to wait, he walked around to Eloise's front and began to release his cock from his breeches. Her rebellious look deepened as he flopped it into his hand, then turned to open resentment and jealousy as he beckoned to Peggy.

'Spank her, Gurney,' he said merrily. 'Come on, Peg; make her watch while she's beaten.'

Eloise opened her mouth to say something, only to have it turn to a startled squeal as Gurney's hand came down hard across her bottom. Peggy giggled but stepped forward, going down on her knees beside Henry. Eloise squeaked again as her bottom bounced under another slap, then watched, wide-eyed and indignant as Peggy opened her mouth and took in Henry's cock.

Henry gave a sigh of contentment as Peggy's soft lips began to work on his penis. He could feel her tongue as well, rolling his cock from side to side in her mouth as they both watched Eloise being spanked. His cock quickly regained its stiffness, swelling to full erection in Peggy's mouth as Eloise's bottom danced under Gurney's firm slaps. Despite her recent orgasm, her pleasure was evident, with her face cheeks flushed near to the colour of those of her bottom.

Resisting the temptation to come in Peggy's mouth, Henry held back, allowing the plump lips around his penis to work up and down his shaft until Gurney finally declared himself satisfied that he had beaten Eloise properly.

'On your knees, then, my fine little puppy,' Henry ordered Eloise as he pulled gently back from Peggy, 'and stick that fine behind high. I want to see your red cheeks and watch your Mrs Brown make moue as I fuck you.'

Eloise obeyed, sinking down from Gurney's lap with a whimper of pleasure and raising her reddened buttocks for inspection. Her face was set in ecstasy, her mouth wide and her eyes half-closed. Her tits swung beneath her, plump and stiff-nippled as she waited on hands and knees. Henry moved behind her, admiring her gorgeous rear view as he decided whether to sheathe his cock in her well-lubricated cunny or the tight brown ring of her anus. Both were impossibly inviting, and he decided to humiliate her further by making her choose.

'Cunt or breech, my little one?' he asked cheerfully. 'Oh, and you can suck my servant's cock while I'm in you.'

'Cunt, please, sir,' Eloise moaned.

'Cunt it is, then!' Henry declared and put the head of his cock to her pink, glistening hole.

'Oh, God, I wish I'd been a whore!' Eloise groaned as her vagina filled with cock.

'Don't worry,' Henry replied. 'The distinction is trivial.'

Eloise made no answer because she had gulped Gurney's cock into her mouth and was sucking on it with an eagerness that bordered on desperation.

'Nothing quite so willing as a well-spanked girl, eh, Gurney?' Henry said as he began to move his cock inside Eloise.

Together they used her, enjoyed the pleasures of her body without reserve. Prompted by Henry, Natalie and Peggy joined in, shyly at first and then with greater vigour as their own pleasure rose. Gurney came quickly, filling Eloise's mouth with come as Natalie stroked his balls and her mistress's neck.

Henry was still working himself in Eloise's vagina and, as Peggy slid beneath his mount to suckle first her breasts and then his dangling balls, he realised that his intent of having the two of them together was at last within reach. Then the plump blonde's soft mouth closed on his scrotum and all such rational thought was lost. With a grunt of ecstasy he came in Eloise, jerking himself frantically into her as his entire sex underwent a pleasure so intense as to reach the boundaries of pain.

Henry withdrew slowly, watching in delight as Peggy immediately buried her face in Eloise's recently vacated vulva. He sighed as he watched one girl lick his sperm from another's vagina, then put his hand to his cock, determined that Peggy also would take her share of penis before the night was out.

Jean Faugres blew his cheeks out, his breath coming white in the cold evening air. The ragged outline of Tours showed in the distance, but he was neither sure he could reach the city by dark nor that he wanted to. Clad only in a shirt, threadbare coat, over-tight breeches and ill-fitting boots, he was aware that he made a ridiculous spectacle. Seething with an anger that was only kept in check by the absence of anything on which to vent it, he began to cast around for a place to sleep.

To his right ran the Loire, broad and placid. To the left a low cliff rose, its pale rock carved with cellars and even crude houses. Flickering light showed in some, promising warmth and food. Selecting one at random, he strode up to it and pounded on the door. For a moment, nothing happened, and then a face showed at the bull's-eye of crude glass in its centre. A cry of shock sounded, immediately followed by a call for some unseen person to fetch dogs.

'I am a traveller. I seek only shelter!' Faugres called out.

Again he heard the demand for dogs, now more urgent. Backing reluctantly away, he abandoned his plan of seeking shelter among the rock hovels and again turned his footsteps towards Tours. As the light faded from the sky, the river road joined a straight, broad track and the peasant hovels stopped abruptly. Ahead, he espied a Château, set high into the cliffs overlooking the river. Many windows were broken, and those that remained intact showed black in clear evidence of desertion.

With a grunt he turned his steps towards a broad flight of yellow stone steps that led up from the riverside to the Château.

* * *

196

Henry awoke with a feeling of disorientation, imagining himself for one moment in his bed in Truscott Hall and wondering why the ceiling had turned blue. With the realisation that it was the wrong ceiling came the memories of the previous night, annoyance at d'Arche, then a deep satisfaction.

He turned his head from side to side. Sure enough, Eloise's red-gold curls lay spread out over the ruined bolster to his right, while Peggy's unruly blonde locks were peeping out from under the edge of the blanket to his left. Both women had their backs to him and both seemed to be soundly asleep. He smiled at the recollection of the previous night's pleasures, his cock stiffening at the thought and as his body began to fully revive. A glance at the window behind his head showed that it was barely dawn.

Reaching down to take his now rigid morning erection in hand, he found himself wondering if it would be possible to make use of his stiffness in either Eloise or Peggy. It would be easy, he decided, with his cock hard and lubricated with saliva, all he would have to do was pull up the girl's skirts, lift her upper leg and enter her. His cock would be inside her before she was properly awake, and once in, he was sure of acceptance. The question was – which one to fuck?

Groping, he took a plump bottom in each hand and squeezed. Peggy responded with a soft groan, Eloise merely shifting her position slightly. Both bottoms were magnificent, full, womanly and ideal material to fill a lover's lap in the position he intended to use. Peggy's was larger and perhaps a little firmer, yet there was something wonderfully succulent about the texture of Eloise's buttocks. Also, while Peggy was likely to be more accepting of his intrusion, it was delightful to think of Eloise waking to the feel of a cock being pushed inside her. It was impossible to chose on the basis of pleasure, yet his exploring fingers had found the hem of

Eloise's dress already ridden up to expose the backs of her legs, while Peggy's seemed to be trapped.

Accepting the choice of expediency, he lifted his hand to his mouth and spat on to his fingers. Turning, he rubbed the spittle on to the tip of his cock, then took hold of Eloise's dress and leg simultaneously. With a brisk motion, he tugged her skirts up and lifted her leg, then jabbed his penis in what he hoped was the right place. The tip bumped against the closed lips of her sex and she gave a little cry of surprise. He grabbed her hips and pushed, feeling the skin of his cock pull taut against her reluctant sex lips. There was a brief moment of pain and then he felt the dampness of her vagina on his penis. Even as she gave a second, louder cry, he was sliding inside her, filling her with a series of sudden, vigorous pushes.

'Ow! What? Who?' she managed. 'Henry!'

He made no reply but began to fuck her, quickly settling into a rhythm as her big, soft bottom bounced in his lap. She quickly began to moan, then gasp as he increased the pace of his movements with the desire to come already building up inside him. A moment later, he felt his cock jerk and gave a long, contented sigh as his semen flooded into her.

In the next room, Todd Gurney was stroking Natalie's long black hair and watching her pretty dusky face as she sucked on his erection. Her mouth was wide, taking in the big cock with an effort, while her eyes were closed in bliss. Gurney had woken to the feel of a timid hand on his thigh and had simply allowed her to do as she pleased, first stroking and kissing his cock to erection and then taking it fully into her mouth.

As before, their inability to exchange more than the most simple sentences made no difference to their lovemaking. No words were necessary for him to enjoy her passion and willingness to please, while in return she seemed to demand only to be allowed to display herself in the act of masturbation and to be held tightly afterwards.

He grunted as his cock jerked and filled the small maid's mouth with come. She made no move to pull back, but swallowed and then continued to suck until he was entirely drained into her mouth. Even as her full lips pulled free of his penis, she gave a little cry and said his name in her high, strongly accented voice and he realised that she had been playing with herself under the blanket all the while she had been sucking.

Henry Truscott stepped out into the courtyard of Château l'Husseau and took in a deep draught of the cool morning air. He felt thoroughly pleased with himself and brimful of confidence. Not only had he succeeded in his aim of bedding Eloise and Peggy simultaneously, but he had also found a dog whip while leaving the Château, a well-made and serviceable implement that he had immediately appropriated. The sight of Gurney checking their powder by the landau did nothing to dispel his cheerful mood and he walked across with a spring in his step.

'A good night I trust, my friend?' he greeted the other, eager to find a way to remark on his successful bedding of the two girls without appearing to boast too openly. 'Not too cold?'

'Fine enough,' Gurney replied distractedly as he closed the cap of the late Captain Jinks's ornamental powder horn.

'I, too –' Henry began and then thought better of it as the trim figure of the Vicomte d'Arche appeared in the doorway of the Château.

'Good morning, Vicomte,' Henry called out instead. 'I trust you enjoyed the accommodation and facilities? The burlesque was fine, was it not?'

'Not altogether,' d'Arche replied coldly. 'Yet I am

prepared to put such things aside for the sake of expediency. Until, that is, we are once more within a compass in which your behaviour may be called to account in the proper fashion.'

'Splendid, splendid,' Henry answered, entirely ignoring the threat. 'So, then, you know the district – what do you advise?'

'Yonder,' d'Arche replied with a nod to the west, 'is the city of Tours. We have little choice but to pass through it, as the Loire and Cher join some small way beyond and thus we are on a peninsula.'

'What of disguising ourselves as nobility and simply driving boldly through?' Henry suggested.

'Me? Wear the garb of a peasant?' d'Arche said, with a shudder of distaste. 'Never; I would rather hang.'

'As well you may,' Henry answered.

'It grates sufficiently to have to flee from a rabble,' d'Arche continued, 'without being forced to impersonate them. No, I may withdraw, but I do so as I am, a vicomte. No, with the treachery of so many supposedly noble Touranjou, our sole concern is that I might be recognised. Therefore I shall feign sleep, with your hat over my face, if you would be good enough to allow me its use.'

'A fair suggestion,' Henry answered, 'which I will accept for want of a better. First, however, I am of a mind to visit the cellar and avail ourselves of a few select bottles. Eloise, my darling, perhaps you would come and assist my choice?'

'Very well,' Eloise answered with a coy look. 'Natalie, Peggy, see to the landau.'

'I also shall accompany you,' d'Arche stated. 'To ensure that you choose only the best of whatever may remain.'

Henry responded with a grunt, having intended at the least to explore the impressive depth of cleavage Eloise was displaying in her now somewhat shrunken vermilion gown. Evidently, he reasoned, the Vicomte d'Arche was no more inclined to face reality in his erotic endeavours than in real life. Shrugging off his annoyance, he made for the cellar steps, closely followed by d'Arche and Eloise.

Wrinkling his nose against the pervading smell of ruined wine, Henry ducked beneath an arch and made for the far side ahead of his companions, only to stop dead in his tracks. A sound had caught his ears, a sound that could only be a human snore. Holding himself absolutely still, he peered into the darkness.

With mounting horror, he realised that a pale oval he had thought merely a reflection was in fact a face, a great bearded face that he had last seen as he pulled a sack down over its features – Jean Faugres. Moving with agonising care, he stepped backwards out of the tunnel, putting his finger to his lips in a frantic gesture as soon as he came in clear sight of Eloise and the Vicomte d'Arche.

'It's that devil Faugres!' he whispered hoarsely in response to their puzzled looks. 'He's asleep in the tunnel!'

'Kill him, before he wakes!' Eloise answered in a terrified hiss.

'What, in cold blood?' Henry demanded. 'Just go, will you, you bloodthirsty bitch?'

'The demoiselle is right,' d'Arche stated. 'Kill the filthy brute!'

'Be assured he would do the same to you,' Eloise added.

'I don't have anything to kill him with; and besides, I feel sure I saw him stir!' Henry protested, making for the stairs.

They emerged from the cellar to find Gurney in the act of helping Natalie to board the landau. Henry ran over and explained the situation, to which Gurney responded with a curt nod.

201

'Get up,' Henry ordered Eloise. 'We're going.'

Eloise hesitated only a moment, but d'Arche did not follow.

'Damn it man, get up!' Henry exclaimed.

'No,' d'Arche replied. 'This man has threatened the person of the demoiselle. If you dare not confront him, even when sleeping, then lend me your pistols and I myself will do what honour demands.'

'We leave, now!' Henry hissed between clenched teeth.

'Sir –' d'Arche began, in his most pompous tone, only to be cut off by the slam of the cellar door.

Henry turned as a great shaggy head emerged from the stairwell. Faugres was rubbing his eyes and blinking in the bright morning light, but as he climbed from the stairwell he focused on Henry and the others and his expression turned from vague puzzlement to rage. Henry grabbed up a pistol and swung round, pointing it directly at the giant's chest. Faugres paused, glaring at Henry but not daring to come on.

As d'Arche scrambled hastily into the landau behind him, Henry obtained his first chance to take in the appearance of Jean Faugres in the light of day. It was not an opportunity in which he took any pleasure. A good head taller than himself, Faugres's body bulged with muscle that the ludicrously ill-fitting clothing only served to enhance. Nor did the giant's face show any fear, but only hatred and contempt. A little whimper of dread from either Eloise or Natalie confirmed that he was not alone in his trepidation, but also served to stiffen his resolve.

Reaching behind him and keeping the pistol firmly trained on Faugres, Henry groped for the landau's door. A hand found his, a hand that seemed impossibly small when compared with Faugres' great, mauling fists. He moved back, found the running board with his foot and stepped up, only then finding that it was Natalie who had guided him. Faugres took a step forward and Henry stiffened his pistol arm as Natalie pulled the door of the landau shut.

He heard the smack of Gurney's whip and the landau began to move. Faugres stood glaring, his great fists clenching and unclenching at his sides. As the landau accelerated, Henry felt a flood of relief. He laughed, as much from nervousness as anything but still managing to convey a note of derision. Faugres raised a fist and took another step forward, then began to lope slowly after the landau. Henry pulled up his arm, very deliberately took aim, put pressure to the trigger and then stopped as Faugres suddenly hurled himself to the side.

Henry laughed, adjusted his aim and pulled the trigger. For just an instant real terror showed on the giant's face, and then an overriding fury as the hammer clicked home against its rest.

'No charge, Jean my boy!' Henry called out as they clattered away down the drive. 'No ball, either!'

Faugres leapt roaring to his feet, but the landau was moving fast and now Henry's laughter was genuinely derisive. Eloise's mocking, silvery tones joined his deeper ones as they swept away and he gave the giant a final insulting hand gesture as the curve of the low cliff cut off their view. Henry was still laughing as they reached the road that led along the river, a humour born as much from relief as from the memory of Jean Faugres's expression.

Tours appeared as they rounded a bluff, a great jumble of houses around a high-walled centre. Within a few minutes, the road had become fully lined with houses on their left and presently they swung away from the river towards the gates of the city proper. A good number of people were already abroad, yet each appeared intent on their own business and none spared more than a curious glance for the landau and its occupants. Following instructions relayed from the vicomte via Eloise, Gurney steered the landau through the outer city, turning left to find the river Cher.

Todd Gurney guided the landau on to the bridge approach, only to find a queue of vehicles stretching most of the way across. Standing in his stirrups, he made out a squat octagonal building, beside which stood two men in uniform of a rich blue with muskets slung over their shoulders. One was speaking to the driver of a wain laden with apples, while the other looked on with an officious expression. As Gurney slowed the landau, a third man stepped from the small building and looked down the line of vehicles, more or less directly at the landau.

He remained still, aware that any unusual action could only draw the attention of the guards. Three choices presented themselves; to turn back, to try and bluff their way through what was evidently some sort of check point, or –

Gurney clapped his knees into the flanks of the carthorse even as he pulled the reins to steer out of the line of vehicles. The team responded, eager to run. Startled people began to turn to look at them as the landau accelerated and then one of the guards was pointing and calling something. Another dashed forward into the open lane to bar their way, raising his hat in a commanding gesture as he did so. Gurney yelled to the horses, ignoring questioning calls from his passengers as they thundered across the wide bridge.

The expression of the man in the road changed from command to terror as he realised that the approaching carriage had no intention of stopping. For a moment, he stood stupefied, even as his colleagues scrambled for their muskets. Then, an instant before he went down under the hooves of the two greys, he leapt to the side and flattened himself against the high wheel of the apple cart.

A yell sounded after them as they tore past the

guards, its meaning clear to Gurney, despite being in French. He paid no attention, but pulled hard on the reins, angling the carthorse towards the road side. The beast responded, the others following. A crack sounded behind him, then another and a musket ball whistled over his head.

The shots served to spur the horses, driving them to a headlong gallop of sheer panic. Gurney clung on, hearing a squeal of alarm from one of the girls as they tore down the broad road to leave the bridge and its guards far behind. Slowly, the horses lost their fear, slowing and then once more becoming controllable.

'I'd not care to do that again, sir,' Gurney said as the landau finally came to a stop.

'Nonsense, man,' Henry answered, 'a more exhilarating ride I have seldom experienced.'

Jean Faugres strode towards Tours, his burning rage far beyond the point at which he might have cared what the citizens thought of his appearance. One thought alone occupied his mind – vengeance. The derisive laughter of Henry and Eloise still rang in his ears, driving him to a state of fury that was made worse by his inability to pursue the landau. Hunger and discomfort added to his woes, all of which he blamed squarely on Eloise and – to an ever greater extent – Henry Truscott.

In the absence of Henry Truscott, he would have been secure in his house in St Romain, not tramping through the cold Touraine without money, food or even his proper clothes. Also, he would undoubtedly have had his pleasure of Eloise – perhaps many times – and the slut would now be awaiting whatever fate he had chosen to impose upon her.

With the thought of his intentions for Eloise, a new element entered his turbulent thoughts – lust. She had been in her vermilion gown, with the upper surfaces of her plump breasts quivering as she sniggered at him.

What bliss, he imagined, to have pulled those fat globes from their restraining velvet, to have heard her cry of shame and defeat as he squeezed them in his hands, to have laid a dog-whip across the big, trembling orbs until their white perfection was criss-crossed with scarlet welts!

He cried out loud with sheer thwarted lust, closing his eyes and clenching his massive fists. A young girl on some morning errand gave him a terrified look and hurried past, then broke into a run.

The city rose before him and rather than cross one or other rivers in futile pursuit of the landau, he entered the old part of the city and was presently stalking down the *Rue des Sulots*, a street of shabby dwellings known for its cheap wine shops and low-grade brothels. Ignoring the slatternly women, most of whom gave him a wide berth in any case, he made for the street's end where the houses pressed against the wall of the city.

He hammered at a door, which opened to reveal a petite, rounded woman whose face, although careworn, still showed beauty.

'Jean!' she exclaimed as she recognised her visitor.

'Lucie,' he responded simply. 'Still here after fifteen years?'

She responded with a resigned smile and beckoned him forward. Ignoring her questions, he pushed inside and explained his needs, which Lucie accepted with a knowing look and a giggle. They went to an upper room, Faugres chivvying her along and then slamming the door shut as soon as they were inside.

'Jean! Not so fast!' she protested as he grabbed her and kissed her fiercely on the mouth.

In answer, he took her by the hair and pressed her to her knees, then held her head firmly in place while he freed his penis from the over-tight breeches.

'Do as you're told but resist,' he instructed. 'Now get your lips around my cock!'

She obeyed, gulping his cock into her mouth. He held

her by the hair, forcing her face into his crotch and listening with delight to the little mewling noises she made as she sucked his cock.

'That's right, suck,' he growled, thinking of not Lucie but Eloise, on her knees with his penis swelling in her mouth.

It was quickly stiff and he pulled back, unwilling to risk ejaculation in her mouth. Still holding her by the hair, he pulled her slowly to her feet, then lowered his face to hers and kissed her. As her mouth opened under his, he put a hand to the bodice of her gown, then, with a sudden violent motion, pushed her back. Lucie fell to the bed, her bodice tearing in his hand to leave both her breasts loose and bare. He laughed and grabbed her ankles, lifting them and wrenching them apart to expose her vulva.

'Jean!' she protested.

'Time I had your cunt, my fine lady,' he snarled. 'Come on, fight!'

Lucie began to struggle as he laid his weight on her, jokingly at first and then with more vigour as his penis probed for the hole in between her legs. Faugres rejoiced in her feeble efforts to dislodge him, all the while thinking of how Eloise would react in Lucie's place, pressed beneath his body with her plump thighs spread and his penis about to be pushed into her helpless cunny. Doubtless she would claw and kick with more vigour, yet as Lucie's desperate thrashing increased, along with the volume of her screams and curses, he felt something of how he had always imagined it would be.

'Never, you filthy, low-born dog!' Lucie screamed as his cock found her hole. 'No, not that: you'll not put it in me, you pig! Get off! Get away! Oh, God! No!'

She gave a final wail of despair as he forced his massive cock into her vagina, feeling the muscles clench against him and then give under the pressure. He groaned as his length slid inside her and she responded with a moan of pleasure.

'Not yet, you fool wench,' he hissed.

Her sighs immediately gave way to noises of distress and she began to beat her fists against his great chest. He began to fuck her, revelling in her futile struggles and pleading as his cock rammed home again and again inside her. Slowly, her resistance subsided, until she lay on the bed like a broken doll, accepting the filling of her vagina with no more than the occasional whimper.

Faugres continued to pump into her. His eyes were closed, and in his mind it was not the amenable Lucie but an unwilling Eloise on whom he was mounted. He would have caught her, wrenched her titties from her bodice, thrown her legs up to expose her cunt and then mounted her and had her, despite her pathetic attempts to resist him. Finally he would have come, deep in her cunt, only to pull free as he did so and drain the remainder of his sperm over her proud, haughty face.

As his fantasy reached its climax, so did he. He was moving frantically inside Lucie, who had began to groan with pleasure, despite herself, and had her legs pulled up in an attitude that suggested anything but reluctance. She cried out as his cock exploded inside her, clutching him to herself with a desperate energy. He continued to pump, draining both his sperm and his frustration into her until he was spent and could only collapse into her arms. For a long moment, they lay inert, until Lucie protested against his weight.

'You're crushing me, Jean,' she said, pushing at his chest, 'and I must douche also.'

He rolled off and then sat upright on the bed as she left the room. Lucie gave him a smile and a peculiar look and scampered from the room. Immediately, Faugres rose. Two long strides took him to the corner of the room, where he pulled up a threadbare rug and then a floorboard. Groping hastily underneath, his fingers found what he was looking for: a leather bag within which were the rounded shapes of coins.

Ten

Keeping to small lanes and tracks, the landau followed the northern boundary of a great forest declared by d'Arche to be the estate of the Château de Chinon. Beyond, the land became more populous and, with no further evidence of open hostility, Henry was emboldened to follow the principal road along the southern bank of the Loire. They passed close under the magnificent battlements and towers of Saumur and then though the town, raising no more than a hostile glance. Nor was there any further difficulty as they approached the city of Angers; indeed, for the most part, the area seemed remarkably deserted.

'It would seem that we are past the worst,' Natalie ventured.

'What of tonight?' Eloise asked. 'Might not an inn be possible?'

'This is Anjou, we are yet a half-day's hard ride from the Vendée, where you might be safe,' d'Arche answered her stiffly. 'Despite appearances, by all accounts the rabble in Anjou is as bad as that in Touraine, so it would seem wiser to spend the night in some deserted place. A wiser choice by far would be to take the road south to Cholet, and by this evening we might be at the estate of my cousin, the Seigneur de Chavanges, where you might rest in both a comfortable bed and security. But, as you have been so obstinate as to throw in your lot with these Englishmen, you should not complain of any resulting discomfort.'

'Do not whine so, Donatien,' she answered him. 'Neither jealousy nor pique become a man of your rank. Henry, I am tired and hungry, might we not risk an inn?'

'I'm not sure I care to,' Henry replied, 'but the horses are fair spent and in need of fodder, while I'd give a round sum for something other than old cheese – and your damned sausages are enough to pull a man's teeth. What do you say, Gurney?'

'Keep the pistols loaded and the nobs out of sight, then visit an inn, that's what I say,' Gurney answered. 'And if milord vicomte is too damn proud to keep low, then he'd best make his own arrangements.'

D'Arche made no reply but the cold look on his face became harder still.

'What of Jean Faugres?' Natalie asked. 'Might he not come up on us?'

'Faugres'll not catch us,' Henry announced confidently. 'Walking, he'll not have crossed the Vienne yet; and besides, how is he to know what road we took, or what inn we chose?'

'And what of the man who raised the rabble against me?' d'Arche demanded. 'Might he not be following?'

'What of it?' Henry laughed after quickly checking himself from revealing his knowledge of Emile Boillot. 'He sounds a meagre fellow, anyway, and not one to concern us.'

'He is an orator,' d'Arche continued, 'and as such more to be feared than any number of beef-bound peasants.'

'An orator? Ha!' Henry exclaimed. 'The fellow's still got pap in his mouth. He's certainly no Fox. Now there's an orator, for all that he's a mad bastard ...'[8]

Emile Boillot paused for breath. His previous attempt to raise a crowd, in St Romain, had been less than successful than he might have hoped. St Romain, though, was small, bucolic and its population had known him since childhood. Angers was very different; large, cosmopolitan and with a hungry mob eager for the fire of his speech.

He had begun by flourishing his letter of authority from the assembly in Paris, which had suitably impressed the crowd. Then, by combining revolutionary rhetoric with descriptions of Eloise's beauty, depravity and cruelty, he had managed to engender anger, lust, envy and hatred. When he had started, few of the crowd had even heard of the de la Tour-Romain family. This had helped him in painting them as the very epitome of all the faults and excesses of the *ancien régime*. Stirring hatred against Donatien d'Arche had been easier still, as the vicomte's reputation for extravagance and callousness had proved well known in the city.

'Citizens!' he called, bracing himself for the final burst. 'Are we to allow these parasites to go free? Are we to sit quietly by while they roll from the country with their crimes still unpunished? They have coin enough to live high in their pockets alone, taxes extorted from the people, while we starve in the streets! Is this just? Is this to be tolerated? I say no!'

A roar of agreement answered his call, and his tiny mouth set into a smile as not dozens, but hundreds of men and women raised their fists in agreement.

'Go out into the country!' he continued. 'They cannot be far, so do not rest until they are dragged back to face trial and execution!'

This time, the roar was louder and Boillot's grin broader still. Whether the mob cared for the principals he had so eloquently outlined he was unsure. What mattered more was their hunger and the thought of the wealth that Eloise was carrying. How much wealth she in fact had, he was unsure, but it hardly mattered. That morning, he had seen black bread on sale for three sous a loaf in the market, and since that moment he had been certain of his ability to raise a vengeful mob to seek out his prey.

Once more he raised his hands, intending to impose some sort of order on the mob to ensure that the search was successful. As the crowd grew slowly quiet, a movement beyond them caught his eye and his face broke into a fierce grin as an elegant landau pulled by an ill-assorted team of four turned into the street.

Jean Faugres grinned to himself as he entered the city of Angers. Twice since leaving Tours he had changed horses, his massive bulk and ferocious appearance quashing any doubts the beasts' owners might have had about the exchanges. After leaving Lucie, he had picked up the story of how the landau had run the bridge and realised that it could only be his quarry. Using most of her money to purchase a horse, he had set off in pursuit, riding hard down the southern bank of the Loire in the hope of overtaking them. He had not, but enquiries had revealed that he was on the right trail and it was his earnest hope that they would stop at Angers.

A noise caught his attention, a wild, roaring sound that rose and fell only to swell again with a new fever. Stopping in puzzlement, he strained his ears, thinking to pick out voices and a mad clattering of hooves. Suddenly, a team of horses burst from a street ahead of him, turning into the main road so sharply that the landau they were pulling came close to tipping up. Two men rode postillion and four figures were in the open rear, one with a gown of an unmistakable rich vermilion. With a curse and a yell of joy, he spurred his own horse forward, even as a mob of hundreds erupted from the street in pursuit of the fugitives.

Henry leant forward to whisper words of encouragement to his exhausted mount. For perhaps an hour they had driven the landau with as much speed as the

212

tiredness of the horses would allow. At first, riding through the well-made streets of Angers, they had gained easily, their horses outpacing the mob. Yet, on crossing the Loire and turning west, they had found themselves in a strip of open country between two rivers and able only to press forward. As Henry had feared, the dust from pursuing horses had quickly appeared.

They had crossed the smaller river only to find themselves on a twisting road that ran along bluffs and offered no better chance of escape. Angers had become a distant line of ragged grey and the dust of their pursuers had drawn gradually closer, until now Henry lay crouched low over the neck of his grey, urging it on and praying for some chance of concealment. Knowing that they were likely to have to fight, he shouted back for the pieces to be loaded.

'There's no ball!' d'Arche answered him.

'Hell!' Henry swore as he realised that what remained of his stock of shot was in his coat pocket.

Gripping the reins desperately in his hand, he began to dig among the contents for a ball. He cursed once more as his thumb caught the pin of a brooch, then a finger brushed the round shape of a pistol ball, then another. Dragging them free, he turned in the saddle and hurled both into the body of the landau. Behind, their pursuers were clearly visible, two dozen or more horsemen. They were strung out along the road, with more on a side turning that disappeared behind the hill. With a sick feeling in his stomach he realised that there could only be one interpretation of their action – an attempt was being made to cut them off.

To the right was a steep drop, to the left a cliff. Trees and marsh lay below, a vineyard above, neither offering refuge. With no other choice, he dug his heels into the flanks of the grey and yelled for more speed. Foam speckled the beast's lips and its eyes held a wild, hunted look, showing all too clearly that it would soon reach the end of its reserves. The others were no better and he found himself casting desperately around for anything that might present the slightest hope.

Nothing came, only the triumphant yells of their pursuers, closer now. They rounded a bluff, then another, to come out on to a hillside that showed empty air stretching away to a far, western horizon. The wide vista seemed to Henry to offer a taunting freedom, yet it was no more than that. Ahead, a road came in from the left, and horsemen were spilling from it. Cut off, he tried to rein the horses in, resolving on a desperate stand among the trees and marshes below them.

'What are you about?' d'Arche's voice demanded from behind him as the landau slowed. 'They –'

The vicomte's voice cut off abruptly and was followed by a report, then another. Henry turned to find the pursuing horsemen almost on them and d'Arche standing with a smoking pistol in either hand. An instant later, a musket crashed and a ball whined overhead. Then horsemen were swarming around them and Henry knew that they were lost.

Snatching the dog-whip from his belt, he struck out blindly as the landau at last came to rest. Red, yelling faces were on every side, showing exultation and anger. Natalie screamed and Gurney roared in anger, to be answered by a curse in French. Expecting to feel the pain of a musket ball or knife at any instant, Henry lashed around himself with the whip. Then a bellowing voice was calling for the men to back away and, to Henry's surprise, they obeyed.

His feeling of relief lasted no more than the space of a heartbeat and then dwindled to dismay as he looked up to find the massive figure of Jean Faugres looking down from the low cliff above them. The giant's face was split into a triumphant grin and he held a musket levelled directly at Henry's chest. With as much dignity as he could muster, Henry slid the whip back into his belt and raised his hands in surrender.

After much shouting and gesticulation, the mob appeared to reach a decision. Surrounded by men with muskets, the landau was led a little further along the cliff road and down a narrow track. This descended into the valley and ended at the ruins of a Château. The landau was brought into a small yard that lay between the lowest level of the once fine building and a narrow water-course. They were ordered to dismount and, with a dozen muskets pointed at them, it seemed futile to argue. Henry allowed himself to be manhandled from the grey and thrust into a tunnel that opened beneath the ruins. The others were pushed in behind him and the iron gate slammed shut and locked, leaving them imprisoned.

A moment later, Emile Boillot appeared and sauntered towards them, his thin face set in a disdainful sneer.

'That's the agitator!' d'Arche exclaimed, seeing Boillot. 'The man who was going to have me hanged!'

'Justice, then, has caught up with you, Citizen Arche,' the lean student remarked as he neared the bars of the gate.

'Justice? How dare you speak of justice?' the vicomte demanded. 'I myself have the sole right to dispense justice within my domaines, as has been my family's privilege since time immemorial!'

'How can a system that is in itself inherently unjust claim the right to dispense justice?' Boillot sneered. 'No, Citizen Arche, I represent a higher justice: the natural justice that condemns your crimes against the French people.'

'I have heard this talk before,' d'Arche stormed, 'and now, as then, I declare that I have committed no crimes but merely taken what was mine by birthright!'

'A statement that is in itself an admission of guilt,' Boillot responded. 'A guilt exceeded only by your companion, the harlot Delatour, beside whom your excesses appear trivial.'

215

'How dare you speak thus of the Demoiselle de la Tour-Romain!' d'Arche responded. 'You know nothing of her!'

'To the contrary,' Boillot responded. 'I was raised in St Romain. Her behaviour has displayed a monstrous wickedness that exceeds even the arrogance and depravity of her father. Indeed, it was while I was in pursuit of her that I took the opportunity to bring justice to you.'

'Is this true, Eloise?' d'Arche demanded as he turned to where she was standing.

'Yes, Donatien, it is true,' Eloise replied softly.

'It's no fault of ours,' Henry cut in defensively. 'How were we to know the rabble-rousing bastard would choose to harass you?'

'It is all one,' Boillot announced imperiously, before the vicomte could answer. 'Tomorrow, you will all be tried for your crimes against France, also against myself and others. You will be found guilty and executed forthwith.'

'Guilty? What do you mean, guilty?' Henry demanded. 'What of fair trial? What of the justice by which you set so much store?'

'You shall be appointed a defence, of course,' Boillot responded. 'Indeed, a defence who is fully acquainted with the events in question – myself.'

'You?' Henry demanded.

'Certainly,' Boillot replied. 'You are guilty, of course – it is beyond doubt – but I shall plead for a quick death for you on the grounds of natural mercy.'

'Guilty of what?' Henry roared.

'Unlawful seizure of a prisoner of the French state, twice; assault upon and attempt to murder various citizens of France; looting; brigandry; horse theft; rape –'

'Rape!' Henry interrupted. 'I'm damned if I –'

'There!' Boillot declared, turning to the crowd behind him. 'A clear admission! When challenged with his

216

crimes, the prisoner denies only one. This is a clear admission of the others!'

'What?' Henry roared. 'By God, I'll wring your scrawny neck, you slimy little toad!'

'Do not stoop to his base level, Mr Truscott.' Eloise spoke from behind him. 'Let us face our end with becoming dignity.'

'I'll be damned if I'll let myself be turned off without a fight!' Henry swore as Boillot turned on his heel and began to walk away. 'Come back here, you little bastard! I should have put an end to your poison in the Bazois!'

'I did suggest it,' Eloise reminded him.

Henry responded with a grunt and sat down on a projection of the wall. Peering glumly through the bars, he watched as Boillot posted three guards armed with muskets. Two of these were local men, the third the giant Jean Faugres.

To avoid the taunts and threats of their captors, they moved back into the darkness of the tunnel, only to find the air thick with dust. A brief investigation showed that this derived from seems of coal in the walls which had evidently been recently worked. Finally, they settled down just far enough from the gate to avoid any missiles that might be thrown.

As afternoon faded to evening, the crowd began to lose interest and dispersed, leaving only their three guards beyond the portal. Nevertheless, these remained vigilant and Henry could think of no means of escape. As a cold dusk set in, another man appeared briefly, guiding the carthorse that had been pulling the landau. Now it was roped to a shallow barge with a covered deck, which the man moored and then went on his way.

Presently, Faugres and one other disappeared from view, leaving a single man with his musket levelled at their door. After a while, he rose and walked over to near the bars.

217

'Greetings, my lords and ladies,' he called with deliberate sarcasm as Henry looked up.

'Yes,' Henry replied.

'This stream is the Louet,' the man informed him nastily, pointing to the water-course behind him. 'Take a good look, for you are to be drowned in it tomorrow, just as soon as you have been tried.'

Henry declined to answer, contenting himself with throwing his tormentor a contemptuous look.

'You will be put in the coal barge,' the man continued, 'along with a goodly ballast of rocks. The hatch will be fastened and it will be sunk. The water is perhaps five feet deep, yet it is enough. Now sleep well.'

The man laughed and tuned his back, leaving them to digest this piece of information.

Night settled over the Louet and the dull marshland beyond it, casting the interior of the coal mine into a darkness so black that Henry found himself unable to see his hand an inch in front of his face. Both Eloise and Peggy had cuddled into him, their bodies warm against his sides, yet the feel of plump breasts and soft arms failed to arouse him.

After a night of fitful sleep, Eloise de la Tour-Romain awoke to a chill dawn. Her body felt cramped and cold, while her mouth and nose seemed filled with the thick coal dust. Of her companions, only Natalie remained asleep. The maid's head was cradled in Todd Gurney's lap, with her dark hair spread out and her face showing a peace very different from Eloise's own feelings. That Jean Faugres had not come for her in the night, she could only ascribe to the extreme dark. Now, pale light showed at the mouth of the mine and, unless by some mercy the giant was asleep, she felt sure that he would not waste the morning. The certainty of his intentions, coupled with the knowledge of their subsequent fate, filled her with sick fear and she found herself unable to tear her eyes away from the patch of ground visible outside the mine.

'At the least we should inspect the gate,' Henry announced suddenly. 'Who knows, it might yield to force, or the lock prove weak or easy to pick. Gurney here is reckoned clean among his crew. Are you not, Todd?'

'Clean enough,' Gurney replied, 'though I'm no dubber.'

Without another word, Todd Gurney started to move towards the gate, only to turn back after no more than a glance. As he rejoined them, Eloise's briefly lifted hopes once more sank down.

'Could you pick it?' Henry asked.

'Dare say,' Gurney answered, 'had I a gilt, or even a nail, but . . .'

'What of whalebone?' Peggy interrupted.

'Could do,' Gurney responded, 'but it'd not be so easy. Faugres sits just to one side, doing rope work, but with his musket cocked and ready.'

'Rope work?' Henry queried.

'Ay, making some devil's device, no doubt,' Gurney answered.

'He's going to come for me,' Eloise said weakly.

As if in answer to her fear, a dull metallic clang sounded from the direction of the gate. Turning, she saw Faugres crouched beyond, his musket tucked beneath his arm as he put a key to the lock.

'Oh, God, he is!' Eloise cried.

'He'll need to shoot me first,' Gurney growled.

'No, no,' Henry interjected in an urgent whisper. 'Go with him, Eloise, and while he's busy we pick the lock!'

'I –' Eloise managed, her mind numb with fear.

'Come on!' Henry urged.

'I couldn't!' Eloise protested. 'I just couldn't!'

'You must!' Henry hissed. 'It's that or be drowned like a rat!'

'How can you ask such a thing?' D'Arche spoke for the first time. 'The demoiselle's virtue is worth more than you could comprehend!'

'Stay quiet, you prattling fop!' Henry snapped. 'Come on, puppy, it's only a cock. Close your eyes and think it's me.'

'I –' Eloise began once more, only to stop abruptly as the gate clicked open.

Faugres crouched beyond with the musket levelled at them as the gate swung back. His features were set in a malign smile, while one great, callused finger beckoned to her to come forward. None of them spoke, but she saw Gurney bunch his fists.

'Please, mistress,' Natalie spoke.

At the terror in her maid's voice, Eloise's mind went back to the Château de St Romain and to how Natalie had clung trembling in her arms after whippings. Turning her head, she found the tiny maid's great brown eyes staring into hers, begging. She rose, swallowing in her fear as she walked slowly towards Faugres. His smile broke into a grin of pure evil as she approached, and he moved back a pace to allow her exit.

'Lock it,' he growled, throwing the key at her feet as she stepped into the cold morning air. 'Then shake the bars.'

Eloise obeyed, trembling violently as she turned the key and then shook the gate to show that it was fast. Then Faugres' hand closed on her wrist with a strength that she knew at once it was useless to resist. A last glance at the gate showed Peggy's face set in horrified fascination, and then Faugres had dragged her to the side.

She had expected to be thrown to the ground and used without preamble but, as her captor exchanged his musket for a piece of rope work, she realised that her ordeal was not to be so quick. An odd relief at the postponement of her violation mixed with a new apprehension of her more immediate fate. Despite the futility of resistance, she struggled and sobbed as Faugres dragged her towards a well-grown apple tree. One branch ran parallel to the ground and several feet clear. More than once she had strapped Natalie to similar branches in the St Romain orchards for whippings – punishments that had always had the added spice of knowing that the naked, wriggling girl might well be seen from the village. Faugres' purpose was immediately clear.

He made quick work of lashing her wrists and strapping her up to the apple branch. Eloise found herself on tiptoe with her hands stretched high above her head to leave her body defenceless. Yet two loops of the rope work remained empty and, as he grabbed one of her ankles, she realised what he intended. He lifted her legs without apparent effort and bound first one ankle into place, then the other, to leave Eloise hanging from the branch by all four limbs. The position had also made her skirts fall, leaving her thighs and buttocks as exposed for whipping as her cunny was for what she had no doubt would come afterwards. Faugres completed her exposure by tearing open the front of her bodice to let her breasts out, then tore an ash sapling of some six feet in height from the ground. Eloise shuddered at the sight of the thing, already imagining how it would feel across the tender skin of her legs and buttocks.

'We play a simple game,' Faugres chuckled. 'When you beg for my mercy and call me sir, then there'll be just six more. After that, I think you know what's going in that fat, aristocratic cunt. Are you going to beg now?'

Eloise could find no words, but managed to shake her head.

'Good,' Faugres laughed. 'I was hoping you'd show some spirit; it'll make it all the more pleasant to break you.'

Eloise shut her eyes tightly as he brought up the switch.

* * *

Using his teeth, Henry worked frantically at the seam of Peggy's bodice. A thread gave, then another as Eloise cried out from beyond the mouth of the coal mine. He was quickly able to draw forth a length of whalebone. Gurney took it and gave a grunt of satisfaction as he tested its strength.

'It'll do, sir,' he announced.

'Good,' Henry replied. 'Now work fast. When the lock springs, I shall go for the musket. Gurney, take Faugres. Vicomte, try the landau; with luck, our possessions remain within, the pistols included. Peggy, Natalie, make for the barge and cast one end loose.'

'And should we fail?' Natalie asked in a small voice.

'Then a musket ball is a better way to die than drowning,' Henry answered. 'Now come.'

Todd Gurney inched forward along the floor of the tunnel, hunched low and with his eyes fixed on the light at the end. At first, he could see only a low wall with the Louet and marshland beyond. Then Faugres and Eloise became visible, the one standing with a switch raised, the other hanging by her wrists and ankles with her dress and petticoats spread out around her naked buttocks and thighs while the dark hair and pink centre of her sex showed in the middle. Three livid welts already decorated the pale skin of her bottom. Beyond them was the barge, with the landau to one side, apparently still loaded with their possessions.

Ducking down, he made a brief inspection of the lock and then inserted the long piece of whalebone. A movement signalled the location of a tumbler, which proved to be the only one. He felt his lips twitch into an involuntary smile as it lifted. Turning the piece of stay on to its long edge, he applied pressure, feeling it bend as the catch pulled slowly clear of the hasp.

A sharp click signalled their freedom and he hurled himself at the gate. Faugres turned at the sound, the vicious stroke he had been aiming at Eloise's bare legs stopping in mid-air. Rushing headlong, Gurney caught the back-hand blow of the sapling on his shoulder and rammed his head into Faugres' midriff.

They went down together, toppling over the wall in a tangle of limbs. Gurney rolled aside as they struck, avoiding a sweep of Faugres' massive arm and then planting his fist hard into the giant's belly. A roar of pain answered his blow and then he was hurled away as Faugres lashed out once more.

Henry dived for Faugres' musket, catching the stock even as a shout from the slope above warned him of the presence of another guard. He rolled and grappled the musket, bringing it around as he sought frantically for his target. To one side, d'Arche had reached the landau and was scrabbling for the pistols and charges. Peggy and Natalie scrambled past, and then a flicker of motion caught his eye. The guard was well up the slope, among trees beyond the ruined Château.

Henry brought the musket up and fired, only to hear the ball skitter away among the branches behind his intended target. The man's face broke into a wicked grin and he brought his own piece up. Henry hurled himself towards the shelter of the mine mouth but no crash of powder came, only a curse. Realising instantly what had happened, he grabbed Faugres' musket, and ran for the ruins. Above him, the guard was trying frantically to re-prime his piece and cursing the wet powder. Henry bounded up a short flight of steps, and then he was on the man and swinging the iron-bound stock of his weapon.

The guard danced back, stumbled on the wet ground and dropped his piece. Henry's musket struck a tree, spending a juddering shock up his arms. The guard rolled and then ran, darting off among the trees.

Henry paused, breathing hard and turned to look

down. Gurney and Faugres stood, toe to toe; the Englishman answered the giant's murderous punches with sharp, well-aimed ripostes. Beyond was the barge, with Peggy working at the painter.

'Go to it, Todd!' Henry called down as Gurney planted a hard jab into Faugres' midriff.

Swallowing air to calm his hammering pulse, he sat down and began to work on the guard's musket. Opening the priming pan, he discovered a sludge of wet black powder, evidently the result of the soaking morning dew. After cleaning it out with his shirt-tail, he carefully replaced it with dry powder from the man's horn, then stood and began to search around for a target. None were apparent, save Faugres, who was too close to Gurney for a shot to be worth the risk. Of the Vicomte d'Arche, there was no sign, nor of the other guard.

Henry started down the slope, intent on holding Faugres off despite the fact that Gurney appeared to be gaining the upper hand. Then, as he reached the upper level of the ruins a man emerged from the structures by the river – the third guard, with a musket in his hands, only yards from the barge and Peggy, closer still to where Eloise hung helpless from the apple tree. Remembering how the man had gloated over their coming drowning, Henry brought his musket up, took careful aim and depressed the trigger. Flame spat and it jumped in his hand. The guard lurched forward as if caught by a giant hand, took one staggering step and pitched forward into the Louet.

Scrambling down among the ruins, Henry emerged in time to see Todd Gurney send a series of crashing blows to Faugres' skull. The giant was half down, and slumped and then fell under the Englishman's fists.

Faugres lay on the ground, apparently senseless, one guard was dead, the other had fled. It was over, completed in minutes. Gurney stepped back, his face bruised and bloody but grinning in triumph.

'One guard's loose,' Henry reported. 'We'd best hurry. Where's d'Arche?'

'No idea, sir,' Gurney replied and immediately loped off towards the barge.

Henry drew in his breath. All around the air was hazy with powder smoke, while a thin mist lay over the river and the marsh beyond. Wondering if Faugres' pockets contained any of his own belongings, he stepped forward, only for the great body to stir on the ground.

'Hell!' he swore and hefted his musket.

Faugres stood slowly, blood streaming from his nose. With a shake of his massive head, he took in the scene around him, Henry Truscott standing with a musket held in his hands like a club, the hawk-faced aristocrat he had seen in the Château l'Husseau behind, in the mouth of the mine. Of Todd Gurney, there was no sign, and Faugres allowed his mouth to break into a grin as he realised that the only man capable of facing him was not there.

He moved forward, intent on Henry's neck, only to realise that the aristocrat in the mine held two pistols. Pausing, his senses still dull from the effect of Gurney's fists, he clenched his massive hands in anger. Of all things, he wanted to get to grips with Henry, yet to move forward was to face death. Then the memory of what Henry had done to him welled up and his anger swept his last vestige of caution aside.

Seeing Faugres' glance, Henry turned, finding the Vicomte d'Arche standing a little way into the mine with his pistols levelled. Turning back, he found Faugres still coming forward, his face set in a deranged grin.

'Shoot him, damn it!' Henry called as Faugres gave a bestial roar and charged forward.

Henry turned again, wondering why the vicomte was delaying. D'Arche stood still, a pistol raised and his face set in an expression of determined malice. Without a word, he pulled the hammer back, even as Henry realised that the pistol was aimed not at Faugres, but at himself.

He leapt frantically to the side as the pistol exploded in his face. Its roar sounded, deafening in his ears as he hit the ground and rolled. Then the blast struck him like a hammer, knocking the breath from his lungs and searing his face. He curled into a tight ball of agony as wave after wave of heat and pressure burned over him, rolling him along the ground like a doll and dragging the air from his lungs. His back struck something, then his head, and for a merciful instant everything went black.

The next thing he was aware of was Eloise's face, with Peggy's close beside, both wearing expressions of alarm and sympathy. Then his head was cradled against the soft pillows of Eloise's chest. As his cock gave a familiar responsive twitch he realised thankfully that whatever injuries he had were superficial.

'What happened?' he croaked.

'Mine exploded,' Gurney remarked, from somewhere beyond Eloise's breasts. 'Don't mix too well, fire and coal dust.'

Of the Vicomte d'Arche there was no sign, nor of Jean Faugres. Neither were mourned although, as Henry worked to transfer their goods from the landau into the coal barge, he found himself constantly expecting either d'Arche's facetious drawl or Faugres's terrifying bellow. Neither came, and the barge was quickly loaded, even Eloise doing her best to help.

Abandoning the landau that had carried them so far, the party pushed off on to the unruffled Louet.

'Do we sail straight for England, then?' Eloise enquired.

'What? This barge'd not make the channel,' Henry

replied in astonishment. 'I'd sooner take to Biscay in a barrel! No, we make for St Nazaire, from where we can take passage in something that'll not sink at the first puff of wind.'

With Gurney using the long gaff as an impromptu skull, they made their way with the current, then raised the clumsy vessel's sail when they had passed the end of the marshy peninsula that separated the stream from the main channel of the Loire.

Jean Faugres dragged himself painfully up the bank of the Louet. Sodden, bruised and stained with coal and mud, he cursed the name of Henry Truscott even as he slumped down among the damp reeds. His hat was gone, blown aside by the blast from the coal mine, while his clothes were torn and filthy.

For a long while he lay still, allowing his strength to return. Then, with a groan of pain, he pulled himself to his feet. Nearby, among the tall reeds, lay the body of the Vicomte d'Arche, which Faugres spared no more than a brief and disinterested glance before trudging off across the marsh. One thought alone occupied his mind – St Nazaire.

Eleven

'What luck, sir?' Gurney asked as Henry returned to their room in the *Auberge Chémoulin.*

They had arrived in the little port of St Nazaire shortly after noon. Leaving Gurney and the girls to arrange a room in the best of the port's three inns, Henry had made for the docks, in the hope of discovering an English trader. Gurney meanwhile had made himself comfortable, seated by the window with one eye on the road leading away to the east and his hand on a bottle of the thin, sharp local wine.

'Some,' Henry answered, 'though not what I had hoped. There are no Englishmen in port, but I met a fellow who plans to sail for Exeter on the morning tide – with a cargo of smoked oysters, as chance has it. He won't leave this evening and drove a fair bargain for our passage. Still, it's Eloise's money, so no matter. Where is she, by the by?'

'Gone into town,' Gurney answered. 'Says she needs a new dress. Always after some old trumpery, that one.'

'She does rather get through her clothes,' Henry stated. 'Still, the land seems peaceful in this part of the world, so I dare say she's safe enough, even with her high and mighty tone. What's that you're drinking?'

'Wine, sir. Filthy stuff, but the beer's worse.'

'I'll see if I can't rustle up some partridge eye for dinner, or even claret: who knows? It seems we're here for the night, in any case.'

Gurney nodded and for a while neither man spoke, Henry slumping into a chair and folding his hand across his stomach while Gurney continued to stare morosely out across the road and the Loire estuary. Finally, Henry seemed to take on new energy, leaning forward to pull at a boot.

'Cheer up, Gurney, old fellow,' he said jovially as he pulled his boot off. 'Plain sailing from now on, eh? I say we order up a pair of aldermen, get beastly drunk and roger the girls silly.'

'Many a slip 'twixt cup and lip, sir,' Gurney answered him, glum at first but then brightening. 'But it seems I can't think of a better way to spend the night.'

'Perhaps with a game of cards to get them stripped and in trim,' Henry added.

'Fine idea, sir,' Gurney responded. 'We'll have them peeled down to their garters before we've so much as doffed our hats.'

Henry laughed, picturing the girls' excited chagrin at having been forced to strip naked while he and Gurney remained dressed.

In the town of Savenay, some miles to the east of St Nazaire, Emile Boillot pushed open the door of a bakery. Scents of fresh bread, sweet pastries and other edibles assailed his nostrils, momentarily making him think of food before his mind snapped back to the task in hand. On learning of the escape, he had ridden from Angers with frantic haste, certain that Eloise and her company must be making for one of the Atlantic ports. Nantes had proved fruitless, although he was sure their trail would be easy to pick up, and so he had pushed on to the small town at which he was assured many English ships called.

'Tell me, citizen,' he asked of the baker who had turned an inquisitive glance to him. 'Has a party of five passed? Three women and two men?'

'Perhaps,' the baker admitted.

'One of the women has bright red hair, another is tiny, no more than the size of a child,' Boillot continued. 'Perhaps they bought something from you?'

'Could be,' the baker continued. 'Maybe they were the ones who were so generous with their money, or then again maybe they weren't.'

With a muttered curse, Boillot slapped down a coin from what remained of his funds.

'No,' the baker announced flatly. 'Not a sign.'

'You're sure?' Boillot demanded.

'I'd have known a party like that,' the baker went on. 'They've not passed.'

'Then thank you, citizen,' Boillot answered and turned for the door.

Stepping into the wan sunlight of the square, he stopped in his tracks. In the narrow street that led east, towering above the villagers as he walked, was Jean Faugres. The giant's clothes were torn and, in places, charred, while what showed of his body was covered with bruises and angry-looking insect bites. His face was a mask of rage, his teeth bared in a furious grimace as he cast about, as if looking for something on which to vent his anger.

Bleary eyed and dizzy with drink, Henry attempted to focus on his cards. He was naked, sat splay-legged on a simple wooden chair in the upper room of the *Auberge Chémoulin*. To one side stood the table at which they had eaten, devouring two roast geese hung with sausages, autumn vegetables and several bottles of wine. Henry's lack of clothes testified to his failure at the game of chance they had chosen to play afterwards, as did the six smarting blemishes on his buttocks. These had been applied by Peggy, who was laughing merrily in her seat next to him, her gown pulled down to reveal her big breasts but otherwise fully clothed.

230

Of the females, Natalie alone had fared badly, showing little effort to win and she now sat on Gurney's knee in nothing more than her knee-length stockings while she held her cards in one hand and stroked her lover's cock with the other. Gurney himself retained only his shirt, while his attention to the game was dropping as his penis grew to erection in Natalie's hand.

Directly opposite Henry sat Eloise, her glorious red-gold hair loose and her face flushed with drink and laughter but without a stitch out of place. The sight of Henry being whipped after loosing the previous hand had had her laughing so much that she had fallen from her chair, and she was still giggling incontinently and giving him bright-eyed, excited glances.

Dealing quickly, he picked up his four cards. At the sight of three nines and a knave he sat back, doing his best to look puzzled and annoyed. Across the table from him, Eloise smiled and giggled, showing the same combination of bad play and extraordinary luck that had so far kept her covered.

Cards were changed and taken up again, Eloise alone declining the opportunity to alter her hand. Henry, on turning up his single exchange, revealed the remaining nine. Finally he had a hand he could be sure of.

'Who will play me?' Eloise enquired brightly.

Both Gurney and Peggy immediately threw their hands down on the table. Natalie laughed and threw her legs up to show off her stockings, indicating that she would be willing to part with them.

'My hat stays in the ring,' Henry declared. 'Indeed, I'll take not six, but twelve cuts of the dog-whip if either of you romps can beat me.'

'So brave,' Eloise responded, 'and all to see a pinch of my nakedness.'

'Sight more than a pinch, if those titties come bare,' Henry retorted. 'Now, do you want to lay or raise the game?'

231

'I shall raise the game,' Eloise responded. 'My nakedness against twenty-four cuts of the dog-whip for Henry; six and her stockings for Natalie.'

'I'll not risk that,' Natalie responded and threw down her cards, two tens and two fives.

'A wise choice, my little one,' Eloise declared. 'So, will the great, brave Henry Truscott risk his hide?'

'I'll go to thirty-six,' Henry answered her. 'That's to have you naked and to put six stripes across your own well-fleshed arse.'

'Then forty-eight if I take that and serve your need, which I am sure is strong,' Eloise retorted.

'You'll serve my need with pleasure, once you're stripped and beaten, as well you know,' Henry said. 'For forty-eight I'll want you in this room, tied and game. I'm like to take you in the breech too. Now show your cards!'

'Not so,' Eloise laughed. 'If you can beat what I have here, Henry, you may indulge every one of your dirty little quirks, just as you like. But first you must raise the stakes.'

'By God, I will!' Henry retorted. 'Here's everything on it: sixty stripes, my coin and everything I carry!'

'Sixty stripes?' Peggy echoed.

'Then let me see what you have, my proud man,' Eloise taunted.

Henry threw his cards to the table, revealing the four nines. Gurney gave him a worried look, as did Peggy; Natalie simply giggled. Eloise smiled her coy knowing smile, her eyes glittering with her mirth as she looked at her hand.

'Oh, my; oh, dear,' she said sweetly. 'What a shame.'

'What have you got, damn you?' Henry demanded.

'Temper, temper,' Eloise chided and laid her cards gently on the table.

With his blood hammering in his temples, Henry craned forward, seeing first an ace, then a king, then a five and finally a seven.

'Nothing,' Eloise said archly, 'and so it seems that you horrid brutes must have your way with me.'

'By God, that's a trick for which you'll pay!' Henry laughed.

'Oh, I do hope so,' she answered.

Strapping the sheet tightly around Eloise's crossed wrists, Henry tied the end off on a beam, leaving Eloise in a helpless and thoroughly shameful position. Her feet were planted wide apart, her body bent at the waist with her arms above her back and her head and breasts hanging down. She could twist her body, but do nothing to protect herself from either hands or cocks. She had stripped, feigning reluctance and shyness until she stood naked and beautiful before them. Once naked, she had kissed Henry and taken his cock in her hand, tugging at it impatiently only to receive a gentle cuff on her bottom and be told to take her position for flogging. Now she waited, every orifice flaunted and her bottom looking plump and tempting in the light of the candles.

'Good to beat 'em in, good to tup 'em in,' Gurney stated admiringly.

'And for sport in general,' Henry answered. 'I may have won this, but I'll show I'm no curmudgeon. Natalie, my sweet, what would you best enjoy from your mistress?'

'I . . . I'm not sure, sir,' Natalie responded shyly.

'I am,' Peggy put in. 'Eloise's trick was to push our faces in her chamber-pot while she beat us, often for as little as catching her ear with a hairbrush.'

'Ho! Ho!' Henry boomed. 'A fine trick and no mistake. Well, Eloise, that shall be your first pleasure – once you've filled a pot, that is. Gurney, feed her another pint of partridge eye while I stoke her cunt to make her ready.'

He reached for his cock, only to have Peggy's soft hand close on it first and begin to tug. Her heavy breasts were pushed against his arm, increasing his pleasure as she stroked him to erection over the sight of Eloise's spread, helpless body. Gurney, meanwhile, took up a freshly opened bottle and lifted Eloise's chin to put it to her lips. She made no resistance, swallowing as best she could but gagging twice as the bottle was emptied down her throat. Plenty spilt, to run down her chin and chest and leave drops of the deep pink liquid hanging from her stiff nipples.

As Eloise swallowed the last of the bottle, Henry decided that he was ready for her. Putting his cock to her vagina, he let Peggy guide it in. Eloise moaned softly as her vagina filled, then began to grunt as Henry fucked her, interspersing the crude, animal noises with pleas for harder and deeper penetration. Already enervated by being stripped and then beaten by Peggy, he quickly felt the urge to come, made difficult only by the volume of drink he had consumed. Yet within the tight sheath of Eloise's vagina, his penis felt exquisitely sensitive, rubbing in her tube of flesh so that he could feel every detail of the head, neck, foreskin and shaft. Concentrating on the feel of his cock and sight of her naked bottom, he worked himself furiously inside her, forcing squeals from her lips. For a moment his cock seemed to swell within her and then he was coming, draining his sperm into the depths of her vagina, which became instantly slick and loose around his erection.

'Up for a wet dock, Gurney?' he asked, pulling slowly out to leave Eloise's cunny wide and oozing sperm.

'I'll take her in the breech, by and by,' his friend replied. 'I've no great liking for a buttered bun and I'd want to watch her piss first.'

Eloise groaned at the news that she was to be buggered, yet still made no protest, merely hanging her head in a gesture that might have been acceptance or simply resignation to the thought of the big man's cock in her back passage.

'Well,' Henry spoke out as he knelt to the level of Eloise's head, 'are you game to fill your pot yet?'

Eloise shook her head, casting a glance at Henry that showed pleasure, drunkenness and exhaustion in equal measures. Henry took one dangling breast in his hand and began to knead, watching Eloise's face as her nipple rubbed in his palm and her soft flesh moved under his fingers. She sighed, her mouth opening slowly in wanton abandonment. Flattening his hand, he began to slap her breasts, gently to make them sway, then more firmly. Her sighs and groans took on a new, more urgent quality as the flesh of the undersides of her breasts began to flush pink. Henry chuckled at her response, watching her breasts sway beneath her as his cock twinged in response.

'Time for your beating, I think, my little puppy,' Henry crowed. 'Where's that dog-whip?'

Taking the dog-whip from Peggy, he stood back behind Eloise. Her bottom was the highest part of her body save for her strapped wrists, the cheeks bulging upward and open, with her pussy a dark wet hole between her chubby thighs. Her muscles were clenching and unclenching, making the flesh of her sex move and her anus wink to a lewd rhythm.

Henry raised his arm, judged the distance and laid the little whip hard across Eloise's bottom. She gave a sharp cry of pain that turned quickly to a whimper as the lash dropped away to leave a long scarlet line across the crests of her upraised buttocks. Again he lashed out, catching her lower so that her bottom jerked at the impact and a wave of flesh spread out over her cheeks and thighs. Once more she cried out, but also kicked her legs so that for a moment her balance went, only to be regained after a frantic dance that made her buttocks wobble and drew a trill of laughter from the audience. Henry struck again, aiming deliberately low to catch her thighs. She yelped and bucked, then finished with another ridiculous little dance on her toes that again drew ribald laughter from the others.

With three deep red welts crossing the goose-pimpled flesh of her rear, Eloise was sobbing and gasping, yet made no complaint or demand for her beating to stop. Once more, Henry brought the dog-whip down hard across her buttocks, the lash tracing a long line over their upper surfaces to leave her yelping and writhing her hindquarters in her pain.

'Two more, my sweet,' Henry stated, 'then it's time for a plug in your beautiful arse!'

Eloise responded with a groan that turned to another yelp as the fifth stroke of the whip landed across her bottom. Again she started her frantic little wiggling dance, only for Henry to lay the sixth stroke across the very fattest part of her bottom before she had had a chance to compose herself. She squealed loudly, then sagged in her bonds, gasping and sobbing out her emotion.

'By God, I'll be ready for another crack myself in a minute,' Henry breathed. 'Doesn't she look well-whipped, though? I always think a bit of decoration becomes a girl's arse. Well, puppy, are you ready to pee?'

For a while, the whipped girl made no response, merely hanging in her bonds and breathing heavily. Henry watched the muscles of her vulva clench, making her vagina close and then open once more, then a slow movement of her bedraggled hair indicated that she was shaking her head.

'More wine!' Henry called.

Natalie took a bottle and put it to her mistress's lips. Eloise drank greedily, gulping the wine from the bottle and spilling a great deal down her chin and on to the floor.

'She'll be ready in a trice,' Henry said as he reached out and squeezed Eloise's belly. 'But what of you, Peggy, while we wait?'

'I'd like my arse kissed,' Peggy declared.

'Fine!' Henry responded. 'Do it, then, Eloise; let's see you kiss your maid's arse!'

Henry and the others watched as Peggy lifted her dress and petticoats to reveal her plump behind. Making a great show of it, she pressed her naked buttocks into Eloise's face, demanding kisses on each cheek. The demoiselle complied, putting her lips to her maid's full buttocks and kissing each before once more hanging her head.

'On Robby Douglas, Peggy!' Henry called out. 'Full between your cheeks, and be sure she gets her tongue well in!'

Peggy gave the faintest of blushes but reached back and hauled her ample bottom-cheeks apart to reveal the wrinkled pink spot of her anus to the onlookers. Eloise groaned deep in her throat, raising her face again to find Peggy's anus inches from her mouth. She started to say something, only to have her face smothered in plump bottom as Peggy moved back. Henry cheered as they heard the unmistakable sound of a kiss being applied to the maid's bum-hole, the others echoing him, save only for Peggy, who sighed in pleasure.

'By God, but she's licking her arse!' Henry exclaimed as Eloise, far from drawing back once she had completed her degrading task, kept her face between Peggy's buttocks. 'She's the bob-tail for me, and no mistake!'

Peggy felt a shiver of pure bliss as Eloise's firm, damp tongue tip began to work at her anus. The others had gone quiet, watching her get her bottom tongued in fascinated silence. Unable to resist, she reached back and hastily pulled up her skirts, her fingers finding the wet flesh of her cunny.

'Lick, please lick,' she gasped as she began to masturbate.

Heedless of everything save the feel of her mistress's tongue against her bum-hole, she rubbed her vulva, working directly against the clitoris with an urgency born not simply from the physical sensation but from the ecstasy of receiving so servile an act from the woman who had before been so firmly in charge of her. Almost before she knew it, her body was tensing in orgasm, with her thigh muscles burning and her back set in a rigid arch. She heard Henry laugh and Gurney cheer as she came with her whole being focused on her anus and the woman whose tongue was probing it.

'I'm going to do it,' Eloise sighed, as soon as her face was clear of Peggy's bottom.

Quickly, Natalie grabbed up the chamber-pot and held it to her mistress's sex. Eloise groaned, a sound mixing pleasure and shame as a little spurt of urine escaped from her tightly clamped pee-hole. For a moment more she held, and then the pee erupted from her vulva in a golden stream, splashing into the chamber-pot and across her thighs. As it did so, she gave a sigh of utter relief.

'Good girl!' Henry called, laughing loudly at the sight of the yellow liquid gushing from the girl's cunny and swirling in the pot. 'Come on, a guinea says she can piss a pint!'

'I'll not take that one,' Gurney responded.

'Then a guinea says she can drink as much as she makes!'

'That I'll chance.'

They watched the pee run from Eloise, still splashing in the pot, but dying slowly, first to a trickle and then a mere dribble that ran down her labia and dripped from the hood of her clitoris to form ripples in the pool beneath her.

'A copious spend,' Henry remarked, peering into the pot. 'You were wise not to take my first wager. Still, I'll stand by my assertion that she can drink down every drop, and better, while your cock's in her breech.'

'It'll be worth a guinea to watch her try, sir,' Gurney responded. 'Now, where's my wench?'

He turned to find Natalie, who was already kneeling beside him.

'It would be kind to ease her passage first,' Peggy suggested as Gurney slipped his half-stiff penis into Natalie's mouth.

'True,' Henry agreed, looking critically at the tight, pink-brown ring of Eloise's anus, 'but with what?'

'Her own juice'll serve, if need be,' Gurney answered. 'I'll take a dip in the cream jar before forcing her breech.'

'There's a little butter,' Peggy suggested. 'Or –'

'Why, the grease from the goose, of course!' Henry interrupted. 'What better way to ease a girl's passage, with the season approaching Christmas? Come on girl, scoop some up and he'll be up her in a trice!'

Peggy walked to the remains of their dinner. She smiled at Henry as she began to scrape the cold grease from the platter on to a knife, a smile of pure mischief. Henry grinned back and accepted the small plate on to which she had loaded the grease, then knelt to get at Eloise's anal opening.

Her bottom was inches in front of his face, a magnificent pear of flesh, criss-crossed with welts from the dog-whip and slick with sweat from her response to the beating. Her vulva was swollen and moist, her cunny a gaping hole, slick with sperm and clearly ready for another helping of penis. Above it, the object of his attention was a bright pink dimple surrounded by the little tucks and bulges of her dun-brown anal ring. The flesh was slightly puffy, and as Henry watched, it opened and closed, as if winking in anticipation of the cock that was shortly to be pushed inside it.

'By God, but she's a ripe one for sodomy,' he

239

murmured as he dipped his finger into the thick goose-grease. 'It's damn seldom you see an arsehole so pretty, or so willing.'

He lifted his finger and applied a blob of grease to Eloise's anus, which contracted in response, only to open like a flower as his finger touched the sensitive flesh. She moaned as he rubbed, and pushed her bottom out, her lust overcoming her reluctance to surrender her rear opening to Gurney's cock.

'In it goes,' Henry said as he popped the first joint of his finger inside Eloise's now well-greased anus.

Her moans became louder as she was penetrated, and Henry felt her ring tighten on his finger, a warm lock of flesh that made him recall how it had felt clamped tight on his cock when he had given her the same treatment his servant was about to. As he lubricated Eloise's anus, Peggy took up the chamber-pot, briefly dipped each of Eloise's breasts in it and then held it up to her mistress's head. Eloise gave a deep sigh, only for Peggy to catch her by her hair and quickly thrust her face into the contents of the chamber-pot. Eloise produced a strange bubbling sound, drawing a fresh peal of laughter from Henry. Peggy then altered her hold of her mistress's red-gold curls and pulled upward. Eloise came up spluttering, her mouth wide open, with drops of pee hanging from her nose and upper lip. Shaking her head in the maid's grip, she sent a shower of droplets across the room.

'Hold it still, Peggy,' Henry instructed. 'I want her to drink it while she's sodomised, not waste it!'

Henry watched as Gurney pulled his erect cock from Natalie's mouth and mounted Eloise, with his shaft resting between her buttocks. She moaned as the head of his cock was put to her goose-greased anus and rubbed in, then gave a sharp squeak as a sudden shove filled her ring. Gurney took her by the hips and began pushing his cock deeper into her rectum, drawing gasps and uncontrolled grunts from her. Soon his cock was right in, embedded to its full length in the soft, fleshy tube of her back passage.

'Drink it down, my dear; it'll do you good!' Henry boomed as Gurney began to bugger Eloise.

Eloise's bestial grunts instantly became rude bubbling noises as Peggy lifted the chamber-pot to immerse her mistress's face. For a moment Eloise continued to blow bubbles, then a gentle lapping sound signalled that she had surrendered even that last vestige of dignity and was drinking her own pee. With a roar of laughter, Henry burst into song:

'So drink, puppy, drink,
And let my puppy drink,
For she's game enough to lap and to swallow!

So drink, puppy, drink,
And she'll drink the pisspot down,
And merrily we'll whoop and we'll hollo!'

As he repeated the song, the others joined in, Peggy with gusto, Natalie doing her best to follow and Gurney interspersing his words with pants and grunts as he buggered Eloise. As Henry sang he watched Eloise drink the contents of the chamber-pot, sucking the pee up and swallowing, only to lose most of each mouthful every time Gurney's cock was rammed home in her back passage. A good deal of piddle went down her throat, but as Gurney's thrusts became harder she began to gag and finally it became evident that she could swallow no more.

'Damn!' Henry laughed as the song trailed off in drunken discordance. 'That's a guinea to you, Todd Gurney, but I still say she'd have done it without a cock in her breech!'

'Dare say,' Gurney grunted in response.

'Put an apple in her cunt to keep her tight and

hungry,' Henry continued, 'and have Natalie put her tongue to our fine lady's cunny; there's no feeling like having a woman come while you're in her breech.'

'Do it, Natalie,' Gurney said in his crude French, the tiny maid immediately running to the table to obey his order.

She came back with a red apple, wider by far than the thickest of cocks.

'That'll never go in!' Henry laughed.

'A shilling says it does,' Peggy retorted.

'Taken, by God!' Henry swore. 'Go on, Natalie, do your best!'

'Grease it, first,' Peggy suggested.

Natalie giggled and pushed the apple into the lump of goose grease that had been used to lubricate Eloise's bottom. Turning it until the red skin was glossy with fat, she then ducked down, putting the apple to her mistress's vagina as Gurney drew back to make room in front of his balls. Eloise squealed as the fruit was pressed to her hole, then gave a gasp of shock as she filled.

'Damn!' Henry swore. 'That's a guinea and a hog down!'

He stepped back; the changing expression on Gurney's face told him that the time for trifling was over, at least for the moment. Natalie was holding the apple into Eloise's vagina and had began to lick, applying her face directly to her mistress's out-thrust clitoris. Gurney's pushes had become more urgent, while Eloise's face was a mask of ecstasy, her mouth slack and open, a dribble of pee and saliva running from her lower lip. Her buttocks began to tighten and she gave a long, drawn-out sigh, signalling to Henry the onset of orgasm.

Gurney growled deep in his throat as Eloise's anus began to spasm on his intruding cock. Since he had met her, the idea of buggering the haughty, aloof

242

noblewoman had appealed to him, as if the act of sodomy alone had the power to make them equal. No girl who had been buggered could afford to give herself airs to the man who had done it, and now his cock was rammed to the hilt in her rectum, sheathed in hot flesh as her bottom-hole contracted rhythmically on the base of his shaft. He could feel the apple in her vagina as well, a hard bump that made her back passage tighter still. Natalie also had a hand on his balls, adding a final thrill to the glorious blend of sensations that were pulling him to orgasm.

As Eloise screamed out her climax, he too came, deep up her bottom, filling her with sperm as spurt followed spurt, until his cock was in a warm pool of fluid. The pulsing of her anus drew out his last drops, and he kept himself deep in her until she had finished.

He pulled free, spreading her buttocks with his thumbs and watching the glistening rod of his penis slide from her everted anus. The head popped out to leave her bum-hole gaping wide with a dribble of come and goose-grease running down to her engorged cunny.

'By God, that's open!' Henry exclaimed. 'A guinea says it can take an apple!'

'Taken, if it stays!' Gurney answered as he stepped back.

'Peggy, choose an apple,' Henry ordered, 'and no bigger than the last.'

Peggy passed the apple to Henry, who applied it to Eloise's anus. The muscle opened, the well-buggered girl pushing out to try and accept it. Gurney watched Eloise's fleshy bum-hole stretch, yawning wide until the apple at last went in.

'My bet, I think!' Henry declared happily.

'Not so,' Gurney retorted. 'It must stay in place!'

Eloise's anus closed on the apple, the wet, pink sphincter creeping shut across the glossy red surface

243

only to stop with an inch or so of apple skin still showing, like the bull's-eye of a target. The whole centre of her bottom was everted, the straining flesh showing the outline of the apple within. As Henry removed his finger, her anus immediately began to open, the muscles of her sphincter evidently unequal to the task.

'Hold it in, damn you!' Henry swore. 'I've got a guinea on that!'

A sudden convulsive clenching of Eloise's anal ring showed that she was trying, yet it was no good and the apple once more began to ooze from her straining bottom-hole.

'By God, I'll not lose this one!' Henry yelled and began to scrabble at his belt.

Pressing his crotch against Eloise's bottom to keep the apple in, he pulled his belt free and hastily fixed the buckle to the loose end of the sheet that bound her wrists. Pulling the thick leather strap hard down between her legs, he pushed the tag end into Eloise's open mouth.

'Hold it in your teeth, you silly bitch!' he called.

Eloise obeyed, gripping the tag hard in her teeth and pulling her head up. Henry stood, triumphant, only to watch the apple exude slowly from Eloise's anus, pushing the belt aside despite her best efforts.

'Hell!' He swore as her anus closed behind the apple. 'You can let go now, Eloise. That's a second guinea to you, Gurney!'

Eloise hung in her bonds, the pain of her position submerged in a mist of pleasure and alcohol. Her wrists, shoulders and thighs seemed numb but nothing more, while her bottom throbbed with a constant sensual ache to remind her of her beating and subsequent buggery. Her mouth was full of the taste of her own urine, which also felt cold on her face and the dangling orbs of her breasts. The apple in her vagina felt enormous, bulging her out to force her clitoris into prominence, while the one in her rectum had threatened to make her lose all control.

The feelings of shame, exposure and frustration – so strong when she had first been strapped up – had faded, lost in a welter of intercourse, buggery, and beating. Her final shred of reserve had dissolved at the moment her pee had erupted into the chamber-pot and at the sure knowledge that she was going to be made to drink it. Now she no longer cared, not that she had licked her maid's anus, not that her cunt and bottom-hole had been stuffed with fruit, not even that a serving man had buggered her and come in her rectum. All of it simply added to her wonderful feeling of total vulnerability, of being helplessly available for any and every delicious degradation.

Henry's cock was once more stiff, a condition assisted by soft strokes of Peggy's hand. Gurney had taken Natalie into the bedroom, and the tiny maid's squeals of pleasure could be clearly heard. Determined to take his fill while he could, Henry moved once more behind Eloise. His cock slid easily into her vagina and he began to ride her bottom, concentrating on the sight of the recently inflicted whip marks in order to inspire him towards a second orgasm.

It began to come faster than he had anticipated, a slowly rising tide of pleasure that grew with each stroke of his cock inside Eloise. She was grunting, and he was about to suggest that Peggy applied a tongue where it would do the most good when a thunderous pounding began on the door.

'Go to hell! I'm parting my beard!' Henry called out and again jammed his cock deep into Eloise.

Her answering grunt was followed by another crash on the door, this time louder.

'I said go to hell, you importunate hick!' Henry roared.

Another crash came in response, then a splintering sound as the catch gave way. Henry turned, furious, expecting the portly innkeeper or someone from a neighbouring room, irate at the noise they had been making. Instead, as his cock slipped from Eloise's vagina, he found himself faced with the massive frame and bearded face of Jean Faugres, a vision of unkempt rage.

'Bastard!' the giant Frenchman screamed as his eyes lit on Henry.

Peggy screamed, Eloise merely producing a moan of what sounded like disappointment. Henry backed away, horrified by the murderous hatred in the man's eyes. Faugres came forward, his great hands clutching convulsively and his teeth bared in an animal snarl. He glanced at Eloise, showing no reaction to the fact that she was bound and naked, then leapt forward.

Henry went back, borne down under his assailant's weight. Striking out frantically, his fist caught Faugres' jaw, yet the blow only served to enrage the Frenchman further. Great hands closed on his neck, abruptly cutting off his cry of alarm. He pushed but to no avail, the giant merely laughing. As his vision began to blacken and blur at the edges, he felt himself picked up, to be held by the neck and shaken. Gurney's yell sounded in his ears, and another female scream.

In front of him, he could see Faugres's face, dim and blurred with red and black shadows, the great mouth open in a triumphant yell. A pang of regret struck him, driven by the realisation, oddly sharp, that Faugres's rage-contorted face would be the last thing he ever saw. The room swirled, all sense of balance vanished and he felt himself falling as his senses slipped away.

His body jarred against something, hard. A sharp pain in one arm brought his senses back and he realised that the great fingers no longer dug into his neck. Shaking his head, he rolled to the side, his face contacting something slimy – the goose carcass. Other details of his surroundings became clear as his vision gradually returned, the splintered debris of the table and a chair, the strewn remains of their meal, and the massive body of Jean Faugres, prone among the debris with the tip of the carving knife jutting from his breast. Beyond, Gurney stood, the silver altar cross they had carried from St Romain clasped in his fist, Peggy and Natalie behind him.

'Thank you, Gurney,' Henry croaked as he pulled himself up on to one fist.

'Wasn't my doing, sir,' Gurney replied. 'He slipped on the plate of goose grease we were using for Miss Eloise's behind.'

'Who says vice doesn't bring a reward?' Henry managed feebly and collapsed back on to the floor.

Shortly after, he had returned to his senses, aided by brandy and the ministrations of Peggy and Natalie. Gurney had meanwhile untied Eloise, only for her to slump to the floor. Even water poured on her head and slaps to her face had done little to revive her senses. With her curls plastered to her skin and her eyes half-closed, she lay limp, her mouth flexed into a happy, torpid smile.

'Drunk as an emperor, sir,' Gurney said unnecessarily.

'Hell!' Henry swore. 'That's all we need, and someone'll be bound to have called the traps.'

'Best be gone, sir,' Gurney put in.

'Come on!' Henry urged, slapping Eloise's cheek.

She responded with an exhausted groan, merely rolling to her side.

'Damn!' Henry declared. 'We'll carry her, then. Come on!'

He grabbed for his breeches, leaving Eloise to her stupor. Dressing with a frantic haste, he yelled instructions to the others, only to find them dressed before his numb fingers had managed to fasten his breeches.

Once more, the door flew open, the innkeeper stepping inside with a look of fury that quickly turned to horror. Another figure was behind him – Emile Boillot. Before either could speak, Todd Gurney's great fists had lashed out, flooring the innkeeper and then sending Boillot sprawling back into the passage. Shouts sounded somewhere down the passage and Gurney strode out of the room. As Henry struggled with the last button of his breeches, he heard a voice raised in anger, then abruptly silenced.

Taking up everything they could carry, they fled from the inn. Angry cries followed them down the street but served only to speed their pace. Gurney was to the fore, Eloise thrown limp across his shoulder and a great bundle of goods in one hand. Peggy and Natalie followed, with Henry at the rear, staggering from both drink and his burden.

Henry looked back over the stern of their vessel, searching for any sign of pursuit. Dawn had come up to reveal the French coast as a dull line on the horizon, while a substantial island lay to the north and west. Several sails were visible, and also the topsails of two larger vessels, one of which was beginning to give him concern. Once clear of the inn, they had left St Nazaire without hindrance, appropriating the boat that they had intended to travel in anyway. Despite what had seemed an easy escape, Henry had no doubt that the vessel would be missed.

His concern increased as they ran up the side of the island. Twice the following vessel came alongside smaller boats, and always in their path. Finally there could be no doubt, as it became evident that the ship was a brigantine of the French navy and intent on overhauling them.

'Hell!' he swore. 'We're done up now, and so near!'

'She's carrying eight, maybe ten guns, sir,' Gurney put in.

'One would be enough to scupper us,' Henry replied. 'Not even that, really, as she has twice our speed and doubtless a fair crew, French or not.'

'Are they going to catch us?' Natalie queried in a small, frightened voice.

'Yes, my dear, I'm afraid they are,' Henry responded. 'Not just yet, but they will.'

'We must fight!' Eloise declared. 'I'd rather die than be taken!'

'Perhaps you're right,' Henry answered. 'Leastwise, I'll not give them the satisfaction of lopping my head off with that infernal device of theirs.'

'What if we were to pull for the lee shore, sir?' Gurney asked. 'We might make it.'

'We'd be like rats in a barrel,' Henry retorted. 'Right under her guns, and they need only put a boat down to catch us. No, make north and west as if nothing were amiss and I'll judge they'll take two hours to catch us. So – Natalie, Peggy, sew us a jack, and be damned quick about it!'

Henry glared up at the French naval officer who was looking down at him from the gunwales of the brigantine. He was a young man and carried an air of officious self-importance, yet seemed mild next to the expression of righteous triumph on the face of the man to his side – Emile Boillot.

'Damn you, sir, are you trying to start another war?' Henry demanded.

'These are they,' Boillot declared to the officer, ignoring Henry completely. 'Take them.'

'What the hell do you mean?' Henry shouted.

'You stand accused of crimes against the French people,' the officer replied. 'Including murder, grievous assault, assisting a known felon –'

'What!?' Henry roared. 'If this is a jest, then it's in damn poor taste, and damn foolish, too. Don't you realise the consequences of pulling over a vessel under British colours?'

For a moment, the officer wavered and began to speak in a less arrogant tone, only to be cut off by Boillot.

'Don't listen to his rodomontade,' the student declared and then turned down to Henry once more. 'Come, Truscott, submit to justice, for it has caught you at last.'

'Truscott? What the hell are you talking about, man?' Henry blustered back. 'Who's this Truscott? I'm Tom Cobley, a Plymouth merchant.'

'Ha!' Boillot began, only to be cut off by a movement of the officer's hand.

'Do you deny the charges, then?' the officer asked, still trying to look stern.

'Deny the charges?' Henry retorted. 'Of course I deny the damn charges.'

'Can you prove this?' the officer continued before Henry could get into the full swing of his tirade.

'Prove it?' Henry yelled. 'Damn you, I've no need to prove anything, to you, nor to any other jumped-up French puppy!'

'It's him, I tell you!' Boillot put in. 'Search the hold, and you'll find the harlot Delatour and her lackeys! Then the truth will be plain!'

'What?' Henry demanded.

'I have reason to believe that you are carrying a woman wanted for crimes against the French state,' the officer replied, now evidently struggling to maintain both his authority and his temper. 'Namely, Eloise de la Tour-Romain. Also her two maidservants.'

'Maidservants?' Henry demanded, abruptly altering his tone from anger to humour. 'Ha, I wish we were. But no, your accusation is preposterous. This is a trading vessel, come to collect St Nazaire oysters, smoked, in barrels.'

'And may we inspect these barrels?' Boillot enquired sarcastically.

'If you must,' Henry replied. 'Despite this gross breach of our sovereign rights, you may come aboard and see for yourself.'

Boillot gave Henry a look, not of doubt, but of puzzlement. The officer called two seamen over, and together they climbed down into the smaller vessel. With Gurney standing silently to one side, Henry motioned the Frenchmen below decks, into a small space stacked with barrels and rich with the heady smell of smoked oysters.

'Be my guest,' Henry said mockingly and gave a sweeping bow that took in the entire hold.

Boillot immediately began to search, peering into every space large enough with increasing puzzlement. The two seamen searched more methodically, but with no greater success. Finally, it became evident that the two Englishmen were the only occupants of the vessel.

'There we are,' Henry declared. 'I trust you are satisfied. And now, if we might resume our journey?'

'They are in the barrels,' Boillot declared. 'Fetch an axe, officer.'

'The barrels are sealed!' Henry expostulated. 'And besides, how would these supposed women breathe, immersed in oysters? I have been generous. I have allowed you to search my vessel, which I was under no obligation to do, but I will not allow you to ruin my stock!'

'See how he blusters!' Boillot declared. 'Search the barrels!'

'My stock!' Henry protested. 'Look, officer, be sensible; the barrels are packed with oysters and sealed! Anyone inside would suffocate.'

'He is right,' the officer said tentatively. 'Monsieur Boillot, are you sure these are the men?'

'Citizen Boillot,' Boillot replied firmly. 'Yes, I am certain. Two Englishmen, one of ordinary size, one tall and strong. I do not know the tall one, but this impudent villain is Henry Truscott, a –'

'I'm Tom Cobley, I tell you,' Henry blustered. 'I've never so much as heard of this Truscott fellow, nor ever before seen this lunatic!'

He indicated Boillot, who returned a look of frustrated outrage at this blatant lie. Reasoning that, with Faugres dead, it was highly unlikely that anybody was aboard the brigantine to gainsay him, he decided on a final bluff.

'Officer,' he said with a sigh, and indicated Boillot. 'This fellow is clearly deranged. I have allowed you to board my vessel; I have allowed you to make a search. It is ludicrous to suppose that three women are on board. So, you have a choice: either allow us to proceed or return us to St Nazaire, where undoubtedly your superior will wish to know why you have risked precipitating an international incident on the whim of a lunatic.'

He stopped, folding his arms and looking directly at the officer while he thanked heaven that, in Boillot's impetuosity, the student had failed to collect his evidence properly before demanding that chase be given. The expression on the officer's face wavered, clearly judging the effect on his career should Boillot's claim prove false.

'I demand they be taken in!' Boillot declared suddenly. 'Do your duty!'

'Well –' the officer began, looking between the furious student and the grim Englishman.

'Do you take orders from every half-grown Jack who gives them?' Henry enquired gently.

The expression on the officer's face changed slowly and Henry knew that he had won.

Henry watched until the brigantine was well clear, only

then returning to the hold. He walked to a barrel, freed his cock into his hand and rolled the foreskin quickly back and forth until the blood began to harden him. Taking hold of the barrel bung, and smiling as his finger touched the deep trough he had cut on the underside, he pulled it out and poked his erection into the hole. The fleshy bodies of smoked oysters parted on either side of his penis head, feeling strangely like a quim, yet cold. Then something else touched the sensitive skin at the very tip of his cock, something of similar texture to the oysters but warm. For a moment he sensed reluctance, only for the divide to open and a moist and muscular mouth to engulf his erection. He gave a sigh of contentment as Eloise began to suck his penis.

Epilogue

Henry Truscott relaxed back into the armchair, allowing his body to go slowly limp, all except his right arm, which was reserved for lifting the nipperkin of ancient port at his elbow. He exhaled a sigh of absolute contentment and slumped another inch down into the armchair. For him, conditions were at the ideal balance of excitement and contentment. Two attractive, hot-blooded women were devoted to him, grateful, only slightly jealous of one another and accommodating – both of his personal foibles and of his penis. Peggy was perfect – sweet, kind, attentive, yet uninhibited and boisterous when the occasion demanded. Eloise continued to show the occasional flash of temper, but knew that the upshot of her tantrums would invariably be a brisk spanking across his knee. Following such spankings, she would be both contrite and submissive, eager to atone for her bad behaviour. Both girls gave willingly and often, sometimes separately, sometimes together.

Putting the nipperkin to his lips, he took a sip of the rich, cherry-sweet liquid, allowing it to flow over his tongue and bathe his senses in a warm symphony of opulent flavours. Life, he decided, was as near perfect as it was going to get, considering that his most pressing problem was the soreness of his cock following its intrusion into more moist, willing female openings than was perhaps advisable. Still, he reflected, it was churlish to grumble.

For most of the day he and a large company of others had been making merry in honour of the wedding that morning between Todd Gurney and Natalie Moreau. It had not been among the most fashionable of the weddings Henry had attended, but it was certainly among the most enjoyable. The ale and cider had flowed freely, and the port almost as much so, until Peggy now lay with her head in his lap, absently nuzzling his cock through his breeches and too drunk to care who was looking on. Eloise had retired to be sick, much to Henry's amusement, and was now being ministered to by old Mrs Catchpole.

As Henry took another sip of port and wondered if he could summon the energy to find somewhere quiet to take Peggy for sex, Mrs Catchpole appeared, her face flushed with excitement.

'Master Henry!' she cried in agitation.

'What's wrong?' Henry demanded.

'It's Miss Eloise,' the old woman announced. 'She's going to have a baby!'

A silence followed, to be broken as suddenly by the crash of the nipperkin on the floor as it fell from Henry's nerveless fingers.

THE END

Notes

1 – Banknotes were originally produced as notes of promise from specific banks. At the end of the eighteenth century, the first official British banknotes were produced in denominations of one and two pounds. In the first year of banknote production, there were nearly 400 convictions for forgery.
2 – In theory, neither the Declaration of the Rights of Man nor the abolition of feudalism endangered either the property or lives of the French nobility. Nevertheless, from July 1789, mob violence had become commonplace and agitators were finding fertile ground among the disaffected peasantry. Among an estimated 80,000 nobles, roughly half fled France, while some 12,000 were either executed or died at the hands of the mob.

Even in the August of 1789, it was clear to the revolutionaries that an invasion of France was to be expected and army recruiting was vigorous.
3 – Towards the end of the eighteenth century, duelling was illegal in that the law regarded a death in a duel as common murder. Nevertheless, public opinion was firmly on the side of duelling as a means of settling disputes of honour and no gentleman could refuse a challenge. Not only were many eminent people involved in duels, even including the Duke of Wellington at a later date, but no jury allowed a conviction for murder as a result of a duel until 1808.
4 – The latter half of 1789 was by no means the most violent part of the French revolution, but it was perhaps the most confusing. The collapse of the *ancien régime* had left a vacuum of authority that was not to be filled until the Assembly had gained full control of the country. Support for the revolution varied greatly from region to region, as did the antagonism of the populace towards its erstwhile rulers. The Church retained control of its land until December of that year.
5 – The guillotine was first used on 25 April 1792 to execute a highwayman named Pelletier. Nevertheless, Dr Guillotine had been attempting to promote it as a method of humane execution for some

years. Beheading was adopted as the standard method of capital punishment by the Assembly on 6 October 1791, as it had previously been reserved for those of noble birth and it was felt that all persons sentenced to death should be treated equally. Such executions were originally intended to be by sword stroke, but when this proved both slow and expensive Dr Guillotine's original proposal of 1 December 1789 was reconsidered.

6 – Burgundy was first auctioned at Christie's in the 1780s and remained a rare wine in Britain until well into the nineteenth century.

7 – Tyburn had been London's principal place of execution since the twelfth century, but after 1783 the facility was transferred to Newgate prison. Executions remained public until well into the nineteenth century.

8 – Charles James Fox (1749-1806), British statesman and orator. Not only was Fox among the most noted liberals of his day, but he had managed to earn a reputation as a dissipated rake by the age of fourteen. He incurred massive gambling debts, fought a famous duel in 1779 and in general remained a model of dissipation of which Henry Truscott would undoubtedly have approved.

NEW BOOKS

Coming up from Nexus, Sapphire and Black Lace

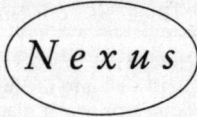

$$\left(\; Nexus \; \right)$$

Giselle by Jean Aveline
October 1999   £5.99   ISBN: 0 352 33440 1
Aside from her extreme beauty, Giselle appears to be an ordinary
country girl when the English photographer Charles discovers her in
Northern France. Yet when he takes her to Paris to recreate her as a
model, he discovers that she has a history. On an island in a flooded
quarry in Avignon, boys and men have already reached her and
corrupted her. All Charles can do is feed her appetite for perverse sex,
and the higher she rises in the world of fashion the lower she falls in
her sexual games with strangers.

House Rules by G.C. Scott
October 1999   £5.99   ISBN: 0 352 33441 X
When Richard meets Helena in Hamburg's red light district, he isn't
prepared for either the forwardness with which she seduces him or his
imminent involvement in her curious business dealings. For Helena
is a designer of fetish clothing, and her colleagues have very forceful
ideas about how a man should be treated.

Bound to Serve by Amanda Ware
October 1999   £5.99   ISBN: 0 352 33457 6
Caroline West is facing up to the absence of her master, Liam, as he
battles to save himself from bankruptcy. When the cruel and
manipulative Clive offers her a means of helping him, on condition
that she becomes his slave for three weeks, she does not hesitate, and
is soon signed over to him. She is then handed over to Lynne, her
former mistress for further, more severe training – treatment which
Caroline soon finds is more and more to her liking. A Nexus Classic.

In For a Penny by Penny Birch
November 1999   £5.99   ISBN: 0 352 33449 5
Penny Birch is back, as naughty as ever. *In for a Penny* continues the story of her outrageous sex life and also the equally rude behaviour of her friends. From stories of old-fashioned spankings, through strip-wrestling in baked beans, to a girl with six breasts, it's all there. Each scene is described in loving detail, with no holding back and a level of realism that comes from a great deal of practical experience.

Maiden by Aishling Morgan
November 1999   £5.99   ISBN: 0 352 33466 5
When Elethrine, Princess Talithea and their maid, Aisla, threaten to spank the sorceress Ea, they are punished by being transported to a distant part of their world. *Maiden* charts their journey home through a series of erotic indignities and humiliations, throughout all of which Elethrine is determined to retain her virginity. What she doesn't realise is that this will involve far more humiliating encounters for her than for her companions.

Bound to Submit by Amanda Ware
November 1999   £5.99   ISBN: 0 352 33451 7
The beautiful and submissive Caroline is married to her new master and the love of her life, James, at a bizarre fetishistic ceremony in the USA. He is keen to turn his new wife into a star of explicit movies and Caroline is auditioned without delay for a film of bondage and domination. Little do they know that the project is being financed by James' business rival and Caroline's former master, the cruel Clive. Clive intends to fulfil a long-held desire – to permanently mark Caroline as his property. Can her husband save her from his mesmeric influence? A Nexus Classic.

The Ties That Bind by Tesni Morgan

October 1999   Price £5.99   ISBN: 0 352 33438 X

When Kim meets devilish stanger Jack Loring at a fancy-dress party, her comfortable world turns upside down. For a start, Jack might have some family ties to Kim, which only makes their mutual attraction all the more problematic. As he demonstrates some kinky new ways of loving her, she's torn between his amoral lust for life and her love for her husband – which will she choose?

In the Dark by Zoe le Verdier

October 1999   Price £5.99   ISBN: 0 352 33439 8

Zoe le Verdier's first collection of stunning short stories, *Insomnia*, pushed the boundaries of women's erotica – but this collection looks set to be even hotter. The author's never been afraid to explore the most explicit female fantasies, from kinky fetishism to sex with a stranger, and her unashamed, powerfully erotic style shows these situations as you've never seen them before.

Bound by Contract by Helena Ravenscroft

November 1999   Price £5.99   ISBN: 0 352 33447 9

Samantha and Ross have been an illicit item for years – rivals as children, and passionate lovers as adults. When Ross becomes involved with the submissive Dr Louisa Richmond, Sam senses his waning interest in her own dominating ways. Reading the classic *Venus in Furs* inspires her to sign a contract to be Ross's slave for a month. She imagines it will rekindle the spark in their relationship – but it becomes altogether more erotic, and totally out of her control.

Velvet Glove by Emma Holly

November 1999   Price £5.99   ISBN: 0 352 33448 7

At the ripe young age of 22, Audrey is an SM Goldilocks in search of the perfect master. Her first candidate, an icy-eyed international banker, is far too hard. Her second, a childhood playmate, is far too soft. A charismatic bar owner seems just right, especially when he saves her from a watcher the bank has set on her trail. But can Audrey trust the man behind the charm? Or will Patrick drag her deeper into submission than even she would care to go?

$$\boxed{Nexus}$$

NEXUS BACKLIST

All books are priced £5.99 unless another price is given. If a date is supplied, the book in question will not be available until that month in 1999.

CONTEMPORARY EROTICA

THE ACADEMY	Arabella Knight	
AMANDA IN THE PRIVATE HOUSE	Esme Ombreux	
BAD PENNY	Penny Birch	
THE BLACK MASQUE	Lisette Ashton	
THE BLACK WIDOW	Lisette Ashton	
BOUND TO OBEY	Amanda Ware	
BRAT	Penny Birch	
DANCE OF SUBMISSION	Lisette Ashton	Nov
DARK DELIGHTS	Maria del Rey	
DARK DESIRES	Maria del Rey	
DARLINE DOMINANT	Tania d'Alanis	
DISCIPLES OF SHAME	Stephanie Calvin	
THE DISCIPLINE OF NURSE RIDING	Yolanda Celbridge	
DISPLAYS OF INNOCENTS	Lucy Golden	
EMMA'S SECRET DOMINATION	Hilary James	
EXPOSING LOUISA	Jean Aveline	
FAIRGROUND ATTRACTIONS	Lisette Ashton	
GISELLE	Jean Aveline	Oct
HEART OF DESIRE	Maria del Rey	
HOUSE RULES	G.C. Scott	Oct
IN FOR A PENNY	Penny Birch	Nov
JULIE AT THE REFORMATORY	Angela Elgar	
LINGERING LESSONS	Sarah Veitch	

THE GOVERNESS AT ST AGATHA'S	Yolanda Celbridge		
THE MASTER OF CASTLELEIGH	Jacqueline Bellevois		Aug
PRIVATE MEMOIRS OF A KENTISH HEADMISTRESS	Yolanda Celbridge	£4.99	
THE RAKE	Aishling Morgan		Sep
THE TRAINING OF AN ENGLISH GENTLEMAN	Yolanda Celbridge		

SAMPLERS & COLLECTIONS

EROTICON 4	Various		
THE FIESTA LETTERS	ed. Chris Lloyd	£4.99	
NEW EROTICA 3			
NEW EROTICA 4	Various		
A DOZEN STROKES	Various		Aug

NEXUS CLASSICS
A new imprint dedicated to putting the finest works of erotic fiction back in print

THE IMAGE	Jean de Berg	
CHOOSING LOVERS FOR JUSTINE	Aran Ashe	
THE INSTITUTE	Maria del Rey	
AGONY AUNT	G. C. Scott	
THE HANDMAIDENS	Aran Ashe	
OBSESSION	Maria del Rey	
HIS MASTER'S VOICE	G.C. Scott	Aug
CITADEL OF SERVITUDE	Aran Ashe	Sep
BOUND TO SERVE	Amanda Ware	Oct
BOUND TO SUBMIT	Amanda Ware	Nov
SISTERHOOD OF THE INSTITUTE	Maria del Rey	Dec

Please send me the books I have ticked above.

Name ....

Address ....

....

....

.... Post code........................

Send to: **Cash Sales, Nexus Books, Thames Wharf Studios, Rainville Road, London W6 9HT**

US customers: for prices and details of how to order books for delivery by mail, call 1-800-805-1083.

Please enclose a cheque or postal order, made payable to **Nexus Books**, to the value of the books you have ordered plus postage and packing costs as follows:

UK and BFPO – £1.00 for the first book, 50p for the second book and 30p for each subsequent book to a maximum of £3.00;

Overseas (including Republic of Ireland) – £2.00 for the first book, £1.00 for the second book and 50p for each subsequent book.

We accept all major credit cards, including VISA, ACCESS/ MASTERCARD, AMEX, DINERS CLUB, SWITCH, SOLO, and DELTA. Please write your card number and expiry date here:

....

Please allow up to 28 days for delivery.

Signature ....